TEN DAYS' WONDER

BY ELLERY QUEEN

LITTLE, BROWN AND COMPANY · BOSTON

1949

Published October 1948
Reprinted October 1948 (twice)
Reprinted December 1948
Reprinted January 1949 (twice)
Reprinted February 1949

Published simultaneously
in Canada by McClelland and Stewart Limited

PRINTED IN THE UNITED STATES OF AMERICA

Contents

PART ONE

....

NINE
DAYS'
WONDER

....

This wonder (as wonders last) lasted
nine daies.

— HEYWOOD, *Proverbes*

The First Day

IN THE BEGINNING it was without form, a darkness that kept shifting like dancers. There was music beyond, tiny, cheerful, baffling, and then it would be vast, rushing on you and, as it rushed, losing its music in sounds so big you flowed through the spaces like a gnat in an air stream, and then it was past and dwindling and tiny music again and there was the darkness shifting again.

Everything swayed. He felt seasick.

That might be a sea sky up there over the Atlantic night with a shadow like a wash cloud and trembly places where stars were. And the music could be singing in the fo'c'sle or the shift of black water. He knew it was real, because when he closed his eyes the cloud and the stars blinked out, although the sway remained and so did the music. There was also the smell of fish and something with a complicated taste, like sour honey.

It was interesting because everything was a problem and having sights and sounds and smells and tastes to worry over gave him a feeling of new importance, as if before he had been nothing. It was like being born. It was like being born in a ship. You lay in the ship and the ship rocked and you rocked with it in the rocking night, looking up at the ceiling of the sky.

You could rock here forever in this pleasant timelessness if only things remained the same, but they did not. The sky was closing in and the stars were coming down and this was another puzzle, because instead of growing as they neared they shrank. Even the quality of the rocking changed: it had muscles in it now and suddenly he thought, Maybe it's not the ship that's rocking, but me.

He opened his eyes.

He was seated on something hard that gave. His knees were pressing against his chin. His hands were locked around his shins and he was rocking back and forth.

Somebody said, "It isn't a ship at all," and he was surprised because the voice was familiar and for the life of him he couldn't remember whose it was.

He looked around rather sharply.

Nobody was in the room.

Room.

It was a room.

The discovery was like a splash of seawater.

He unclasped his hands and put them down flat against something warm and grainy yet slithery to the touch. He did not like it and he raised his hands to his face. This time his palms were offended as if by mohair and he thought, I'm in a room and I need a shave but what's a shave? Then he remembered what a shave was, and he laughed. How could he possibly have had to think what a shave was?

He lowered his hands again and they felt the slithery stuff and he saw that it was a sort of blanket. At the same instant he realized that during his reflections the darkness had gone away.

He frowned. Had it ever been there at all?

Immediately he knew it had not. Immediately he knew the sky had never been, either. It's a ceiling, he thought, scowling, and a damned scabby ceiling at that. And those stars were phonies, too. Just fugitives of sunstreaks sneaking in through the tears in an exhausted window shade. Somewhere a voice was bellowing "When Irish Eyes Are Smiling." There was also sloshing water. And that smell was fish, all right, fish frying in lard. He swallowed the sour-sweet taste and he realized that the taste was also an odor and that both were in chemical combination in the air he was breathing. No wonder he felt like heaving. The air was aged, like cheese.

Like cheese with socks on, he thought, grinning. Where am I?

He was sitting up on a bed of fancy iron which had once been painted white but now was suffering from a sort of eczema, facing a slash of undecided glass. The room was comically small, with banana-colored walls. And, he thought, grinning again, the banana's peeling.

That's three times I've laughed, he thought; I must have a sense of humor. But where the hell am I?

There was a grand oval-backed chair with carving and a mumpy green horsehair seat, an X of wire holding its elegant legs together; a man with long hair who looked as if he were dying stared at him from a tilted calendar on the wall; and the back of the door poked a chipped china clotheshook at him, like a finger. A finger in a mystery, but what was the answer? Nothing was on the hook, nothing was on the chair, and the man in the picture looked as familiar as the voice which had said it wasn't a ship, only both remained just out of reach.

The man on the bed with his big knees sticking up was a dirty bum, that's what he was, a dirty bum with a beat-up face who hadn't even bothered to take his dirty clothes off, the dirty bum; he sat there wrapped in his own dirt as if he liked it. And this was a pain.

Because I'm the man on the bed and how can I be the man on the bed when I never saw the dirty bum before?

It was a sticker.

It was a sticker when you not only didn't know where you were but who you were, either.

He laughed again.

I'll flop back on this alleged mattress and go to sleep, he thought, that's what I'll do; and the next thing Howard knew he was a ship again under a covering of stars.

ತಿ

WHEN HOWARD AWOKE for the second time it was all different, no gradual being born again, no ship fantasy or any of that nonsense; but an opening of the eyes, a recognition of the foul room, of the Christ on the calendar, of the broken mirror, and he was out of the functional bed in a bound and glaring at his remembered image.

Nearly everything flashed back in place in his head: who he was, where he came from, even why he had come to New York. He remembered catching the Atlantic Stater at Slocum. He remembered trudging up the ramp from the smelter of Track 24 into the oven of Grand Central Station. He remembered phoning the Terrazzi Galleries and asking what time the doors opened for the Djerens exhibition, and the annoyed European voice saying in his ear, "The exhibition of Mynheer Djerens expired as of yesterday." And he remembered opening his eyes in this garbage can. But between the voice and the room hung a black mist.

Howard got the shakes.

He knew he was going to get them before he got them. But he didn't know they were going to be so bad. He tried to control himself. But muscle-tightening only made them worse. He went to the door with the chipped-china hook.

I can't have slept very long this last time, he thought. They're still sloshing water around out there.

He opened the door.

The hall was an odorous memorial to departed feet.

The old man pushing the mop looked up.

"Hey, you," said Howard. "Where am I?"

The old man leaned against the mop and Howard saw that he had only one eye. "I was out West one time," the old man said. "I traveled in my day, cully. There was this Red Injun sitting outside a wide place in the road. Nothing for miles around, see, just this one little old shack, and a mountain back there. Kansas, I think it was —"

"More likely Oklahoma or New Mexico," said Howard, finding himself holding up the wall. That fish had been eaten, no doubt, but its corpse haunted the place tantalizingly. He'd have to eat, and soon; that's the way it always was. "What's the point? I've got to get out of here."

"This Injun, he was sitting on the dirt with his back against this shack, see —"

Suddenly the old man's eye shifted to the center of his forehead and Howard said, "Polyphemus."

"No," said the old fellow, "I didn't know his name. The thing is, right over this Red Injun's head, nailed to the wall, was a sign on it with great big red sort of lettering. And what do you think it says?"

"What?" said Howard.

"Hotel Waldorf," said the old fellow triumphantly.

"Thanks a lot," said Howard. "That really sets me up, old-timer. Now where the hell am *I*?"

"Where the hell would you be?" snarled the old man. "You're in a flophouse, my friend, a flophouse on the Bowery, which was good enough for Steve Brody and Tim Sullivan but it's too good for the likes of you, you dirty bum."

The slop pail flew. It took off like a bird. Then it landed on its side with a musical splash.

The old man quivered as if Howard had kicked, not the pail, but him. Standing there in the gray suds, he looked about to cry.

"Give me that mop," said Howard. "I'll clean it up."

"You dirty bum!"

Howard went back into the room.

∽

He sat down on the bed and cupped his palms over his mouth and nose, exhaling hard, because he was hoping hard.

But he hadn't been drinking, after all.

His hands dropped.

His hands dropped and there was blood all over them.

Blood all over his hands.

∽

Howard tore at his clothes. His fawn gabardine was ripped and wrinkled, grease-smeared, stiff with filth. He reeked like the pens on Jorking's farm beyond Twin Hills. As a boy he had taken the long way round to Slocum Township just to avoid Jorking's pigs. But now it didn't matter; it was even pleasant, because it wasn't what you were looking for.

He searched himself like a louse-ridden monkey.

And suddenly he found it. A big, brown-black clot. Part of the clot was on his lapel. The other part was on his shirt. The clot was making the shirt stick to the suit. He tore them apart.

The raw edge of the clot was fibrous.

He jumped off the bed and ran over to the slice of mirror. His right eye resembled an old avocado pit. There was a scarlet trench across the bridge of his nose. The left side of his lower lip was blown up like a piece of bubble gum. And his left ear was a caricature in purple.

He had picked a fight!

Or had he?

And he had lost.

Or had he won?

Or had he won and lost, too?

He held his shaky hands up to his functioning eye and peered at them. The knuckles of both were gashed, scraped, oversize. The blood had run into the blond hairs, making them stand up stiff, like mascaraed eyelashes.

But that's my own blood.

He turned his hands palms up and relief washed over him in a wave.

There was no blood on the palms.

Maybe I didn't kill anybody after all, he thought gleefully.

But his glee dribbled away. There was that other blood. On his suit and shirt. Maybe it wasn't his. Maybe it was someone else's. Maybe this time it had happened.

Maybe . . . !

This is going to push me over, he thought. If I keep thinking about it, by God I'll go right over.

The pain in his hands.

He went through his pockets slowly. He had left home with over two hundred dollars. The inventory was perfunctory; he had no real hope of finding anything and he was not disappointed. His money was gone. So was his watch, with the miniature gold sculptor's mallet his father had given him to wear as a fob the year he went to France. So was the gold fountain pen Sally had given him last year for his birthday. Rolled. Maybe after he'd checked into this opium den. It sounded plausible; they'd never have given him a room without payment in advance.

Howard tried to conjure up "desk clerk," "lobby," "Bowery" — how it had all looked the night before.

Night before. Or two nights before. Or two weeks before. The last time it had taken six days. Once it had been for a mere couple of hours. He never knew until afterwards because the thing was like a streak of dry rot in Time, unmeasurable except by what surrounded it.

Howard went drearily to the door again.

⁊

"WHAT'S THE DATE?"

The old man was on his knees in the slop, soaking it up with his mop.

"I said what's the date."

The old man was still offended. He wrung the mop out over the pail stubbornly.

Howard heard his own teeth grinding. *What is the date?*

The old man spat. "You get tough, brother, I'll call Bagley. He'll fix your wagon. He'll fix it." Then he must have seen something in Howard's good eye, because he whined, "It's the day after Labor Day," and he picked up the pail and fled.

Tuesday after the first Monday in September.

Howard hurried back into the room and over to the calendar.

The year on it was 1937.

Howard scratched his head and laughed. Cast away, that's what I am. They'll find my bones on the bottom of the sea.

The Log!

Howard began to look for it, frantically.

He had started The Log immediately after his first baffling cruise through time-space. Making a nightly report to himself enabled him to fix the conscious part of his existence, it provided a substantial deck for his feet from which to look back over those black voyages. But it was a curious log. It recorded only the events, as it were, on shore. For the intervals he passed on the timeless sea the pages stood smooth and blank.

His diary was a collection of fat black pocket notebooks. As he filled one he put it away in his writing desk at home. But he always carried the current one.

If they'd lifted that, too — !

But he found it in the outside breast pocket of his jacket, under the Irish linen handkerchief.

The final entry told him that this latest voyage had lasted nineteen days.

∾

HE FOUND HIMSELF staring through the dirty window.

Three stories above the street.

Enough.

But suppose I just break my leg?

He plunged out into the hall.

∾

ELLERY QUEEN SAID he wouldn't listen to a word until later because a story told under stress of pain and hunger and exhaustion, while it might interest poets and priests, could only prove a waste of time to a man of facts. So pure selfishness demanded that he strip Howard, toss him into a hot tub, scrape off his beard, doctor his wounds, provide him with clean clothing, and push a breakfast into him consisting of a large glass of tomato juice mixed with Worcestershire and tabasco, a small steak, seven pieces of hot buttered toast, and three cups of black coffee.

"Now," said Ellery cheerfully, pouring the third cup, "I recognize you. And now you can probably think with at least a primitive efficiency. Well, Howard, when I last saw you, you were bashing marble. What have you done — graduated to flesh?"

"You examined my clothes."

Ellery grinned. "You were a long time in that tub."

"I was a long time walking up here from the Bowery."

"Broke?"

"You know I am. You looked through my pockets."

"Naturally. How's your father, Howard?"

"All right." Then Howard looked startled and pushed away from the table. "Ellery, may I use your phone?"

Ellery watched him go into the study. The door didn't quite close after him and Ellery was reluctant to make a point of closing it. Apparently Howard was putting through a long-distance call, because for some time there was no sound from beyond the door.

Ellery reached for his after-breakfast pipe and reviewed what he knew of Howard Van Horn.

It wasn't much and what there was of it lay darkly behind a war, an ocean, and a decade. They had met on the *terrasse* of the café at the corner where the Rue de la Huchette meets the Boulevard St. Michel. This was prewar Paris: Paris of the Cagoulards and the *populaires;* of the incredible Exposition, when Nazis with elaborate cameras and guidebooks infested the Right Bank, shouldering their way *Uebermensch*-wise through pale refugees from Vienna and Prague, going to view Picasso's mural, *Guernica,* with every appearance of tourist passion; Paris of the raging Spanish argument, while across the Pyrenees Madrid lay dying of nonintervention. A decaying Paris, and Ellery was there looking for a man known as Hansel, which is another and dated story and therefore will probably never be told. But since Hansel was a Nazi, and few Nazis were believed to come to the Rue de la Huchette, that was where Ellery looked for him.

And that was where he found Howard.

Howard had been living on the Left Bank for some time, and Howard was unhappy. The Rue de la Huchette did not share the confidence of other Parisian quarters in the impregnability of the Maginot Line; there were disturbing political atmospheres; it was all upsetting to a young American who had come abroad to study sculpture and whose head was full of Rodin, Bourdelle, neoclassicism, and the purity of Greek line. Ellery recalled that he had felt rather sorry for Howard; and because a man who is watching the world go by is less conspicuous if he is two, he permitted Howard to share his *terrasse* table. For three weeks they saw a great deal of each other; until one day Hansel came strolling out of fourteenth century France, which is the Rue St. Séverin, into Ellery's arms, and that was the end of Howard.

In the study Howard was saying, "But, Father, I'm okay. I wouldn't lie to you, you mugg." And then Howard laughed and said, "Call off the dogs. I'll be home right off."

In those three weeks Howard had spoken at length and with terrible adoration of his father. Ellery had gathered the impression that the elder Van Horn was a great iron-chested figure, hero-sized, a man of force, dignity, humanity, brilliance, compassion, and generosity — a veritable father-image; and this had amused the great man, because when Howard took him to his impressive *pension* studio, Ellery saw that it was thronged with sculptures, worked directly in the stone on a solid geometric basis, of such looming deities of maleness as Zeus, Moses, and Adam. It had seemed significant at the time that Howard did not once mention his mother.

"No, I'm with Ellery Queen," Howard was saying. "You remember, Father — that wonderful guy I met in Paris before the war . . . Yes, Queen . . . Yes, the same one." And, grimly: "I decided to look him up."

During that Parisian idyl, Howard had struck Ellery as rather pitifully provincial. He came from New England — Ellery never did learn from just where in New England; but it was not far, he had gathered, from New York. Apparently the Van Horns lived in one of the town's great houses: Howard, his father, and his father's brother; no women were mentioned, and Ellery supposed that Howard's mother had been dead for many years. His boyhood had been surrounded by a high wall of tutors and governesses; he learned a great deal of the world through the eyes of paid adults, which is to say, he learned nothing. His only contact with reality was the town he lived in. It was not wonderful, then, that in Paris Howard should have been uneasy, bewildered, and resentful. He was too far from Main Street . . . and, Ellery suspected, from papa.

Ellery remembered thinking that Howard would have interested a psychiatrist. He was structurally the big-boned, muscular, rugged, bony-headed, square-jawed, thick-skinned man of action — bold, adventurous, and masterful, the typical hero of popular fiction. Yet, caught up in the ferment of Europe at the most tempestuous moment in its history, he kept stealing wistful glances, as it were, over his big shoulder at fireside and father an ocean away. The father creates the son in his own image, Ellery had thought, but not always with the expected result.

Ellery had got the feeling that Howard was in Europe not because he wanted to be but because Diedrich Van Horn expected him to be. Howard would have been far happier, Ellery knew, in a Boston fine arts class or, as the town's sole authority in such matters, acting as consultant to the Mayor's Planning Committee on the propriety of allowing that foreign sculptor to go ahead with those undraped females planned for the pediment of the proposed Civic Recreation Center. Ellery had thought with a grin that Howard would have made the perfect adviser in such a situation, for he invariably blushed when they passed the *clandestin* at the corner of the Rue de la Huchette and the Rue Zacharie, and he had once summarized his feelings about Europe by pointing earnestly to the *Poste de Police* across the street from it and bursting out: "I'm no prude, Ellery, but by God that's going too far, that's pure decadence!" Ellery recalled thinking at the time that Howard could not have been too familiar with the sociological facts of life as it was lived in his own home town. He had often thought since of Howard hacking soberly away at his father's image in that splendid Left Bank studio, an overgrown and troubled young soul. He had been very fond of Howard.

"But that's silly, Father. You tell Sally she's not to worry about me. At all."

But all this had been ten years ago. Another Sculptor had been at work on Howard's physiognomy in the intervening decade, and Ellery was not thinking of the unknown artist who had given it such an expert going-over with his fists. There were secretive corners to Howard's mouth now and an older, warier glint in his undamaged eye. Things had happened to young Van Horn since their last meeting. He would not be abashed by a bordel now; and there was a note in his voice as he spoke to his father which Ellery had not heard ten years before.

Ellery experienced a sudden very odd feeling.

But before he could examine it, Howard came out of the study.

ᴄᴡᴐ

"FATHER HAD ALL the cops in the East out looking for me," grinned Howard. "Doesn't speak very well for Inspector Queen's profession."

"The East is a big place, Howard."

Howard sat down and began to examine his bandaged hands.

"What was it?" asked Ellery. "The war?"

"War?" Howard looked up, really surprised.

"You're so obviously suffering from a painful — and I should think a chronic — experience. It wasn't the war?"

"I wasn't even in it."

Ellery smiled. "Well, I've given you your opening."

"Oh. Yes." Howard scowled, jiggled his right foot. "I don't know why I should think you'd be interested in my troubles."

"Let's assume I am."

Ellery watched him struggle with himself.

"Come on," he said. "Get it off your chest."

Howard blurted: "Ellery, two and a half hours ago I was going to jump out of a window."

"I see," said Ellery, "you changed your mind."

Howard went slowly red. "I'm not lying!"

"And I'm not the least bit interested in dramatics." Ellery knocked out his pipe.

Everything in Howard's battered face tightened and blued.

"Howard," said Ellery, "I don't know of anyone who hasn't toyed with the notion of committing suicide at one time or other. But you'll notice that most of us are still around." Howard glared at him. "You think I'm one hell of a confidant. But Howard, you started the wrong way. Suicide isn't your problem. Don't try to impress me." Howard's glance wavered, and Ellery chuckled. "I like you, you ape. I liked you ten years ago when I thought you were a fine kid who'd been thoroughly screwed up by a dominating and overindulgent father — and stop making with the jaw, Howard, I'm not talking your father down; what I just said is true of most American fathers — what differences exist are only in degree, varying according to the individual.

"I say I liked you then, when you were a damp-muzzled pup, and I like you now, when you're obviously a full-grown dog. You're in trouble, you've come to me, and I'll help all I can. But I can't do a thing if you strike attitudes. Heroics are going to get in the way. Now have I wounded you to the soul?"

"Damn you."

They both laughed, and Ellery said briskly, "Wait till I reload my pipe."

❧

EARLY ON THE morning of September 1, 1939, Nazi warplanes roared over Warsaw. Before the day was out the Republic of France had decreed general mobilization and martial law. Before the week was out Howard was homeward bound.

"I was glad of the excuse," Howard confessed. "I'd had a bellyful of France, refugees, Hitler, Mussolini, the Café St. Michel, and myself. I wanted to crawl under the comforter in my own little bed and sleep for twenty years. I was even sick of sculpture; when I got home I chucked my chisel away.

"Father came through, as usual. He didn't ask any questions, and he didn't throw anything up to me. He let me work it out alone."

But Howard had not worked it out. His bed was not the slumbrous womb he had looked forward to; Main Street unaccountably seemed more foreign than the Rue du Chat Qui Pêche; he found himself reading newspapers and news magazines and listening to the radio report Europe's agony; he began to avoid mirrors. And he discovered that he resented violently some of his uncle's isolationist observations. There were quarrels at the Van Horn dinner table, with Howard's father the rather troubled mediator.

"Uncle?" said Ellery.

"My Uncle Wolfert. Father's brother. He's something of a character," said Howard, and he let it go at that.

And then Howard sailed on his first cruise on the black sea.

"It happened the night father married," said Howard. "It was a surprise to all of us — I mean the marriage; I remember Uncle Wolf making a typical snide remark about old fools in their second childhood. But father wasn't so old, and he'd fallen in love with somebody pretty wonderful — he hadn't made any mistake.

"Anyway, he married Sally and they left for their honeymoon and that same night I was standing in front of my bureau mirror ripping off my tie — undressing to hit the hay — when the next thing I knew I was choking over a piece of fly-specked blueberry pie in a truckmen's diner four-hundred-odd miles away."

Ellery very carefully put a match to his pipe again. "Teleportation?" he grinned.

"I'm not kidding you. It was the next thing I knew."

"How long a time had elapsed?"

"Five and a half days."

Ellery puffed. "Damn this pipe."

"Ellery, I had no recollection of a thing. One minute I was taking off my tie in my own bedroom, the next minute I was sitting on a stool in a diner over four hundred miles away. How I'd got there, what I'd done for almost six days, what I'd eaten, where I'd slept, whom I talked to, what I said — nothing. A blank. I had no sensation of the passage of time. I might just as well have died, been buried, and been resurrected."

"That's better," said Ellery to his pipe. "Oh, yes. Unsettling, Howard, but not uncommon. Amnesia."

"Sure," said Howard with a grin. "Amnesia. Just a word. Did you ever have it?"

"Go on."

Three weeks later it happened again.

"The first time nobody knew about it. Uncle Wolfert didn't give a damn where I was or how long I stayed away, and father was off on his honeymoon. But the second time father and Sally were back home. I was gone twenty-six hours before they found me, and I didn't snap out of it for another eight. They had to tell me what happened. I came to thinking I'd just stepped out of my shower. But it was a full day and a half later."

"And the doctors?"

"Naturally father had every doctor he could lay his hands on. They couldn't find a thing wrong with me. Brother Queen, I was scared, and no fooling."

"Of course you were."

Howard lit a cigaret, slowly. "Thanks. But I mean scared." He frowned as he blew out the match. "I can't describe . . ."

"You felt as if all the normal rules were suspended. But only for you."

"That's it. All of a sudden I felt absolutely alone. Sort of — sort of fourth-dimensional stuff."

Ellery smiled. "Let's get off the auto-analysis. The attacks kept recurring?"

"Right up to and through the war. When Pearl Harbor was blasted, I was almost relieved. To get into uniform, get going, do things . . . I don't know, it looked like a possible answer. Only . . . they wouldn't take me."

"Oh?"

"Turned down, Ellery. By the Army, the Navy, the Air Force, the Marine Corps, and the Merchant Marine — in that order. I guess they didn't have much use for a guy who staged his own private blackouts at the most unpredictable times." Howard's puffed lip curled. "I was one of Uncle Sam's pet four-effs."

"So you had to stay home."

"And it was rugged. People in town gave me an awful lot of queer looks. And the boys home on leave sort of avoided me. I guess they all thought because I was the son of . . . Anyway, I fought the war working on the night shift at a big aircraft plant up home. Half-days I messed around with clay and stone in my studio at the house. I didn't show myself much. It was too tough trying to shrink up so I wouldn't be noticed."

Ellery glanced over the powerful body sprawled in the armchair, and he nodded.

"All right," he said crisply. "Now let's have some details. Tell me everything you know about these amnesia attacks."

"They're periodic and sporadic. Never any warning, although one doctor claimed that they seemed to occur when I've been unusually excited, or upset. Sometimes the blackout lasts only a couple of hours, sometimes three or four weeks. I snap out of them in all sorts of places — at home, in Boston, in New York, once in Providence. Other times on a dirt road in the middle of nowhere. Or any old place. I never have the faintest recollection of where I've been or what I've done."

"Howard." Ellery's tone was casual. "Did you ever come to on a bridge?"

"On a bridge?"

"Yes."

It seemed to Ellery that Howard's tone was as deliberately casual as his own.

"I did once, at that. Why?"

"What were you doing when you became conscious of yourself? I mean on the bridge."

"What was I," Howard hesitated, "doing?"

"That's right."

"Why . . ."

"You were about to jump off, weren't you?"

Howard stared at him. "How the hell did you know that? I never even told that to the doctors!"

"The suicide pattern suggests itself strongly. Any other such episodes? I mean waking up to find yourself about to take your own life?"

"Two other times," said Howard tightly. "Once I was in a canoe on a lake; I came to as I hit the water. The other time I was just about to step off a chair in a hotel room. There was a rope around my neck."

"And this going-to-jump-out-of-a-window business this morning?"

"No, that was conscious." Howard jumped up. "Ellery —"

"No. Wait. Sit down." Howard sat down. "What do the doctors say?"

"Well, I'm perfectly sound organically. There's no medical history that would account for the attacks — epilepsy, or anything like that."

"Have they put you under?"

"Hypnosis? I think they have. You know, Ellery, they've got a cute trick of hypnotizing you and then, before they bring you out of it, they'll order you not to remember having been put under — to wake up thinking you'd simply fallen asleep." Howard grinned grimly. "I have an idea I'm not a very easy hypnotic subject. I'm sure it hasn't happened more than once or twice, and then unsatisfactorily. I don't co-operate."

"They haven't offered anything constructive?"

"There's been a lot of learned talk, and I suppose some of it means something, but they certainly haven't been able to stop the attacks. The last psychiatrist father sicked onto me suggested that I may be suffering from hyperinsulinism."

"Hyper-what?"

"Hyperinsulinism."

"Never heard of it."

Howard shrugged. "The way it was explained to me, it's the exact opposite of the condition that causes diabetes. When the pancreas or whatever it is doesn't manufacture — the M.D. used the word 'elaborate' — enough insulin, you have diabetes. When it elaborates too much insulin, you have the big fancy word and it can cause, among other things, amnesia.

"Well, maybe that's it and maybe it isn't. They're not sure."

"You must have been given sugar-tolerance tests?"

"Inconclusive. Sometimes I reacted normally, sometimes I didn't. The truth is, Ellery, they just don't know. They say they could find out all right if I'd really co-operate, but what do they expect? A piece of my soul?"

Howard glared at the rug.

And Ellery was silent.

"They admit it's perfectly possible for me to have periodic, temporary attacks of amnesia and still be organically and functionally okay. Helps, doesn't it?" Howard squirmed in the armchair, rubbing the back of his neck. "I don't give a damn any more what the doctors say, Ellery. All I know is, if I don't stop walking into these black holes, I'll . . ." He sprang to his feet. Then he walked over to the window and stared out at Eighty-seventh Street. "Can you help me?" he said, without turning around.

"I don't know."

Howard whirled. He was very pale. "Somebody's got to help me!"

"What makes you think I can help?"

"What?"

"Howard, I'm not a doctor."

"I'm fed up with doctors!"

"They'll locate the cause eventually."

"And what am I supposed to do in the meantime? Go off my trolley? I tell you I'm close to it right now!"

"Sit down, Howard, sit dc   "

"Ellery, you've got to help me. I'm desperate. Come home with me!"

"Come home with you?"

"Yes!"

"Why?"

"I want you near me when the next one comes. I want you to watch me, Ellery. See what I do. Where I go. Maybe I'm leading a . . ."

"Double life?"

"Yes!"

Ellery rose and went to the fireplace to knock out his pipe again. And he said: "Howard, come clean."

"What?"

"I said come clean."

"What do you mean!"

Ellery glanced at him sidewise. "You're holding something out on me."

"Why, I'm doing nothing of the sort."

"Yes. You won't co-operate with the only people who can really help you find a cause — and consequently a cure — for this condition, the doctors. You're not an 'easy' subject for diagnosis or treatment. You admit you've told me things you haven't told any of the medical men. Why me, Howard? We met ten years ago — for three weeks. Why me?"

Howard did not answer.

"I'll tell you why. Because," said Ellery, straightening, "I'm an amateur snoop, Howard, and you think you've committed a crime during one of your blackouts. Perhaps more than one crime. Perhaps one in each episode."

"No, I —"

"That's why you won't help the doctors, Howard. You're afraid of what they might find out."

"No!"

"Yes," said Ellery.

Howard's shoulders drooped. He turned around and put his bandaged hands in the pockets of the jacket Ellery had given him and he said, in a hopeless sort of way, "All right. I suppose that's what's behind it."

"Good! Now we have a basis for discussion. Any concrete reason for your suspicion?"

"No."

"I think you have."

Howard suddenly laughed. He withdrew his hands and held them up. "You saw them when I got here. That's the way they were when I came to in that flophouse this morning. You saw my coat, my shirt."

"Oh, is that it? Why, Howard, you were in a fight."

"Yes, but what happened?" Howard's voice rose. "It's not being sure that's getting me down, Ellery. Not knowing. I've got to know! That's why I wish you'd come home with me."

Ellery took a little walk around the room, sucking on his empty pipe.

Howard watched him, uneasily.

"Are you considering it?" Howard asked.

"I'm considering," said Ellery, stopping to lean against the mantel-piece, "the possibility that you're still holding something back."

"What's the matter with you?" cried Howard. "I'm not!"

"Sure, Howard? Sure you're telling me everything?"

"My God in His sweet heaven, man," shouted Howard, "what do you want me to do — take my skin off?"

"Why the heat?"

"You're calling me a liar!"

"Aren't you?"

This time Howard did not shout. He ran over to the armchair and flung himself into it, angrily.

But Ellery persisted: "Aren't you, Howard?"

"Not really." Howard's tone was unexpectedly calm. "Naturally, we girls have our secrets. I mean secrets." He even smiled. "But Ellery, I've told you every damned thing I know about the amnesia. You can take it or leave it."

"At this point," said Ellery, "I'm inclined to leave it."

"Please."

Ellery looked at him quickly. He was sitting on the very edge of the armchair, grasping the arms, not smiling now, not angry, not calm — not any of the things he had done and been for the half-hour past.

"There are some things I can't tell, Ellery. If you knew, you'd understand why. Nobody could. They involve — " Howard stopped and slowly got up. "I'm sorry I've bothered you. I'll send these duds back as soon as I get home. Would you stake me to the fare? I haven't a dime."

"Howard."

"What?"

Ellery went over and put his arm around Howard's shoulders. "If I'm to help I've got to dig. I'll come up."

∽

Howard telephoned home again to tell the elder Van Horn that Ellery was coming up for a visit in a couple of days.

"I thought you'd whoop," Ellery heard Howard say with a laugh. "No, I don't know for how long, Father. I imagine for as long as Laura can keep him interested in her cooking."

When he came out of the study, Ellery said to him: "I'd leave with you now, Howard, but it's going to take me a day or so to get away."

"Sure. Naturally." Howard was feeling good; he was almost bouncing.

"Also, I'm writing a novel . . ."

"Bring it with you!"

"I'll have to. I'm committed by contract to deliver the manuscript by a certain date, and I'm behind schedule now."

"I suppose I ought to feel like a skunk, Ellery — "

"Learn to have the courage of your emotions," chuckled Ellery. "Can you provide a typewriter in decent working order?"

"Everything you'll need, and the best quality. What's more, you can have the guest house. You'll have privacy there, yet you'll be near me — it's only a few yards from the main house."

"Sounds good. Oh, and by the way, Howard. It won't be necessary to tell your family why I'm coming up. I'd prefer an atmosphere as free from tensions as possible."

"It's going to be pretty tough fooling the old gent. He just said to me on the phone, 'Well, it's about time you decided to hire a bodyguard.' He was kidding, but father's shrewd, Ellery. I'll bet he's figured out already why you're coming."

"Just the same, don't say any more about it than you can help."

"I could tell them you had to finish your novel and I offered you a chance to do it far from the madding crowd." Howard's good eye clouded over. "Ellery, this may take a long time. May be months before the next attack — "

"Or never," said Ellery. "Hasn't that ever occurred to you, my fine Denmarkian friend? The episodes may stop as suddenly as they started." Howard grinned, but he looked unconvinced. "Say, how about your putting up with dad and me here at the apartment until I can get away?"

"Meaning you're worried about how I'll get home."

"No," said Ellery. "I mean yes."

"Thanks, but I'd better be getting back today, Ellery. They've been frantic."

"Of course. — You're sure you'll be all right."

"Positive. I've never had two attacks less than three weeks apart."
Ellery gave Howard some money and walked him downstairs
to the street.

∞

THEY WERE SHAKING hands before the open door of the taxi when
Ellery suddenly exclaimed: "But Howard, where the devil do I go?"

"What do you mean?"

"I haven't the remotest idea where you live!"

Howard looked startled. "Didn't I tell you?"

"Never!"

"Give me a piece of paper. No, wait, I've got a notebook — did
I transfer all my things to your suit? Yes, here."

Howard tore a page out of a fat black notebook, scribbled on it,
and was gone.

Ellery watched the taxi until it turned the corner.

Then he went back upstairs, thoughtfully, the piece of paper still
in his hand.

Howard's already committed a crime, he thought. *It's not the
"possible" crime of his amnesic state that he dreads. It's a remembered crime, committed in his conscious state. This crime, and the
circumstances surrounding it, are the "things" Howard can't "tell"
— the "secrets" which, in all conscious sincerity, he protests are
irrelevant to his emotional problem. But it's the guilt feeling involving precisely that crime that's sent him desperately to me.
Psychologically, Howard is seeking punishment for it.*

What was the crime?

That was the first question to be answered.

And the answer could only lie in Howard's home, in . . .

Ellery glanced at the sheet of paper Howard had scribbled on.
He very nearly dropped it.

The address Howard had written was:

Van Horn
North Hill Drive
Wrightsville

∞

WRIGHTSVILLE!

The squatty little railroad station in Low Village. Steep square-cobbled streets. The round Square, its ancient horse trough supporting the bird-stippled bronze of Founder Jezreel Wright. The Hollis Hotel, the High Village Pharmacy-that-used-to-be, Sol Gowdy's Men's Shop, the Bon Ton Department Store, William Ketcham — Insurance, the three gilt balls above the shop front of J. P. Simpson, the elegant Wrightsville National Bank, *John F. Wright, Pres.*

Wheel-spoke avenues . . . State Street, red-brick Town Hall, the Carnegie Library and Miss Aikin, the tall obsequious elms. Lower Main, the *Wrightsville Record* building with the presses on display beyond the plate-glass windows, old Phinny Baker, Pettigrew's real estate office, Al Brown's Ice Cream Parlor, The Bijou Theater and Manager Louie Cahan . . .

Hill Drive and Twin Hill Cemetery and Wrightsville Junction three miles down the line and Slocum Township and *The Hot Spot* on Route 16 and the smithy with the neon sign and the distant peaks of the Mahoganies.

Old scenes flashed across his memory as he sank frowning into the worn leather armchair Howard had just vacated.

Wrightsville . . .

Where had Howard Van Horn been while Ellery observed the tragedy of Jim and Nora Haight develop? [1] That had been early in the war, when Howard was living at home, by his own admission, working in an aircraft factory. Why, during Ellery's revisit to Wrightsville not long after the war, in the case involving Captain Davy Fox, hadn't he run across Howard's trail then? [2] True, Ellery had mixed with few Wrightsvillians during that investigation. But on his first visit, on the Haight business, he had received a great deal of local publicity; Hermione Wright had seen to that. Howard couldn't possibly have remained ignorant of his presence in town. And North Hill Drive was a mere extension of Hill Drive, where the Wrights and the Haights lived and where Ellery had occupied,

---

[1] *Calamity Town*, by Ellery Queen; Little, Brown & Co., 1942.
[2] *The Murderer Is a Fox*, by Ellery Queen; Little, Brown & Co., 1945.

first the Haight cottage, then a guest room in the Wright house next door — perhaps ten minutes from the Van Horn place by car, certainly no longer. Now that Ellery thought of it, the very name "Van Horn" had a Wrightsville ring. He was sure he had heard old John F. mention Diedrich Van Horn on several occasions as being one of the *points d'appui* of the town, a civic-minded, philanthropic millionaire; and so, he seemed to recall, had Judge Eli Martin characterized him. Howard's father could not have been one of the Wright-Martin-Willoughby set or Ellery would have met him; but that was understandable — they constituted the traditional society of Wrightsville. So the Van Horns must be of the industrial element, the tycoons, the Mitsubishis of the community — the Country Club crowd, between the traditional caste and whom the fence was unscalable. Still, Howard must have known that Ellery was living in town; and since he had not come forward, it seemed clear that he had deliberately avoided his old acquaintance of the Rue de la Huchette. Why?

Ellery was not seriously disturbed by the question. Howard was newly in the grip of his malady in those days. Probably he had been too frightened to face the ordeal of renewing their acquaintanceship. Or very likely he had been immobilized by feelings of guilt still buried deep.

Ellery refilled his pipe. What really bothered him was that he was Wrightsville-bound on a case for the third time. It was a disheartening coincidence. Ellery disliked coincidences. They made him uneasy. And the longer he thought about it, the uneasier he became.

If I were superstitious, he thought, I'd say it was Fate.

Strangely enough, in each of the previous Wrightsville investigations, circumstances had nudged him into the same unsatisfying speculations. He wondered, as he had wondered before, if there might not be a pattern in all this, a pattern too large to be discerned by the human eye. Certainly it was odd that, while he had brought the Haight and the Fox cases to successful solutions, the nature of each had compelled him to suppress the truth, so that the world outside regarded his Wrightsville ventures as among his more conspicuous failures.

And now this Van Horn business . . .

Damn Wrightsville and all its works!

Ellery thrust Howard's address into a pocket of his smoking jacket and loaded his pipe irritably.

But then he caught himself wondering what had ever happened to Alberta Manaskas and if Emmy DuPré would invite him this time to discuss the Arts in the coolth of the evening, and he grinned.

The Second Day

AS THE TRAIN scuttled away toward Slocum Ellery thought, It isn't so different.

There weren't so many horse droppings in the gravel and some of the stoop-shouldered frame houses around the station had disappeared; the latticework of a block of stores going up made an unfamiliar arabesque in the old fresco; the smithy with the neon sign was now a garage with a neon sign; Phil's Diner, which had been a reconditioned castoff of the Wrightsville Traction Company, was a grand new thing of blue-awninged chrome. But through the open doorway of the stationmaster's office the bald dome of Gabby Warrum shone in welcome; it seemed as if the same dusty-footed, blue-jeaned urchin sat on the same rusty hand truck under the station eaves chewing the same bubble gum and staring with the same relentless vacancy; and the surrounding countryside had not changed in contour, only in coloration, for this was Wrightsville putting on its war paint for the Indian summer.

There were the same fields, the same hills, the same sky.

Ellery caught himself breathing.

That was the sweet thing about Wrightsville, he thought, setting his suitcase down on the platform and looking around for Howard. It struck even the passer-by as home. It was easy to understand why Howard in Paris ten years before had seemed provincial. Whether like Linda Fox you liked Wrightsville, or like Lola Wright you loathed it, if you had been born here and raised here you took Wrightsville with you to the fourth corner and the seventh sea.

Where's Howard?

Ellery wandered to the east end of the platform. From here he could see up Upper Whistling Avenue, which ambled through Low Village to within one square of the Square and then turned elegant and marched sedately into the land of milk and honey, even unto the place of the Canaanite. He wondered if Miss Sally's Tea Roome in town was still serving pineapple marshmallow nut mousses to the Wrightsville *bon ton;* if you could still smell the delectable olio of pepper, kerosene, coffee beans, rubber boots, vinegar and cheese in Sidney Gotch's General Store; if at Danceland in the Grove on Saturday nights careworn mothers still beat the brush seeking their young; if . . .

"Mr. Queen?"

Ellery turned around to find a terrifying station wagon beside him with a smiling girl behind its wheel.

Someone he'd once met in Wrightsville, no doubt. She had a vaguely familiar look.

But then he saw D. VAN HORN gilt-lettered on the door.

Howard hadn't mentioned a sister, damn him! And a pretty one at that.

"Miss Van Horn?"

The girl looked surprised. "I ought to feel crushed. Didn't H̶ ̶-ard mention me?"

"If he did," quoth Mr. Queen gallantly, "I was out to lunch /hy didn't he say he had a beautiful sister?"

"Sister." She threw back her head and laughed. "I'm not H vard's *sister,* Mr. Queen. I'm his mother."

"Beg pardon?"

"Well . . . his stepmother."

"You're *Mrs.* Van Horn?" exclaimed Ellery.

"It's the family joke." She looked mischievous. "A /ve been in awe of you so long, Mr. Queen, I just couldn't re cutting you down to my size."

"In awe of *me?*"

"Howard said you were nice. Don't you kno ou're a famous personality, Mr. Queen? Diedrich's got all yo ooks — my husband thinks you're the greatest mystery writer in the world — but I've had a secret crush on you for years. I once saw you in Low Village driving through with Patricia Wright in her convertible, and I thought she was the luckiest girl in America. Mr. Queen, is that your suitcase over there?"

ᏬᎵᏬ

IT WAS AN agreeable start to any case, and Ellery hopped in beside Sally Van Horn feeling very important, very male, and absurdly envious of Diedrich Van Horn.

As they drove away from the station, Sally said: "Howard was so miserable at the prospect of driving into town with his face all mashed up that I made him stay home. I'm sorry now I didn't make him come! Imagine not even mentioning me."

"Simple justice compels me to exonerate the knave," said Ellery. "Howard mentioned you emphatically. It's just that I wasn't quite prepared — "

"To find me so young?"

"Er, something like that."

"It throws most people. I suppose it's because marrying Dieds gave me a son older than I am! You don't know my husband, do you?"

"Never had the pleasure."

"You don't think of Dieds in terms of *years*. He's immense and powerful and so wonderfully young. And," Sally added with the lightest touch of defiance, "handsome."

"I'm sure of that. Howard's disgustingly like a Greek god himself."

"Oh, there's no resemblance between them at all. They're built along the same lines, but Dieds is black and ugly as an old butternut."

"You just said he was handsome."

"He is. When I want to make him mad I tell him he's the *ugliest* handsome man I ever saw."

"There seems," chuckled Ellery, "to be a slight paradox involved."

"That's what Diedrich says. So then I tell him he's the handsomest ugly man I ever saw, and he beams again."

Ellery liked her. It was not hard to grasp how a man of solidity and character, as he judged Diedrich Van Horn to be, could have fallen in love with her. Although he took Sally to be twenty-eight or twenty-nine, she had the look, the figure, the laugh, the glow of eighteen. At Van Horn's age, and with a vigor probably untapped through many years of loneliness, this could be an irresistible magnet. But Howard's father, from all reports, was also a man of seasoned horse sense; Sally's youth might pull him emotionally, but he would want — and know he wanted — more in a wife than a companion of his bed. Ellery saw how Sally might have seemed to satisfy this want, too. Her look was also gracious, her figure was rich as well as young, her laugh had wisdom, her glow a promise of fire. She was intelligent and, for all her warm quick friendliness, Ellery felt a certain reserve under the surface. Her frankness was natural and charming, like a child's; and yet her smile seemed old and sad. In fact, Ellery thought as they chatted, Sally's smile was the most provocative thing about her, the supreme contradiction in a personality that appealed by contradiction. He wondered again where he had seen her before, and when . . . The more he studied her, as she drove along, talking pleasantly and unaffectedly, the more he was able to understand how Van Horn could have abdicated his bachelordom without a regret.

"Mr. Queen?" She was looking at him.

"Sorry," said Ellery quickly. "I'm afraid I didn't catch that last."

"You've been looking at Wrightsville and probably wishing I'd stop twittering in your ear."

Ellery stared. "We're on Hill Drive!" he exclaimed. "How on earth did we get here so fast? Didn't we drive through town?"

"Of course we did. Where were you? Oh, I know. You were thinking of your novel."

"Heaven forbid," said Ellery. "I was thinking of you."

"Of me? Oh, dear. Howard didn't warn me about *that* part of you."

"I was thinking that Mr. Van Horn is undoubtedly the most envied husband in Wrightsville."

She glanced at him swiftly. "What a nice thing to say."

"I mean it."

Her glance went back to the road and he noticed that her cheek was growing pink. "Thank you . . . I don't always feel myself adequate."

"Part of your charm."

"No, seriously."

"I said it seriously."

"You did?" She was astonished.

Ellery liked her very much.

"Before we get to the house, Mr. Queen—"

"Ellery," said Ellery, "is the preferred term."

The pink deepened, and he thought she was uncomfortable.

"Of course," Ellery went on, "you can keep on calling me Mr. Queen, but I'm going to tell your husband the very first thing that I've fallen in love with you. Yes! And then I'm going to bury myself in that guest house Howard waved before my nose and work like mad substituting literature for life . . . What were you about to say, Sally?"

He wondered as he grinned at her which nerve he had touched. She was thoroughly upset; he thought for a silly moment that she was going to burst into tears.

"I'm sorry, Mrs. Van Horn," said Ellery, touching her hand. "I'm really sorry. Forgive me."

"Don't you dare," said Sally in an angry voice. "It's just me. I've got an inferiority complex a mile long. And you're very clever" —Sally hesitated, then she laughed—"Ellery."

So he laughed, too.

"You were digging."

"Shamelessly. Can't help it, Sally. Second nature. I have the soul of Peeping Tom."

"You suspect something about me."

"No, no. Just jabbing in the dark."

"And?"

Ellery said cheerfully: "I'll let you tell me, Sally."

That odd smile again. But then it faded out. "Maybe I will." And after another moment: "I have the queerest feeling I could tell you things that . . ." She broke off abruptly. He said nothing.

Finally, in an altogether different tone, Sally said: "What I began to say was . . . I wanted to talk to you about Howard before we reach home."

"About Howard?"

"I suppose he's told you — "

"About his attacks of amnesia?" said Ellery pleasantly. "Yes, he did mention them."

"I wondered whether he had." She stared straight ahead as the station wagon began to climb. "Naturally, Howard's father and I don't talk about it much. To Howard, I mean . . . Ellery, we're scared to death."

"Amnesia is commoner than people realize."

"You must have had gobs of experience with odd things like that. Ellery, do you think it's anything to — well, worry about? I mean . . . really?"

"Of course, amnesia isn't normal and the cause should be ascertained — "

"We've tried and tried." Her distress was quick and she made no attempt to hide it. "But the doctors all say he's an antagonistic subject — "

"So I gathered. He'll snap out of it, Sally. Many amnesia cases do. Well, for heaven's sake, there's the Wright place!"

"What? Oh. Does it bring back memories?"

"In droves. Sally, how are the Wrights?"

"We don't see much of them — they're the Hill crowd. You know, I suppose, that old Mr. Wright is dead?"

"John F.? Yes. I was awfully fond of him. Simply have to look up Hermione Wright while I'm here . . ."

Somehow, the subject of Howard's amnesia failed to come up again.

⧯

ELLERY HAD EXPECTED opulence, but in the Wrightsville manner, which is homely and rooted in the past. So he was completely unprepared for what he found.

The station wagon turned off North Hill Drive between two

monoliths of Vermont marble to glide over a tailored private drive lined with spaced Italian cypresses, the most beautiful English yews Ellery had ever seen, and a parade of multicolored shrubs which even to his unhorticultural eye looked like the rarer products of a rich man's nursery than the random efforts of Nature. The drive took a spiral rising course, past rock gardens and terraces, and it came to an end under the porte-cochere of a great modern house at the very top of the hill.

To the south lay the town, hugging the floor of the valley from which they had just come, a cluster of toy buildings dribbling squiffs of smoke. To the north crouched the Mahoganies. Westward, and beyond the town to the south, stretched the broad farmlands which give Wrightsville its rural complexion.

Sally switched off the ignition. "How splendid it all is."

"What?" asked Ellery. She was full of surprises.

"That's what you were just thinking. How tremendously splendid."

"Well, it is," grinned Ellery.

"Too much so."

"I didn't say that."

"I'm saying it." Again she was smiling that odd smile. "And we're both right. It is. Too much so, I mean. Oh, not that it's vulgar. It's like Dieds himself. Everything in perfect taste — but gigantic. Dieds never does things normal size."

"It's one of the most beautiful places I've ever seen," Ellery said truthfully.

"He built it for me, Ellery."

He looked at her. "Then it's not one bit too tremendously splendid."

"You're a love," she said, laughing. "Actually, it shrinks as you live in it."

"Or you expand."

"Maybe. I never told Dieds how scared I was, how lost I felt in it at first. You see, I came originally from Low Village."

Van Horn had built this magnificence for her and she came from Low Village . . .

Low Village was where the factories were. There were a few blocks of misshapen brick houses in Low Village; but most of the dwellings were rotted frame, pinched and mean, with broken porches. Occasionally one saw a house with a clean face and dainty underpinning; but only occasionally. Through Low Village ran Willow River, a narrow saffron-charged ditch fed by the refuse of the factories. The "foreigners" lived in Low Village: the Poles, the French Canadians, the Italians, the six Jewish families, the nine Negro families. Here were the whore houses and the 60-watt storefront gin mills; and on Saturday nights Wrightsville's radio cars patrolled its cobbled crooked streets restlessly.

"I was born on Polly Street," Sally said with that funny smile.

"Lucky Polly Street." Polly Street!

"You're such a dear. Oh, here's Howard."

Howard came bounding up to crush Ellery's hand and seize his suitcase. "Thought you'd never get here. What did you do, Sally, kidnap him?"

"It was the other way around," said Ellery. "Howard, I'm just mad about her."

"And I about him, How."

"Say, is this a thing already? Sal, Laura's in a tizzy about the dinner. It seems the mushrooms didn't come with the order — "

"Oh, dear, that's a catastrophe. Ellery, excuse me. How'll take you over to the guest house. I saw to everything myself, but if you want something you can't find there's an intercom in the sitting room there; it connects with the kitchen in the main house. Oh, I've got to run!"

∽

ELLERY WAS DISTURBED by Howard's appearance. He had last seen Howard on Tuesday. This was only Thursday, and Howard looked years older. There was a muddy trench under his undamaged eye, his mouth was crimped with tension, and in the bright afternoon his skin looked yellow-gray.

"Did Sally explain why I didn't meet the train?"

"Don't apologize, Howard. You were inspired."

"You really like Sal."

"Crazy about her."

"It's right here, Ellery."

The guest house was a field-stone gem in a setting of purple beeches, separated from the terrace of the main house by a circular swimming pool with a broad marble apron on which stood deck chairs and umbrella tables and a portable bar.

"You can set your typewriter up on the edge of the pool and jump in between adjectives," said Howard, "or if you want real privacy . . . Come take a look."

It was a two-room-and-bath house, done in rustic lodge style, with big fireplaces, massive hickory furniture, white goat rugs, and monk's-cloth hangings. In the sitting room stood the handsomest desk Ellery had ever laid eyes on, an emperor's affair of hickory and cowhide, with a deep-bottomed swivel chair to match.

"My desk," said Howard. "I had it hauled down from my rooms at the other house."

"Howard, you overwhelm me."

"Hell, I never use it." Howard went to the far wall. "But this is what I wanted to show you." He drew the hanging which covered the wall. And there was no wall. It was one great window

Far below, with a green shag rug between, lay Wrightsville.

"I see what you mean," murmured Ellery, sinking into the swivel chair.

"Think you can write here?"

"It'll be tough." Howard laughed, and Ellery went on casually, "Everything's all right, Howard?"

"All right? Sure."

"Don't get coy with me. No recurrence?"

Howard straightened a stag head which needed no straightening. "Why do you ask? I told you I never — "

"I thought you were looking a little brown around the edges."

"Probably a reaction from that beating." Howard turned busily. "Now the bedroom's in there. Stall shower in the bathroom. Here's a standard typewriter, portable's in the corner there, and you'll find paper, pencils, carbons, Scotch . . ."

"You'll spoil me permanently for the Spartan life of Eighty-seventh Street. Howard, this is magnificent. Really it is."

"Father designed this shack himself."

"A great man, sight unseen."

"The best," said Howard nervously. "You'll meet him at dinner."

"I'm looking forward to it."

"You don't know how he wants to meet you. Well . . ."

"Don't walk out on me, you ape."

"Oh, you'll be wanting to sluice down, maybe rest up a bit. Come on back to the house when you feel like it and I'll show you around."

And Howard was gone.

For some time Ellery teetered gently in the swivel chair.

Something had gone wrong between Tuesday and today. Very wrong indeed. And Howard didn't want him to know.

Ellery wondered if Sally Van Horn knew.

He decided that she did.

♕

HE WAS NOT surprised when he found, not Howard, but Sally waiting for him in the living room of the main house.

Sally had already changed. She was wearing a Vogueish black dinner dress with a swirl of black chiffon over an extreme *décolletage* — contradiction again, he thought, in its most attractive form.

"Oh, I know," she said, coloring. "It's indecent, isn't it?"

"I'm torn between admiration and contrition," Ellery exclaimed. "Was I to dress for dinner? Howard didn't mention it. As a matter of fact, I didn't bring dinner clothes with me."

"Dieds will fall on your neck. He hates dinner clothes. And Howard never dresses if he can help it. I only put this on because it's new and I wanted to impress you."

"I'm impressed. Believe me!" Sally laughed. "But what does your husband think?"

"Dieds? Heavens, he had it made for me."

"A great man," said Ellery reverently, and Sally laughed again, enabling him to go on without seeming to make a point of the question, "Where's Howard?"

"Up in his studio." Sally made a face. "How's in one of his moods, and when he gets that way I send him upstairs to his own quarters like the spoiled brat he is. He has the whole top floor and he can grouse there to his heart's content." She added lightly, "I'm afraid you're going to have to overlook a great deal in Howard's behavior."

"Nonsense. My own isn't recommended by Emily Post, especially when I'm working. You'll probably ask me to leave in three days. Anyway, I'm grateful. It gives me the opportunity to monopolize you."

He said it deliberately, looking her over with his admiration showing.

He had felt from the moment of their meeting at the station that Sally was an important factor in Howard's problem. Howard was emotionally involved with his father. The sudden intrusion of this desirable woman between them, monopolizing the father's interest and affections, had reacted traumatically on the son. It seemed significant that Howard's first attack of amnesia, according to his own story, had occurred on his father's wedding night. Ellery had watched very closely for signs of tension between Howard and Sally in the few moments of their meeting under the porte-cochere, and he had seen them. Howard's exaggerated spirits, his ultra-casual manner of speaking to Sally before Ellery — and his avoidance of ocular contact — were clearly defensive expressions of an inner conflict. Sally, being a woman, had been more circumspect, but Ellery had no doubt that she was aware of Howard's feelings about her. *Against her.* It suggested to Ellery that if she were a woman of a certain sort she might seek relief in a completely uninvolved male object. Was she that sort?

So he looked her over obviously.

But Sally said: "Monopolize me? Oh, dear, I'm afraid it wouldn't be for long," and smiled.

"Afraid?" murmured Ellery, smiling back.

She said levelly: "Dieds just got home. He's upstairs brushing, up, excited as he can be. Would you like a cocktail now, Ellery?"

It was an invitation to refuse. So Ellery said: "Thanks, but I'll wait for Mr. Van Horn. What a wonderful room!"

"Do you really like it? Suppose I show you around until my husband comes down."

"Love it."

Ellery liked Sally very much indeed.

The room *was* wonderful. They all were. Great rooms designed for lordly living and furnished in heroic taste by someone who loved the richness of natural woods and had a dramatic feeling for the sweep of a wall, the breadth of a fireplace, the juxtaposition of simple colors, the affinity of a window for what grew beyond . . . rooms for giants. But what Ellery found even more wonderful was their mistress. The Low Village girl moved through this splendor splendidly. As if she had been born to it.

Ellery knew Polly Street. Patricia Bradford had given him a sampling of its sour poverty during his first visit to Wrightsville, when she was still Patty Wright the sweater girl, his sociological guide to her town. Polly Street was the meanest slum in Low Village, a butchered alley of grim cold-water flats and work-stupefied factory hands. Its men were silent and beaten, its women defeminized, its adolescents hard-eyed, its babies dirty and undernourished.

And Sally came from Polly Street! Either Diedrich Van Horn was a sculptor himself, molding flesh and spirit as his son molded clay; or this girl was a chameleon, taking on the color of her surroundings by some mysterious natural process. Ellery had seen Hermione Wright walk into a room and diminish it by her grandeur; but Hermione was a lout's wench compared with Sally for sheer functional association.

෴

AND THEN DIEDRICH VAN HORN came quickly down the staircase with outstretched hand and a "Hello!" that caromed off the hand-hewn beams.

His son followed him, shuffling.

In an instant the son, the wife, the house grouped themselves around Van Horn, reshaped, reproportioned, integrated.

He was an extraordinary man in every way. Everything about him was oversize — his body, his speech, his gestures. The great room was no longer too great; he filled it, it had been built to his measure.

Van Horn was a tall man, but not so tall as he seemed. His shoulders were actually no broader than Howard's or Ellery's, but because of their enormous thickness he made the younger men look like boys. His hands were vast: muscular, wide-heeled, two heavy tools; and Ellery suddenly remembered a remark of Howard's on the *terrasse* of the Café St. Michel about his father's beginnings as a day laborer. But it was the elder Van Horn's head which fascinated Ellery. It was large and bony, of angular contour and powerful brow. The face beneath was at once the ugliest and the most attractive male face Ellery had ever seen; it struck him that Sally's remark about it had been, not a conversational whimsy, but the exact truth. What made it seem so ugly was not so much the homeliness of its individual features as their composite prominence. Nose, jaw, mouth, ears, cheekbones — all were too large. His skin was coarse and dark. In this disproportioned, unlovely composition were set two remarkable eyes, of such size, depth, brilliance, and beauty they illuminated the darkness in which they lay and transformed the whole into something singularly harmonious and pleasing.

Van Horn's voice was as big as his body, deep and sexual. And he spoke with his body as well as with his voice, not disconnectedly but in unconscious rhythm, so that one was drawn and held; it was impossible to escape him.

Shaking hands with Ellery, putting a long arm quickly around his wife, pouring cocktails, telling Howard to touch off the fire, sitting down in the biggest chair and hooking his leg over one arm — whatever Diedrich Van Horn did, whatever he said, were important and unavoidable. Simply, the master was in his house; he made no point of it — he was the point.

Seeing him in the flesh, in relation to his son and his wife, what they were became inevitable. Anything Van Horn turned his vitality upon would eventually be absorbed by it. His son would worship and emulate and, unable to resolve his worship or rival his object, would become . . . Howard. As for his wife, Van Horn would create her love out of his, and he would preserve it by engulfing it. Those he loved attached themselves to him, helplessly. They moved when he moved; they were part of his will. He reminded Ellery of the demigods of mythology, and Ellery uttered a voiceless apology to Howard for having been merely amused in Howard's *pension* studio ten years before. Howard had not been romanticizing when he had chiseled Zeus in his father's image; unconsciously, he had been sculpturing a portrait. Ellery wondered if Diedrich had the gods' vices as well as their virtues. Whatever his vices might be, they would be anything but trivial; this man was quite above pettiness. He would be just, logical, and immovable.

And Sally had been right; you didn't think of him in terms of years. Van Horn must be over sixty, Ellery thought, but he was like an Indian — you felt that his coarse black hair would neither thin nor gray, that he would never stoop or falter; you could think of him only as a force, prime and unchanging. And he would die only through some other force, like lightning.

৶

THE TALK WAS all about Ellery's novel, which was flattering but advanced nothing.

So at the first opportunity Ellery said: "Oh, by the way. Howard told me the other day about these amnesia attacks and how they've absolutely baffled him. Personally, I don't think they're alarming, but I was wondering, Mr. Van Horn, if you had any idea what causes them."

"I wish I had." Diedrich put his big hand briefly on his son's knee. "But this boy is a hard customer, Mr. Queen."

"You mean I'm like you," said Howard.

Diedrich laughed.

"I've told Ellery how unco-operative he's been with the doctors," said Sally to her husband.

"If he were a little younger, I'd whale the tar out of him," growled Van Horn. "Dearest, I should think Mr. Queen is starved. I know I am. Isn't dinner ready?"

"Oh, yes, Dieds. I was waiting for Wolfert."

"Didn't I tell you? I'm sorry, darling. Wolf is going to be late. We won't wait for him."

Sally excused herself quickly and Diedrich turned to Ellery.

"My brother has the bad habit of all bachelors. He never gives a thought to the feelings of the cook."

"Not to mention the family," remarked Howard.

"Howard and his uncle don't get along very well," chuckled Diedrich. "As I've told my son, he doesn't understand Wolfert. Wolfert is conservative —"

"Reactionary," corrected Howard.

"Careful with money —"

"Stingy as hell."

"Admittedly a hard man to beat in a business deal, but that's no crime —"

"It is the way Uncle Wolfert does it, Father."

"Son, Wolf's a perfectionist —"

"Slave driver!"

"Will you let me finish?" said Diedrich indulgently. "My brother is the kind of man, Mr. Queen, who expects instant obedience from people, but on the other hand he drives himself harder than anyone under him —"

"He doesn't make thirty-two bucks a week," said Howard. "He has something to drive himself for."

"Howard, he's done a lot for us, running the plants. Let's not be ungrateful."

"Father, you know perfectly well that if you didn't sit on him he'd institute the speed-up system, hire labor spies, abolish seniority, fire anyone with guts enough to talk back to him —"

"Why, Howard," said Ellery. "Social consciousness? You've changed since the Rue de la Huchette."

Howard snarled something, and they all laughed.

"My point is that my brother's essentially an unhappy man, Mr. Queen," Diedrich went on. "I understand him; I can't expect this pup to. Wolfert's a bundle of fears and frustrations. Afraid of living. That's what I've always tried to teach Howard: Look trouble in the eye. Don't let things fester. Do something about them. Which reminds me — if I'm to keep from wasting away I'd better do something about this dinner situation. Sally!"

Sally came in with a handsome plastic apron over her gown and her cheeks round with laughter. "It's Laura, Dieds. She's gone on strike."

"The mushrooms," exclaimed Howard. "By God, the mushrooms — and Laura's a fan of yours, Ellery. This is a crisis."

"What about the mushrooms?" demanded Diedrich.

"I thought I had it all straightened out this afternoon, darling, but now she says she *won't* serve her steak without mushroom sauce to Mr. Queen, and the mushrooms didn't come — "

"Hang the mushrooms, Sally!" roared Diedrich. "I'll fix that steak myself!"

"You'll sit here and pour another cocktail," said Sally, kissing her husband on the top of his head. "Steak is expensive."

"Strikebreaker," said Howard.

Sally gave him a look on her way out.

०৮৩

THE DINNER GOT on Ellery's nerves; and this was baffling, because it was a tasty, nourishing, and excellently served dinner in a dining room whose prodigious fireplace spoke of charcoal fires and spits in the royal manner, with a great china service designed by a gourmet to preactivate the taste buds and handmade silver utensils forged by a Vulcan of the art. Diedrich mixed his own salad in a colossal wooden bowl which could only have been hollowed out of the heart of a sequoia tree; and for dessert there was an unbelievable something which Sally called an "Austrian tart" — surely the great-grandmother of all tarts, Ellery thought innocently, since it was as vast as the centerpiece and every bite an orgy. And the talk was animated.

Still, there was an undercurrent.

There shouldn't have been. The talk was as nourishing as the food. Ellery learned a great deal about the Van Horns' beginnings. The brothers, Diedrich and Wolfert, had come to Wrightsville as boys, forty-nine years before. Their father had been a hell's-fire-and-brimstone evangelist who traveled from town to town calling down eternal damnation upon sinners.

"He meant it, too," chuckled Diedrich. "I remember how scared Wolf and I used to be when he really got going. Pa had eyes that I swear turned red when he was bellowing and a long black beard that was always beaded with spit. He used to beat the hell out of us — spare-the-rod business. He got a lot more fun out of the Old Testament than the New; I've always thought of him as Jeremiah, or old John Brown, which isn't fair to either of 'em, I guess. Pa believed in a God you could see and feel — especially feel. It wasn't till I grew up that I realized my father had created God in his own image."

Wrightsville was merely a way station on the evangelist's road to salvation, but "he's still here," said Diedrich. "Buried in Twin Hill Cemetery. He dropped dead of apoplexy during a Low Village prayer meeting."

Evangelist Van Horn's family remained in Wrightsville.

It took an unusual man, thought Ellery, to rise from Low Village to the crest of North Hill Drive and to go back to Low Village for his wife.

And why did Howard have so little to say?

"We were pretty darned near the poorest folks in town. Wolf got a job in Amos Bluefield's feed store. I couldn't take Amos or the indoors. I went to work with a road gang."

Sally was pouring from the silver coffee pot very carefully. It certainly wasn't her husband's autobiography that was troubling her; there was unmistakable evidence of her pride in Diedrich. It was Howard, halfway down the field-long board. Sally was feeling Howard's half-smile silence as he played tricks with his dessert fork and pretended to listen to his father.

"One thing led to another. Wolf was ambitious. He studied nights, correspondence courses in bookkeeping, business administration, finance. I was ambitious, too, but in a different way. I had to get

out among people. I learned about the other things from books —
read every chance I got. Still do. But it's a funny thing, Mr. Queen:
Aside from technical books, I never found a syllable outside of my
father's Bible, Shakespeare, and certain studies of the human mind
that I could apply to my own life. What good is learning something
if it doesn't help you live?"

"It's a fairly well-debated question," laughed Ellery. "Apparently,
Mr. Van Horn, you agree with Goldsmith that books teach us very
little of the world. And with Disraeli, who called books the curse
of the human race and the invention of printing the greatest mis-
fortune that ever befell man."

"Dieds doesn't really believe what he's saying," said Sally.

"But I do, dear," protested her husband.

"Blah. I wouldn't be here, sitting at this table, if not for books."

"Take that," murmured Howard.

Sally said: "Why, How, are you still with us? Let me refill your
cup."

Ellery wished they would stop.

"I had my own road-construction company at twenty-four. At
twenty-eight I owned a couple of pieces of Lower Main property
and I'd bought out old man Lloyd's — he was Frank Lloyd's grandfather — lumberyard. Wolfert was plugging away in a Boston
brokerage house by then. The World War came along and I spent
seventeen months in France. Mostly mud, as I recall it, and cooties.
Wolf wasn't in it — "

"He wouldn't be," said Howard, with the bitterness of a man who
hadn't been, either.

"Your uncle was exempted because of a weak chest, son."

"I notice it hasn't bothered him since."

"Anyway, Mr. Queen, my brother came up from Boston to run
things for me during my hitch overseas, and — "

"Big of him," commented Howard.

"Howard," said his father.

"Sorry. But you did come back to find that he'd pulled a few
miracles by way of lumber contracts for the army."

"That'll be enough, son." Diedrich said it pleasantly enough, but

Howard drew his lips in and said no more. "But Wolf *had* done pretty well, Mr. Queen, and after that we naturally stuck together. We went bust in the '29 crash together and we built it all up again together. This time it stuck, and here we are."

Ellery gathered that "here" was a rhetorical allusion both to the eagle's nest on North Hill Drive and what he had come to suspect was Van Horn's dictatorship among Wrightsville's plutocracy. And as the big man went on, from casual references Ellery found his suspicion strengthened. Apparently the Van Horns owned lumberyards, sawmills, machine shops, the jute mill, the paper mill in Slocum, and a dozen other plants scattered over the county, besides controlling interests in Wrightsville Power & Light and the Wrightsville National Bank — this last a development of John F.'s death. And Diedrich had recently bought up Frank Lloyd's *Record,* modernized it, liberalized it, and it was already a fighting power in state politics. The great upsurge in the Van Horns' fortunes seemed to have come just before, during, and since World War II.

It was all factual, unstudied, and inoffensive, and Ellery was just beginning to relax when, suddenly, Wolfert Van Horn came in.

இ

WOLFERT WAS A one-dimensional projection of his brother.

He was as tall as Diedrich, and his features were as ugly and as overlarge, but where Diedrich had breadth and thickness Wolfert was a thin crooked line. He seemed all length and no substance. There was no blood in him, no heat, no grandeur. If his brother was a sculpture, Wolfert was a scratch-pen caricature.

He came into the dining room with a sort of swoop, like a starving bird alighting on carrion. And he fixed Ellery with a frigid, avian glance.

This man gave off acerbity as Diedrich gave off sweet, warm strength. But even this was given stingily; Ellery had the ridiculous feeling that he had been granted one glimpse into hell, and then the man's elongated face split in what he intended as a smile and was instead a contortion of foxy lips and horsy dentures. He offered a hand, too, and it was all bones.

"So this is our Howard's famous friend," said Wolfert. His voice had a thin, acid bite. The way he said "our Howard" soured any hope of a *rapprochement* between them; his "famous" was a sneer, and "friend" an obscenity.

Unhappy and frustrated — yes, thought Ellery; and dangerous, too. Wolfert resented Diedrich's son; he resented Diedrich's wife; one felt he resented Diedrich. But it was interesting to observe how differently he expressed his various resentments. Howard he ignored; Sally he patronized; toward Diedrich he deferred. It was as if he despised his nephew, was jealous of his sister-in-law, and feared and hated his brother.

Also, he was a boor. He did not apologize to Sally for being late to her dinner; he ate bestially, with his elbows planted challengingly on the table; and he addressed himself exclusively to Diedrich, as if they had been alone.

"Well, you got yourself into it, Diedrich. Now I suppose you'll ask me to get you out."

"Into what, Wolfert?"

"That Art Museum business."

"Mrs. Mackenzie called?" Diedrich's eyes began to sparkle.

"After you left."

"They've accepted my offer!"

His brother grunted.

"Art Museum?" Ellery said. "When did Wrightsville acquire an Art Museum, Mr. Van Horn?"

"We haven't, yet." Diedrich was beaming. Wolfert's skeletal wrists continued to fly about.

"It's been quite a thing," Howard remarked suddenly. "Going on for months, Ellery. A group of the old biddies — Mrs. Martin, Mrs. Mackenzie, and especially — "

"Don't tell me," grinned Ellery. "And especially Emmeline DuPré."

"Say! You know the unphysical culturist of our fair city?"

"I have had that honor, Howard — numerously."

"Then you know what I mean. They're a Committee, capital C, and they rammed a Resolution, capital R, through the Selectmen, and everything was all set for Wrightsville to become the capital of all the County's Culture, capital C again, only they forgot art museums take lettuce and lots of it."

"They've had a horrible time trying to raise funds." Sally was looking at her husband in an anxious way.

Diedrich kept beaming, and Wolfert kept stuffing himself.

"But, Father." Howard sounded puzzled. "How the devil are you mixed up in it?"

"I thought," said Sally, "you'd made your contribution, Dieds." Diedrich merely chuckled.

"Oh, come *on,* darling. You've done something heroic again!"

"I'll tell you what he's done," said Wolfert in a chewy voice. "He's guaranteed to make good the deficit."

Howard stared at his father. "Why, they're hundreds of thousands of dollars short."

"Four hundred and eighty-seven thousand," snapped Wolfert Van Horn. He threw down his fork.

"They came to me yesterday," Diedrich said placatively. "Told me the fund-raising campaign was a bust. I offered to make up the deficit on one condition."

"Dieds, you didn't tell me a thing about this," wailed Sally.

"I wanted to save it, dear. And besides, I had no particular reason to think they'd accept my terms."

"What terms, father?"

"Remember, Howard, when the Museum was first suggested? You said you thought an appropriate architectural plan would be to run a pediment or frieze or whatever you call it across the entire face of the building in which there'd be life-size statues of the classical gods."

"Did I say that? I don't remember."

"Well, I do, son. So . . . that was my condition. That, and the proviso that the sculptor of those statues must be the artist who signs his stuff 'H. H. Van Horn.'"

"Oh, *Dieds,*" breathed Sally.

Wolfert got up, belched, and left the room.

Howard was extremely pale.

"Of course," drawled his father, "if you don't want the commission, son . . ."

"Want it." He was whispering.

"Or if you think you're not qualified — "

"Oh, I can do it!" said Howard. "I can do it!"

"Then I'll send Mrs. Mackenzie a certified check tomorrow."

Howard was shaking. Sally poured a fresh cup of coffee for him.

"I mean I think I can do it . . ."

"Now don't start that silliness, Howard," said Sally quickly. "What exactly would you sculpt? What gods would you plan on?"

"Well . . . the sky god, Jupiter . . ." Howard looked around; he was still dazed. "Anybody got a pencil?"

Two pencils clattered before him.

He began sketching on the cloth.

"Juno, queen of heaven — "

"There'd be Apollo, wouldn't there?" said Diedrich solemnly. "The sun god?"

"And Neptune," cried Sally. "God of the sea."

"Not to mention Pluto, god of the Lower World," said Ellery, "Diana of the chase, martial Mars, bucolic Pan — "

"Venus — Vulcan — Minerva — "

Howard stopped, looking at his father. Then he got up. Then he sat down. Then he got up again and ran out of the dining room.

Sally said, "Oh, Dieds, you fool, you've got me b-blubbing," and she ran around the table to kiss her husband.

"I know what you're thinking, Mr. Queen," said Diedrich, holding his wife's hands.

"I'm thinking," smiled Ellery, "that you ought to apply for a medical license."

"Kind of expensive medicine," chuckled Van Horn.

"Yes, but Dieds, I know it's going to work!" said Sally in a muffled voice. "Did you see Howard's face?"

"Did you see Wolfert's face?" And the big man threw back his head and roared.

WHILE SALLY WENT upstairs after Howard, Diedrich took Ellery into his study.

"I want you to see my library, Mr. Queen. Incidentally, whatever you can use in here, I mean in writing your novel — "

"That's very kind of you, Mr. Van Horn."

Ellery wandered about this kingly study, a cigar in his teeth and a brandy in his hand, looking. From the depths of a huge leather chair his host quizzically watched him.

"For a man who's found so little in books," remarked Ellery, "you've certainly done a lot of hunting."

The great shelves displayed a magnificent collection of first editions and special bindings. The titles were orthodox.

"You have some extremely valuable items here," murmured Ellery.

"A typical rich man's library, eh?" said his host dryly.

"Not at all. There are too few uncut pages."

"Sally's cut most of them."

"Oh? And, by the way, Mr. Van Horn, I promised your wife this afternoon that I'd tell you I'm completely in love with her."

Diedrich grinned. "Come right in."

"I gather it's a common complaint."

"There's something about Sally," said Diedrich thoughtfully. "Only sensitive men see it — Here, let me refill your glass."

But Ellery was staring at one of the shelves.

"I told you I was a fan of yours," said Diedrich Van Horn.

"Mr. Van Horn, I'm thrown. You have them all."

"And these I've read."

"Well! There's hardly anything an author won't do to repay this sort of kindness. Anybody I can murder for you?"

"I'll tell you a secret, Mr. Queen," said his host. "When Howard told me he'd asked you up here — and to work on a novel — I was as excited as a kid. I've read every book you ever wrote, I've followed your career in the papers, and the greatest regret of my life was that during your two visits to Wrightsville I couldn't get to meet you. The first time — when you stayed with the Wrights — I was in Washington most of the time hunting war contracts. The second time — when you were here on that Fox business — I was in Washington again, this time by request of — well, it doesn't matter. But if that's not patriotism, I don't know what is."

"And if this isn't flattery — "

"Not a bit of it. Ask Sally. And incidentally," smiled Diedrich, "you may have fooled Wrightsville in both those cases, but you didn't fool me."

"Fool you?"

"I followed the Haight and Fox cases pretty closely."

"I failed in both of them."

"Did you?"

Diedrich grinned at Ellery. Ellery grinned back.

"I'm afraid I did."

"Not a chance. I told you, I'm a Queen expert. Shall I tell you what you did?"

"I've told *you*."

"I hesitate to call my honored guest a cockeyed liar," chuckled Diedrich, "but you solved the murder of Rosemary Haight — and it wasn't young Jim, even though he did pull that fool stunt of making a break at Nora's funeral and running that newspaper woman's car — what was her name? — off the road in his escape. You were protecting somebody, Mr. Queen. You took the rap."

"That wouldn't give me a very good character, would it?"

"Depends. On whom you were protecting. And why. The mere fact that you did a thing like that — you being what you are — is a clue."

"Clue to what, Mr. Van Horn?"

"I don't know. I've beaten my brains out about it for years. Mysteries bother me. I guess that's why I'm such a sucker for them."

"You have my type of mind," remarked Ellery. "Labyrinthine. But go on."

"Well, I'd bet a whole lot that Jessica Fox didn't commit suicide, either. She was murdered, Mr. Queen, and you proved it, and what's more you proved who murdered her . . . I *think* . . . and you withheld the truth about that, too, for I suppose the same reason."

"Mr. Van Horn, you should have been a writer."

"What I don't get in the Fox case — what I didn't get in the Haight case, for that matter — is where the truth *might* lie. I know all the people involved in both cases, and I'd swear none of 'em's the criminal type."

"Doesn't that answer your question? Things were what they seemed and I failed to establish otherwise."

Diedrich was looking at him through the smoke of his cigar. Ellery looked back, politely. Then Diedrich laughed.

"You win. I won't ask you to violate any confidences. But I did want to establish my right to be known as the number one Queen fan of Wrightsville."

"I won't even react to that one," murmured Ellery, "on advice of counsel."

Diedrich nodded with enjoyment, pulling on his cigar. "Oh, and just to reassure you, you're not going to be pestered while you're here. I want you to use this house as if it were your own. Please don't stand on the slightest ceremony. If you don't feel like eating with us at any time, just tell Sally and she'll have Laura or Eileen serve you in the guest house. We have four cars and you're welcome to use any one of them if you feel like getting away from us, or running over to the public library, or just running."

"This is really handsome of you, Mr. Van Horn."

"Selfish. I want to be able to brag that your book was written on Van Horn property. And if we bother you, Mr. Queen, it'll be a bad book and then I shan't have so much to brag about. D'ye see?"

While Ellery was laughing, Sally came in, straight-arming a sheepish Howard before her. Howard was loaded down with reference books and his bruised face was alive again.

For the remainder of the evening they sat listening to his enthusiastic plans for recreating the gods of ancient Rome.

∾

It was after midnight when Ellery left the main house to return to the cottage.

Howard walked him out to the terrace, and they had a few minutes alone together.

The moon was being coy and beyond the terrace lay overlapping darknesses. But someone had turned the lights on in the guest house and it poked fingers into the garden like a woman exploring her hair. A breeze played on the invisible trees and overhead the stars stirred, as if they were cold.

They stood side by side smoking cigarets in silence.

Finally Howard said: "Ellery, what do you think?"

"About what, Howard?"

"About this Art Museum deal."

"What do I think?"

"You don't go for paternalism, do you?"

"Paternalism?"

"Father buying me a museum to make sculptures for."

"That's bothering you?"

"Yes!"

"Howard." Ellery paused to grope for the right words; talking to Howard called for a diplomat's tact. "Cellini's saltcellar was made possible by Francis the First. In a very real sense Pope Julius was every bit as important to the Sistine ceiling, the *Moses* in Vincoli, and the *Slaves* at the Louvre, as Michelangelo. Shakespeare had his Southampton, Beethoven his Count Waldstein, van Gogh his brother Théo."

"You put me in distinguished company." Howard stared into the gardens. "Maybe it's because he's my father."

"Etymologically, *patron* and *father* come from the same womb."

"Don't be cute. You know what I mean."

"Do you feel," asked Ellery, "that if you weren't Diedrich Van Horn's son, you wouldn't get this commission?"

"That's it. It would be put on the usual competitive basis—"

"Howard. I saw enough of your work in Paris to tell me you have considerable talent. In ten years you can't help but have grown as an artist. But let's assume you're no good—no good at all. As long as we're discussing this frankly . . . What's wrong with the patronage system in art is that too often the creation of the art work depends on the whim of the patron. But when the whim is there, a positive good results."

"You mean if my sculpture is good."

"Even if your sculpture is not so good. Hasn't it occurred to you that unless you do those statues, your father won't come across with those fantastic funds necessary to make the Art Museum a reality? It's brutal, certainly; but we live in a brutal world. You're making it possible for Wrightsville to acquire an important cultural institution. That's something to work for. I hope it doesn't sound stuffy, Howard, but the fact is your job is to do the finest sculpture you're capable of — not so much for your own sake or your father's as for the sake of the community. And if you should pull off a really bang-up job, why, the fact that you're home talent will give the project an added and very strong local appeal."

Howard was silent.

Ellery lit another cigaret, fervently hoping his argument sounded more convincing than it felt.

Finally, Howard laughed. "There's a flaw in that somewhere, but I'm damned if I can find it. It sounds good, anyway. I'll try to keep it in mind." And then he said, in a different way, "Thanks, Ellery."

He turned to go into the house.

"Howard."

"What?"

"How are you feeling?"

Howard stood there. Then he turned back, patting his swollen eye. "I'm just beginning to appreciate how smart my old man is. This Art Museum business drove all that out of my head! I'm feeling fine."

"Still want me to hang around?"

"You're not thinking of leaving!"

"I simply wanted to find out how you feel about it."

"For God's sake, stay!"

"Of course. Incidentally, there are certain disadvantages to the housing arrangement. You on the top floor of the main house, me over there at the cottage."

"You mean in case I get another attack?"

"Yes."

"Why not bunk with me? I have the whole top floor — "

"Then I wouldn't have the privacy I need for that blamed novel, Howard. I'll be doing a lot of night work. Wish I didn't have that contract commitment . . . Do the attacks often come in the middle of the night?"

"No. As a matter of fact, I can't recall a single one coming on while I was asleep."

"Then my job is not to turn in myself until you're snoring. That simplifies it. During the day I'll work where I can keep an eye on the front door here. At night I won't go to bed until I'm reasonably certain you're in dreamland. Is that your bedroom? Where the light is, up on the top floor?"

"No, that's the big window of my studio. My bedroom is to the right of that. It's dark now."

Ellery nodded. "Go to bed."

But Howard did not move. He was slightly turned away and his face was in shadow.

"Something else on your mind, Howard?"

Howard stirred, but no sound came from him.

"Then hit the sack, slug. Don't you know I can't until you do?"

"Good night," said Howard in a very odd voice.

"Good night, Howard."

Ellery waited until the front door closed. Then he crossed the terrace and slowly made his way around the star-specked pool to the cottage.

⌇

HE TURNED OFF the lights in the cottage, came out to sit down on the porch. He sat smoking his pipe in the dark.

Apparently Diedrich and Sally had gone to bed: the second floor of the main house showed no lights. And after a moment the light in Howard's studio went out. Another moment, and a window to the right lit up. Five minutes later that window, too, darkened. So Howard had turned in.

Ellery sat there for a long time. Howard would not fall asleep easily.

What was bothering Howard today, tonight? It wasn't the amnesia. It was something new, or a fresh development or something old; something which had occurred in the last two days. Whom did it involve? Diedrich? Sally? Wolfert? Or someone Ellery had not met?

The strain between Howard and Sally might be part of it. But there were other stresses. Between Howard and his unlovely uncle. Or the older stress, the stress of love, between Howard and his father.

The dark big house faced him imperturbably.

Dark and big.

It was a big house to hate in. Or to love in.

It came suddenly to Ellery that this was something re-experienced, this sitting in the Wrightsville night puzzling over a problem in Wrightsville relationships. The night he had rocked on the porch of the Haight cottage after Lola and Patty Wright had gone . . . the night he had sat in the slide swing on the porch of Talbot Fox's house . . . both down the Hill there, somewhere in the darker darkness. But he'd had his teeth into something then. This . . . this was like trying to take a bite out of the darkness itself.

Maybe there was nothing. Maybe there was just Howard's amnesia, for clear and unmysterious cause. And all the rest imagination.

Ellery was about to knock out his pipe and go in to bed when his hand stopped in mid-air and every muscle stiffened with alarm.

Something had moved out there.

His eyes had become accustomed to the darkness and he could make out degrees of it. It had dimensions now, gray spots and dappled spots, jigsaw pieces of the night.

Something had moved in that lighter fragment, in the gardens beyond the pool, just short of the ghostly blue spruce.

He was positive no one had come out of the house. So it could not be Howard. It must have been someone there all the time — all the time he and Howard had stood on the terrace talking, all the time he had sat here alone before the cottage, smoking and thinking.

He strained, squinting, trying to get through the shadows.

He remembered now that there was a marble garden seat on that spot.

With this he tried to take apart the darkness. But the more he looked, the less he saw.

He was about to call out when a shower of light fell on the pool and the garden. The cloud had backed away from the moon.

Something was on the garden seat. A great lump of a thing that spilled over to the ground.

As his eyes readjusted themselves, he saw what it was.

It was a figure draped in cloths, or a cloak; a female figure, to judge from the fullness around the legs.

It was still now.

For a moment he recognized it. It was Saint-Gaudens's sculpture of *Death*. The seated female with swathing garments, even her head covered and a face in darkness with one arm showing, the hand supporting the chin.

But then the resemblance dissolved in shifting draperies as the moonlight struck life from the stone. And the figure, incredibly, rose, and it became an old, a very old, woman.

She was so old that her back described the semicircle of an angry cat. She began to move, and her movements were secretive, with something ancient in them.

And as she inched along, hovering over the earth, sounds came out of her. They were thin, faint sounds, with the haunting quality of whispers drifting on the wind.

"*Yea, though I walk through the valley of the shadow of death . . .*"

And then she vanished.

Utterly.

One moment she was there. The next she was not.

Ellery actually rubbed his eyes. But when he looked again, there was still nothing to be seen. And then another cloud concealed the moon.

He cried out: "Who is that?"

Nothing answered.

A trick of the night. There'd been nothing there. And the words he had "heard" had been the echo of some racial memory in his brain. Talk of sculpture . . . the still deathly blackness of the house . . . concentrated thought . . . self-hypnosis . . .

Because he was Ellery, he felt his way around the pool toward the now-invisible garden seat.

He placed his hand on it, palm down.

The stone was warm.

∽

ELLERY WENT BACK to the cottage, put the light on, rummaged in his suitcase, found his flashlight, and returned quickly to the garden.

He found the bush she had stepped behind an instant before the moon went out.

But nothing else.

She was gone, and there was no answer anywhere. He searched the grounds for a half-hour.

The Third Day

SALLY'S VOICE WAS so taut with tension that he thought Howard had had another attack.

"Ellery! Are you up?"

"Sally. Something wrong? Howard?"

"Heavens, no. I took the liberty of walking in. I hope you don't mind." Her laugh was pitched too high. "I've brought you your breakfast."

He washed quickly and when he came out into the living room in his robe he found Sally striding up and down, smoking a cigaret jerkily. She threw it immediately into the fireplace, snatched the lid off a large silver tray.

"Sally, you're a darling. But this wasn't at all necessary."

"If you're anything like Dieds and Howard, you like a hot breakfast the first thing. Coffee?"

She was very nervous. She kept chattering.

"I know I'm awful to do this. Your first morning here. But I didn't think you'd mind. Dieds has been gone for hours, and Wolfert. I thought if you didn't mind wasting your time sleeping so late, you wouldn't mind my barging in on you with coffee and ham and eggs and toast. I know how anxious you must be to get to your novel. I promise I shan't make this a habit. After all, Dieds did lay the law down about your not being disturbed and I'm a dutiful wife . . ."

Her hands were trembling.

"It's all right, Sally. I wouldn't have made a start for hours. You don't know how many things a writer has to do before he can recapture the slimy thread of his story. Like cleaning his finger-nails, reading the morning newspaper . . ."

"That makes me feel better." She tried to smile.

"Have a cup of this coffee. It'll make you feel better still."

She accepted the second cup which had been on the tray. He had noticed its presence at once.

"I was hoping you'd ask me, Ellery." Too light.

"Sally, what's the matter?"

"I was hoping you'd ask me that, too."

She set her cup down; her hands were really shaking badly. Ellery lit a cigaret and got up and walked around the table and put the cigaret between her lips.

"Lean back. Close your eyes, if you'd like."

"No. Not here."

"Then where?"

"Anywhere but here."

"If you'll wait till I dress—"

Her face was haggard; something hurt. "Ellery, I don't want to take you away from your work. It isn't right."

"You wait, Sally."

"I wouldn't have dreamed of doing this if—"

"Now stop it. I'll be out in three minutes."

Howard said from the doorway: "So you went to him after all."

Sally twisted in the chair, her hand on the back. She was so pale Ellery thought she was going to faint.

Howard's cheeks were gray.

Ellery said calmly, "Whatever it is, Howard, I'd say offhand Sally was right to come to me, and you're wrong to try to hold her back."

The swollen part of Howard's lower lip gave his mouth a bitter twist.

"Okay, Ellery. Get your clothes on."

WHEN ELLERY CAME out of the cottage, he saw a new convertible drawn up under the porte-cochere of the main house. Sally was at the wheel. Howard was just stowing a hamper away.

Ellery walked over to them. Sally was wearing a deer-brown suède suit and she had bound her hair with a silk scarf, turban-fashion; she had made up rather heavily; her cheeks had color.

She avoided his eyes.

Howard seemed most particular about the hamper. He didn't look up until Ellery was seated beside Sally. Then he squeezed in beside Ellery and Sally started the car.

"What's the hamper for?" Ellery asked cheerfully.

"I had Laura put up a picnic lunch," said Sally, very busy shifting gears.

Howard laughed. "Why don't you tell him why? It's so if anybody calls up, the help can say we've gone on a picnic. See?"

"Yes," said Sally in a very low voice, "I'm getting quite clever at this."

She took the curves of the winding drive angrily. At the exit to North Hill Drive she turned left.

"Where are we going, Sally? I've never been in this direction."

"I thought we'd run up to Quetonokis Lake. It's in the foothills of the Mahoganies there."

"Good place for a picnic," commented Howard.

Sally looked at him then, and he flushed.

"I've taken along some coats," he said gruffly. "It's kind of chilly up there this time of year."

And after that there was no conversation whatever, and Ellery was grateful.

∽

UNDER ORDINARY CIRCUMSTANCES the drive north would have been a jaunt.

The country between Wrightsville and the Mahoganies has flexible contours — a hilly land with life of its own, stone fences running and little crooked bridges named Sheep Run and Indian Wash and McComber's Creek rattling over moving water and the heave of green, clover-flecked, overlapping meadowlands, like deep-sea swells, in which schools of cows shift placidly, feeding. Here are the great dairies of the state; Ellery saw hospital-like barns, the flash of stainless steel vats, slow herds grazing, all the way up to the foothills.

And the road was a clean wake foaming toward the mountains.

But they darkened this road with their cargo of secrets; it was a sinful cargo, piratical and contraband, of that Ellery had no doubt.

The character of the country changed as the convertible climbed. Scrub pine appeared, outcroppings of granite. The cows became sheep. Then the sheep disappeared, and the fences, and there were lone stands of trees, and then clumps, and then patches of woods, and finally a great and continuing forest. The sky was nearer here, a cold clear blue, like a different sea, with clouds sailing it swiftly. And the air was sharp; it had teeth.

They rolled through the woods past immense dark glens where the sun never came under great pine and spruce and hemlock, and everywhere were the granite bones of the mountain. A giant country; and it made Ellery think of Diedrich and he wondered if some relentless harmony of subject and mood had not made Sally choose this place for her confession.

And there was Quetonokis Lake, a blue wound in the mountain's flank, stanched by its green hair, and lying quietly.

Sally ran the car up to a moss-sprayed boulder on the lake's edge, turned off the ignition.

There was laurel all about, sumac, and the spicy breath of pine. Birds flew off, settled on a log in the lake. They poised for flight.

Ellery said: "Well?" and they rose.

He offered a cigaret to Sally but she shook her head; her gloved hands were still on the wheel, gripping it. Ellery glanced at Howard; but Howard stared at the lake.

"Well?" said Ellery again. He put the cigarets back into his pocket.

"Ellery." It came out crookedly, and Sally wet her lips to try again. "I want you to know this is all my doing. Howard was dead against it. We've been arguing in corners and in snatches for two days. Ever since Wednesday, Ellery."

"Tell me about it."

"Now that we're here I don't know how to begin." She was not looking at Howard, but she stopped and waited.

Howard said nothing.

"Howard. May I tell Ellery about . . . you? First?"

Ellery could feel the wood in Howard. His body was as rigid as the trees. And suddenly it came to Ellery that what he was about to hear was at least one root of Howard's great trouble. Perhaps the biggest root, the root that plunged deepest into his neurosis.

Sally began to cry.

Howard slumped in the leather seat and his lips loosened under the pull of his misery. "Don't do that, Sally. I'll tell him myself. Just don't do that!"

"I'm sorry." Sally fumbled in her bag for a handkerchief. She said, muffled: "It won't happen again."

And Howard turned to Ellery and said, quickly, as if to get it over with: "I'm not Diedrich's son."

∽

"No ONE KNOWS it outside our family," Howard said. "Father told Sally when they got married. But Sally's the only outsider." His lip curled. "Except me, of course."

"Who are you?" asked Ellery, as if it were the most ordinary question in the world.

"I don't know. Nobody knows."

"Foundling?"

"Corny, isn't it? It's supposed to have gone out with Horatio Alger. But it's still happening. I'm it. And let me tell you something: When it happens to you, it's the most wonderfully new thing in the world. It never happened before to anybody. And you pray to God it'll never happen to anybody again."

This was said matter-of-factly, almost impatiently, as if it were the least important of the elements of the problem. By which Ellery knew that it was the most deeply imbedded.

"I was an infant. Only a few days old. In the traditional way I was left on the Van Horn doorstep, in a cheap clothesbasket. There was a piece of paper pinned to my blanket with the date of my birth on it — just the birth date, no other message. The basket's up in the attic somewhere; Father won't part with it." Howard laughed.

Sally said: "It's such a tiny basket."

Howard laughed.

"And there was no clue?" Ellery asked.

"No."

"How about the basket, the blanket, the piece of paper?"

"The basket and the blanket were of very cheap quality — standard stuff, Father says; he found that they were sold everywhere in town. The paper was just a piece torn off a sack."

"Was your father married?"

"He was a bachelor. He didn't marry till he married Sally, a few years ago . . . It was just before the First War," Howard said, looking at the birds, who had settled back on the log again. "How Father finagled it I don't know, but he managed somehow to get a court order of adoption — I guess they weren't as strict about adoptions in those days. He got a first-class nurse to take care of me; I suppose that helped. Anyway, he gave me the name of Howard Hendrik Van Horn — Howard after his father, the old fire-eater, and Hendrik after his grandfather. And then the War came along and he got Wolfert down from Boston and went off.

"Wolfert wasn't very nice to me," said Howard with another laugh. "I seem to remember him walloping me all over the place, and the nurse crying and arguing with him. She stuck only till Father got back from the trenches. After that, there was another nurse. Old Nanny. Her name was Gert, but I always called her Nanny. Original, wasn't I? She died six years ago . . . Of course, there were tutors afterward, when father got more prosperous. All I can remember are giants, lots of giants. Their big faces came and went.

"I didn't know I was somebody else till I was five. Dear Uncle Wolf told me."

Howard paused. He took out a handkerchief and wiped the back of his neck and then he put the handkerchief away and went on.

"I asked Father that night what it meant, if he was going to send me away, and he picked me up and kissed me and I guess he explained it all to me and reassured me, but for years afterward I went around afraid somebody would come and take me away. Every time I saw a strange face coming I'd hide.

"But I'm getting away from the point. There was a big row that night between Father and Uncle Wolfert. About Wolfert's having told me I'd come in a basket out of nowhere and that Father wasn't my father. I was supposed to be in bed asleep, but I remember hearing angry voices and creeping down the stairs and sneaking a look through a pair of . . . portieres, I guess they were. Father was madder than I've ever seen him since. He was yelling that he'd intended to tell me himself, when I was a few years older, that it was his job and he'd have known how to do it right, and what did Wolfert mean by scaring the hell out of me when his back was turned? Uncle Wolfert said something — something pretty nasty, I guess — because Father's face got like a rock and he made a fist . . . you know how big his hand is, but it looked to me then like one of those old Civil War cannon balls piled up at the Soldiers' Monument in Pine Grove . . . made a fist and hit Wolfert with it smack in the mouth."

Howard laughed once more.

"I can still see Wolfert's head snapping back on his skinny neck and a flock of teeth spraying out of his mouth, the way they used to do it in the slapstick comedies in the movies when I was a kid, only these were real teeth. His jaw was broken and he was in the hospital for six weeks; they thought for a while an important nerve or vertebra or something in his neck had been injured and that he'd be paralyzed for life or die. It wasn't, and he didn't, but father's never hit anybody since."

And so Diedrich was carrying his own burden of guilt around, which his brother had doubtless been exploiting for twenty-five years. But this was relatively trivial; even the strong carry such guilt feelings with them; the important part of the story was

Howard's part, and what it explained about his neurosis. The powerful attachment between Howard and Diedrich had been born out of Howard's fears concerning his origin, fears bred by Wolfert and fixed in Howard's unconscious mind traumatically by the violence of the whole episode. Knowing he was not Diedrich's child, and not knowing whose child he was, Howard clung to Diedrich and made of him the colossal father-image he was later to hammer out of stone, the symbol of his security and the bridge between him and the hostile world. So that when Sally came along, and the father married her . . .

"The only reason any of this is important," Howard was saying earnestly, "is that, if you're to understand what happened later, and the spot we're in, you've got to know what Father means to me, Ellery."

"I think I know," said Ellery, "what your father means to you."

"You can't possibly. Everything I am, everything I have, I owe to him. Even my name! He took me in. He provided the finest of care, at times when it meant real sacrifices. And always with his brother needling him and telling him what a sucker he was. He gave me an education. He's encouraged my yen to be a sculptor, from the time when I messed around with those kid modeling-clay sets. He sent me abroad. He took me back in. He's made it possible for me to continue my work without economic pressure. I'm one of his three heirs. And he's never once thrown anything up to me, about my failure to produce anything recognizably successful, about my laziness at times . . . anything. You yourself saw what he did last night — bought me a museum — so I'd have a practical immediate outlet for whatever talent I possess. If I were Judas I couldn't hurt him or let him down. I mean, I wouldn't want to. He's my reason for being. I owe him everything."

"Don't you mean, Howard," said Ellery with a smile, "that he's acted exactly like what he is — your father?"

Howard said angrily: "I didn't expect you to understand it," and he jumped out of the car, walked over to the boulder, and sat down on the moss to kick at a stone, miss it, pick it up, flip it at the log.

The birds rose again.

"That's Howard's part of the story," said Sally. "Now let me tell you mine."

ERORY MOVED OVER in the seat and Sally turned around and tucked her legs under her. This time she accepted a cigaret. She smoked for a moment, her left arm resting on the wheel. It was as if she were groping for the sesame word. Howard glanced over at her, and then he glanced away.

"My name was Sara Mason," she began hesitantly. "Sara without the *h*. Mama was very particular about that. She'd seen it spelled that way in the *Record* and she thought it had elegance . . . It's Dieds who started calling me Sally," she smiled faintly, "among other things.

"My father worked in the jute mill. Jute and shoddy. I don't know if you know what a jute mill can be like. Before Dieds bought it it was a hellhole. Dieds made it into something decent. It's very successful now — the jute's used for so many things, even goes into phonograph records, I think — or is it the shoddy? I never can remember. Anyway, Dieds took the whole place over and reorganized it. One of the first things he did was to fire my father."

Sally looked up. "Papa was just no good. The job he had in the mill was one that's usually given to girls — unskilled, not very hard. But he couldn't make good at that, either. He'd been everything — he'd had a pretty good education — and he'd been a failure at everything. He drank, and when he drank he'd beat up Mom. He never beat me — he didn't get the chance. I learned very early how to stay out of his way." She smiled the same faint smile. "I'm the prize example of Darwin's theory. I had a raft of sisters and brothers, but I'm the only one who survived. The others died in infancy and early childhood. I imagine I'd have died, too, if Papa hadn't died first. And Mom."

"Oh," said Ellery.

"They died a few months after Papa lost his job at the mill. He never did get another job. One morning he was found in Willow River. They said he'd blundered in the night before, drunk, and just drowned. Two days later, Mama was taken to Wrightsville Hospital to be delivered of her umpteenth baby, prematurely. The baby was born dead and Mom died, too. I was nine years old."

It was a typical Polly Street case history, Ellery reflected. But he was beginning to be puzzled. In none of this was the germ of the Sally beside him. Sociologically, there are few miracles. How had grubby little Sara Mason become Sally Van Horn?

She smiled again. "It's really no mystery, Ellery."

"You're a very annoying female," snapped Ellery. "Well, how?"

"Dieds. I was a minor, penniless, the only relatives I had were one in New Jersey, a cousin of Mom's, and the other in Cincinnati, a brother of Papa's; and they didn't want me. Well, they were both very poor, with large families; I can't blame them. I was headed for the Slocum Orphanage as a ward of the County when Dieds heard about me. He was a trustee of the hospital and he was told about Mom's dying and leaving a brat . . .

"He'd never seen me. But when he found out who I was — the orphan of Matt Mason, whom he'd fired . . . I used to ask him why he bothered. Dieds would always laugh and say it was love at first sight. His first sight of me was the day he came to see me at Mrs. Plaskow's house on Polly Street; she was the neighbor who took me in. I can still see Mrs. Plaskow, a big, stout, motherly woman with gold-rimmed eyeglasses. It was a Friday night and Mrs. Plaskow was lighting candles — they were Jews, and I remember she explained to me that the Jews lit candles on Friday nights because sundown Friday was the beginning of the Jewish sabbath and had been for thousands of years — and I remember being terribly impressed when there was a knock at the door and little Philly Plaskow opened it and there was this huge man looking around at the candles and at the kids and saying, 'Which one is the little girl whose mother died?' Love at first sight!" Sally smiled again, a little secretively. "I was a dirty, frightened brat with skinny arms and legs and a chest you could have played chopsticks on. I was so frightened I fought back. An alley cat." This time she laughed. "I think that's what did it. He tried to take me on his lap and I battled him off — scratched his face, kicked his shins — while

Mrs. Plaskow started to cry and the Plaskow kids all danced around screaming at me . . ." Her expression changed. "I remember how strong he was, how big and warm and wonderful-smelling . . . smelling even more wonderful than the fresh-baked bread on the kitchen table. And I found myself shrieking and wetting his tie while he kept stroking my hair and talking quietly to me. Dieds is a fighter himself. He goes for fighters."

Howard got up and came over to the car and said hoarsely: "Let's get on with this, shall we?"

"Yes, Howard," said Sally; and then she said: "Well, he made an arrangement with the County authorities. He set up a fund for me — I don't have to go into the details. I was brought up in private schools, with kind and understanding and progressive people, the right private schools. On Dieds's money. They were schools in other states. Eventually I went to Sarah Lawrence. Abroad. I'd become interested in sociology." She said lightly: "I have a couple of degrees, and I did some rather interesting work in New York and Chicago. But I always wanted to come back to Wrightsville and work here —"

"In Polly Street."

"In all the Polly Streets. And that's what I did. I'm still doing it, in fact. We have staffs of experienced people now, day schools, clinics, a complete social service program. Chiefly on Dieds's money. Naturally, I saw a great deal of him . . ."

"He must have been very proud of you," murmured Ellery.

"I suppose it started out that way, but . . . then he fell in love with me.

"I don't think I can quite describe how I felt when he told me. Dieds had always corresponded with me. He'd made flying trips to see me when I was at school. I'd never thought of him as a father . . . more like a big strong protecting angel of a very masculine type. Would it sound awfully silly if I said, 'like a god'?"

"No," said Ellery.

"I'd kept every letter he ever wrote me. I had snapshots of him tucked away in hiding places. At Christmas I'd get enormous boxes of the most wonderful things. On my birthday there was always something exquisite — Dieds has fantastically good taste, almost a woman's sense of the unusual. And at Easter, gobs and gobs of flowers. He was everything to me, everything that was good, kind, strong, and oh, a comfort, a place to put your head when you were lonely. Even when he wasn't there.

"And I'd got to know other things about him: that only a year or so after he'd established that big fund that was to care for me and educate me, for instance, he went broke. In the 1929 market collapse. It wasn't an irrevocable trust; he could have taken the money and used it — heaven knows he needed it. But he wouldn't touch it. Things like that.

"When he asked me to marry him, my heart flopped right up into my mouth. I got actually dizzy. It was too much. Too terribly much. There was so much . . . much feeling in me that I felt I couldn't stand it. Physically. All the years of adoring, of worshiping, and now this."

Sally stopped and then she said, very low: "I said yes and cried for two hours in his arms."

Suddenly she looked into Ellery's eyes.

"You've got to realize, really understand, that Diedrich created me. Whatever I am, he shaped with his hands. It wasn't just money and opportunities. He took a creative interest in my progress. He directed my schooling. His letters were wise and adult and terribly right. He was my friend and my teacher and my confessor, chiefly by remote control, but the lessons sank in somehow that way, maybe more than they'd have done if I'd seen him frequently. He was so vital to me that in my own letters to him I told him things other girls hesitate to tell their own mothers. I never found Dieds wanting. He was always there with just the right word, the right touch, the right gesture.

"If not for Dieds," said Sally, "I'd be a Low Village slattern married to a struggling factory hand trying to bring up a brood of undernourished kids — uneducated, ignorant, dried up, full of pain, and without hope."

She shivered suddenly, and Howard reached into the back of the car, fished out a camel's-hair coat, and came quickly around to put the coat about Sally's shoulders. He let his hand remain on her shoulder and to Ellery's amazement her hand came up and rested on his, tightening, tensing the leather across her knuckles.

"And then," said Sally, looking steadily into Ellery's eyes, "and then I fell in love with Howard and Howard fell in love with me."

ᕬᕬ

THE PHRASE, *They're in love,* kept repeating itself stupidly in his head.

But then order came, and things dropped magically into place, and Ellery was astounded only by his own blindness. He had been wholly unprepared for this because he had been so sure he understood the nature of Howard's neurosis. His analysis had convinced him that Howard hated Sally, hated her because she had stolen Howard's father-image. What he had failed to take into account, obviously, was the cunning and complex logic of the unconscious process. He saw now that *it was precisely because Howard hated Sally that he had fallen in love with her.* She had come between him and his father. By falling in love with her, he took her away from his father — *not in order to have Sally, but to regain Diedrich.* To regain Diedrich, and possibly to punish him.

Ellery knew that Howard and Sally knew nothing of this. Consciously, Howard loved; consciously, he suffered the torments of the guilt which was the consequence of his love. It was probably because of this guilt that Howard had concealed, concealed; concealed his relationship with his father's wife even as he begged Ellery to come to Wrightsville to help him; tried to conceal it again when Sally herself wanted to come to Ellery with the truth. If not for Sally, Howard would never have come.

That's the way it looks to me, Ellery thought, *and it makes sense, but this is over my depth; I can't fish in these waters, I haven't the equipment. I must try to get Howard receptive to a first-class psychiatrist, lead him there by the hand, and then go home and forget the whole involved business. I mustn't tamper, I mustn't tamper, I may do Howard serious injury.*

Sally's was a different, simpler case. She loved Howard, not as a roundabout means to an antipathetic emotional end, but for himself. Or perhaps despite himself. But if her case was simpler, the remedy there was even more difficult. Happiness with Howard was out of the question; his love was spurious; with the accomplishment of its object the counterfeit would reveal itself for what it was. And yet . . . How far had it gone?

Ellery asked: "How far has this gone?"

He was angry.

Howard said: "Too far."

∽

"I'LL TELL IT, Howard," said Sally.

Howard said again: "Too far," and he sounded hysterical.

"We'll both tell it," said Sally quietly.

His lips worked and he half turned away.

"But I'll start, Howard. Ellery, it happened this past April. Dieds had flown down to New York to see his lawyers about something, on business . . ."

Sally had found herself irritatingly restless. Diedrich would be gone for several days. There was work she might have done in Low Village, but unaccountably she found no taste for it that day. And they really wouldn't miss her . . .

On impulse Sally had decided to jump into her car and drive up to the Van Horn lodge.

The lodge was higher in the Mahoganies, near Lake Pharisee, in summer a favorite vacation ground for the well-to-do. But in April it was deserted. There would be no deliveries, but food supplies were kept in the lodge the year round, stored in quick-freeze lockers. She could stop on the way and buy bread and milk for a couple of days. It would be cold, but there was always a mountain of cut firewood; and the fireplaces were wonderful.

"I'd felt the need to be alone. Wolfert was always grim company. Howard was . . . Well, I wanted to get off by myself. I told them I was driving into Boston to do some shopping. I didn't want anyone to know where I was going. Laura and Eileen were there to take care of them . . ."

Sally had driven off, fast.

Howard said huskily: "I saw Sally leave. I'd been messing around in the studio, but . . . Well, father's going away, and Sally's leaving me alone with Wolfert . . . I felt I had to get away, too. I suddenly thought," Howard said, "of the lodge."

Sally had just carried an armful of firewood into the lodge when Howard filled the doorway. Around them was the silence of the woods. They had stared at each other for a long, long time. Then Howard had crossed the room, and Sally had dropped the logs, and he had taken her in his arms.

"I don't remember what possessed me," Howard mumbled. "How it happened. What I was thinking. If I was thinking anything at all. All I knew was that she was there, and I was there, and that I had to put my arms around her. But when I did, I knew I loved her. I'd loved her for years, I just knew that."

Did you, Howard?

"I knew it was Fate that took me to the lodge when I thought all the time she was on the road to Boston."

Not Fate, Howard.

Sally said: "I was sick," and she was sick as she said it. "I was sick and I was well, too, more alive than I'd ever been in my life-time. Everything was spinning around, the cabin, the mountain, the world. I closed my eyes and thought, 'I've known this for years. For years.' I knew then that I'd never loved Diedrich, not really, not the way I loved Howard. I'd mistaken gratitude, tremendous feelings of indebtedness, hero worship, for love. I knew it then, in Howard's arms, for the first time. I was frightened, and I was happy. I wanted to die, and I wanted to live."

"And so," said Ellery dryly, "you lived."

"Don't blame her!" cried Howard. "It was my fault. When I saw her I should have turned and run like a rabbit. I made the break. I wore her down. I was the one who made the love, who kissed her eyes, stopped her mouth, carried her into the bedroom."

Now we show the wound, now we pour salt on it.

"He's been punishing himself like that ever since it happened. It's no use, Howard." Sally's voice was very steady. "It's never just one; it's two. I loved you and I allowed myself to be carried away by you, because for the moment it was right. Right, Howard! Only for the moment, but for the moment it was right. For the rest of time . . . Ellery, there's no justification for it; but that's what happened. People should be stronger than Howard and I were able to be. I think we were both caught off guard; there *are* times when you are, no matter what defenses you've built up beforehand. And it wasn't a momentary thing, a bad thing in itself. I did love him; he did love me." She said: "We still love each other."

Oh, Sally.

"It was completely irrational. We didn't think; we felt. We stayed in the lodge overnight. The next morning we saw it as it was."

"We had two choices," muttered Howard. "To tell Father or not to tell Father. But we hadn't talked long before we saw that we didn't have two choices at all. We had only one choice — and that's no choice."

"We couldn't tell him." Sally clutched Ellery's arm. "Ellery, do you see that?" she cried. "We couldn't tell Dieds. Oh, I know what he'd have done if we'd told him. Being Dieds, he'd have given me a divorce, he'd have offered to settle a fortune on me, he wouldn't have uttered a single word of complaint or anger; he'd have been . . . Dieds. But Ellery, he'd have died inside. Do you see that? No, you can't. You can't know what he's built up around me. It's not just a house. It's a way of living, it's the rest of his life. He's a one-woman man, Ellery. Dieds never loved a woman before me; he'll never love another. I'm not saying that boastfully; it really has nothing to do with me, what I am, what I've done or not done. It's *Dieds*. He's chosen me as his center and he's revolved his whole reason for being about me. If we'd told him, it would have been a death sentence. Slow murder."

"It's a pity," began Ellery, "that — "

"I know. That I didn't think of all that the day before. I can only say . . . I didn't. Till it was too late."

Ellery nodded. "Very well, you didn't. It happened, and you two decided to keep it from him. Then?"

"There's more to it than that," said Howard. "There's what we owe him. It would have been bad enough if I'd been his real son and he'd met Sally under normal circumstances, when she was an adult, and married her. But—"

"But you felt that he'd created you where without him you'd have been nothing, and Sally felt the same way," said Ellery, "and I quite understand all that. But what I want to know is: What did you do about it? Because it's obvious you did do something about it, and what you did only made a worse mess. What was it?"

Sally bit her lip, deeply.

"What was it?"

She looked up suddenly. "We decided then and there that it was over. That it must never be revived. We must try to forget it. But whether we forgot it or not, it must never under any circumstances happen again. And above all, Diedrich must never know.

"It's never happened again," Sally said, "and Dieds doesn't know. We buried it. Only . . ." She stopped.

"Say it!" Howard's shout rang over the lake, startling birds everywhere; they rose in clouds, wheeling away and up and disappearing.

For a moment Ellery thought something disastrous was going to happen.

But the color of convulsion faded out of Howard's face and he thrust his hands into his pockets, shivering.

When he spoke, Ellery could hardly hear him.

"It worked for a week. Then . . . It was being in the same house with her did it. Eating at the same table. Having to put on an act twelve hours a day . . .

You could have gone away.

"I wrote Sally a letter."

"Oh, no." *Oh, no!*

"A note. I couldn't talk to her. I had to talk to somebody. I mean . . . I had to say it. I said it on paper." Howard suddenly choked up.

Ellery shaded his eyes.

"He wrote me four letters in all," said Sally. She sounded small and faraway. "They were love letters. I'd find them in my room, under my pillow. Or in the make-up drawer of my vanity. They were love letters and from any one of them a child could have told what had happened between us that day and night at the lodge . . . I'm not telling the exact truth. They were franker than that. They told everything. In detail."

"I was crazy," said Howard hoarsely.

"And of course," said Ellery to Sally, "you burned them."

"I didn't."

Ellery vaulted from the car. He was so angry he wanted to walk back through the woods, down the white road, past the sheep and cows and bridges and fences the forty-five miles back to Wrightsville, to pick up his things and head for the station and take a train back to New York and sweet sanity.

But after a moment he walked back to the car.

"I'm sorry. You didn't burn them. Just what did you do with them, Sally?"

"I loved him!"

"What did you do with them?"

"I couldn't! They were everything I had!"

"What did you do with them?"

She twisted her fingers. "I had an old japanned box. I'd had it for years, since my school days. I'd bought it in an antique shop somewhere because it had a false bottom and I could keep my secret best picture of — "

"Of Diedrich."

"Of Diedrich." Her fingers became still. "I'd never told anyone about the false bottom, not even Dieds. I thought it would sound too silly. I kept jewelry in the box proper. Well, I put the four letters in the false bottom. I thought they'd be safe there."

"What happened?"

"After the fourth letter I came to my senses. I told Howard he must never write another. He never did. Then . . . a little over three months ago . . . it was in June . . ."

"We had a robbery at our house," laughed Howard. "A little old robbery."

"A thief broke into my bedroom," Sally whispered, "one day

when I was at the hairdresser's in town, and he stole the japanned box."

Ellery touched his eyelids with his two forefingers. His eyes felt hot and grainy.

"The box was jammed with expensive jewelry — things Dieds had given me. I knew that's what the thief had been after, and he'd simply picked up the whole box and made off with it, not knowing there was something in the false bottom I'd have given every diamond and emerald in the box to get back. And burn."

Ellery said nothing. He leaned on the car.

"Of course, Dieds had to be told."

"He called in Chief of Police Dakin," Howard said, "and Dakin . . ."

"Dakin." *That shrewd Yankee, Dakin.*

". . . and Dakin after weeks and weeks managed to round up all the missing jewelry. In various pawnshops — in Philadelphia, Boston, New York, Newark — a piece here, a piece there. But there were all sorts of conflicting descriptions of the thief — he was never caught. Father said we were," Howard laughed again, "lucky."

"He didn't know how Howard and I waited, waited, for that japanned box to turn up," said Sally tensely. "But it didn't, it didn't. Howard kept saying the thief had thrown it away as being of no value. It sounded reasonable. But . . . suppose he hadn't? Suppose he'd found the false bottom?"

A cluster of swollen clouds swam up over the lake. They had dark hearts and they looked against the sky like great microbes viewed against a blue field in a microscope. The lake swiftly darkened and some drops of cold rain fell, stippling the water. Ellery reached for a coat and thought irrelevantly of the hamper.

"It was worrying about those letters that brought on this last amnesia attack," Howard muttered. "I'm sure of it. The weeks passed and the box didn't turn up and everything seemed all right and all the time I felt as if I were being eaten through by acid inside. The day I went into New York for the Djerens exhibition I was just looking for something to take my mind off things. I didn't give a damn about Djerens; I don't like his work — he's like Brancusi, and Archipenko, and I'm strictly a neoclassical boy. But he was an escape. You know what happened.

"It's a funny thing that I snapped before the blow fell, and since I've been all right."

"Let's stick to the line," said Ellery tiredly. "I take it the thief's got in touch with you. Was it Wednesday?"

It must have been Wednesday; he recalled thinking that something serious had happened on the day before his arrival.

"Wednesday." Sally was frowning. "Yes, Wednesday, the day after Howard saw you in New York. I got a phone call — "

"*You* got a phone call. You mean the caller asked for you? By name?"

"Yes. Eileen answered and then said some man wanted to talk to me, and — "

"Man?"

"Eileen said it was a man. But when I got on the phone I wasn't sure. It might have been a woman with a deep voice. It had a funny sound. Hoarse, whispery."

"Disguised. And how much did this man-woman ask for the return of the letters, Sally?"

"Twenty-five thousand dollars."

"Cheap."

"Cheap!" Howard glared at him.

"I imagine your father would pay a lot more than that, Howard, to keep those letters from being published. Don't you?"

Howard did not reply.

"That's what he — or she — said," said Sally drearily. "He said he'd give me a couple of days to raise the money and that he'd phone again with instructions about how to get it to him. He said if I refused, or tried to double-cross him, he'd sell the letters to Diedrich. For a lot more."

"And what did you say to that, Sally?"

"I could hardly talk. I thought I was going to be stupid and faint. But I managed to hold on to myself, and I said I'd try to raise the money. And then he hung up. Or she."

"The blackmailer called again?"

"This morning."

"Oh," said Ellery. Then he said: "Who answered the phone this time?"

"I did. I was alone."

The rain was falling hard now on the lake, and Howard said peevishly, "You'd better put the top up, Sally." But Sally said, "Not much is coming through the trees; it's just a shower," and then she looked at Ellery and said, "Howard had gone into town this morning to get a copy of the architect's Museum plans — he'd driven in just after Dieds and Wolfert. I . . . had to wait until How got back. Then we . . . talked and then I brought you your breakfast."

"What instructions were you given this morning, Sally?"

"I didn't have to bring the money myself. I could send a representative. But only one person was to come. If I told the police, or tried to have somebody watch the meeting, he'd know, he said; he wouldn't show up, the deal would be off, he'd contact Dieds at his office."

"Where is this meeting to take place, and when?"

"In Room 1010 at the Hollis Hotel — "

"Oh, yes," murmured Ellery. "And that's the top floor."

" — tomorrow, Saturday, at two P.M. Whoever brings the money will find the door to 1010 unlocked; he said to walk right in and wait there for further instructions."

And now they were both looking at him with such a concentration of anxieties that he turned aside again. He walked to the edge of the lake. The rain had stopped; the clouds had marvelously vanished; the birds were back; there was a fresh wet feel to the air.

Ellery came back.

"I take it you're intending to pay."

Sally looked bewildered.

"Intending to pay?" growled Howard. "You don't seem to get it, Ellery."

"I get it. I also have a thorough acquaintance with blackmail and blackmailers."

"But what else can we do?" cried Sally. "If we don't pay, he'll take the letters to Diedrich!"

"You've quite made up your minds that you'll do anything to keep Diedrich from finding out?" They didn't answer. Ellery sighed. "That's the diabolical thing about blackmail, isn't it? Sally, do you have the twenty-five thousand?"

"I have it." Howard reached inside his tweed jacket and took out a long, very fat, plain manila envelope. And he held it out to Ellery.

"Me?" said Ellery in a perfectly flat voice.

Sally whispered, "Howard won't let me go, and I don't think he ought to go — it'll be a great nervous strain and he might pull another amnesia attack in the middle of it. Then we'd be in the soup for fair. And besides, we're both so well known in town, Ellery. If we were noticed . . ."

"You want me to act as your intermediary tomorrow."

"Would you?"

It came out in a little exhausted puff, like the last gasp of a deflating balloon. There was nothing left in her, not anger or guilt or shame or even despair.

It hardly matters how this turns out. She'll never be the same. It's all over for her. From now on it's Diedrich, first and last. And he'll never know, and after a while she may even be happy with him after a fashion.

And Howard, you've lost. You've lost what you don't even know you've been trying to win.

"What did I tell you?" cried Howard. "This was all for nothing, Sal. You couldn't expect Ellery to do it. Especially Ellery. I'll simply have to do it myself."

Ellery took the envelope from him. It was unsealed; there was a rubber band around it. He removed the band and looked inside. The envelope was filled with sharp new bills, five-hundred dollar bills. He glanced at Howard inquiringly.

"The exact amount. Fifty five-hundreds."

"Sally, didn't he say anything about having the money in small denominations?"

"He didn't say."

"What difference does it make?" snarled Howard. "He knows

we'd never try to trace the bills. Or catch him. All he'd have to do is talk."

"Dieds would never believe him!" She hurled it at Howard. And then she was silent again.

Ellery put the rubber band back around the envelope.

"Let me have it," said Howard.

But Ellery was stowing the envelope away. "I'll need it tomorrow, won't I?"

Sally's lips were parted. "You'll *do* it?"

"On one condition."

"Oh." She braced herself. "What, Ellery?"

"That you crack open that hamper before I starve to death."

⁘

ELLERY SOLVED A difficult problem in histrionics by pleading "the novel" as an excuse for not appearing at the dinner table. He had already lost the better part of a day, he explained, and if he was to honor his commitment, authors being notoriously honorable about commitments to publishers, he would have to push along. He managed to convey, by the delicate edge on his tone — he did not pronounce the words themselves — that his schedule would be further impaired by a certain nonliterary pursuit on the morrow.

This was all deliberate; Ellery felt a desperate need for solitude. If Sally suspected his real reason, she gave no sign; as for Howard, all the way back to North Hill Drive he dozed. Sleep, Ellery recalled, was another form of death.

Back at the cottage, with the door closed, Ellery flung himself on the ottoman before the picture window and communed with Wrightsville. Let Howard face his father; let Sally face her husband. But then he reflected that both had had plenty of practice; apparently they were good at it.

Ellery felt especially badly about Sally's role in this unpleasantness, and he wondered just what his feeling comprised. Largely disappointment, he decided: she had betrayed his estimate of her. He recognized that in this feeling there was a large content of pique; she had bruised his self-esteem. He had thought Sally an unusual woman; he had erred; she was simply a woman. The Sally he had thought she was might conceivably have surrendered herself in the excitement of discovering that she loved, not her husband, but another man; but the other man could not have been a Howard. (It occurred to him that the other man *might* have been an Ellery; but this thought he dismissed at once as illogical, unscientific, and unworthy.)

It struck Ellery that he didn't think much of Howard Van Horn, neurosis or no neurosis.

Since this brought him to Howard, his thoughts turned in natural sequence to the fat envelope in his breast pocket; and this led him to consider the nature and identity of the thief-blackmailer he was to meet the next day. But wherever his brain turned, it was confronted by an unanswerable question.

ᴄᴡᴐ

ELLERY AWOKE TO find that he had been asleep. The sky over Wrightsville was darkening; popcorn lights were jumping up in the valley below; as he turned over on the ottoman he saw windows in the main house materialize.

He didn't feel well. There were the tangled Van Horns, and there was his frowning briefcase. No, he didn't feel well.

Ellery got off the ottoman, groaning, fumbled for the switch of the desk lamp. The great acreage of the desk repelled him.

But when he had opened the case, removed the typewriter's shroud, flexed his fingers, rubbed his chin, reamed his ear, and gone through all the other traditional preparations the punctilio of his craft prescribed, he found that, *mirabile dictu,* work could be fun.

Ellery discovered himself in that rarest of auctorial phenomena, the writing mood. His brain felt greased, his fingers mighty.

The machine jumped, rattled, and raced.

At some indeterminate point in timelessness a buzzer buzzed. But he ignored it, and later he realized it had stopped. The worshipful Laura, no doubt, beckoning from the kitchen of the main house. Food? No, no.

And he worked on.

"Mr. Queen."

There was an insistence in the voice which made Ellery recall that it had actually repeated his name two or three times.

He looked around.

The door stood open and in the doorway stood Diedrich Van Horn.

∽

IN A FLASH it all came back to him: the drive north, the woods, the lake, the tale of the adulterers, the blackmailer, the envelope in his pocket.

"May I come in?"

Had something happened? Did Diedrich know?

Ellery raised himself from the swivel chair stiffly, but smiling.

"Please do."

"How are you tonight?"

"Stiff."

Howard's father closed the door, rather pointedly, Ellery noticed with alarm. But when he turned around, he was smiling, too.

"I knocked for two minutes and called out to you several times, but you didn't hear me."

"I'm so sorry. Won't you sit down?"

"I'm interrupting."

"I'm all gratitude, believe me!"

Diedrich laughed. "I often wonder how you fellows manage it, this sitting on your bottom hour after hour punching out words. It would drive me crazy."

"What time is it, anyway, Mr. Van Horn?"

"After eleven."

"My God."

"And you haven't had your dinner. Laura was practically in tears. We caught her trying to reach you over the intercom and threatened to tell you she got all your books from the public library. I don't know that Laura got the point, but she stopped trying to bother you."

Diedrich was nervous. He was nervous and worried. Ellery didn't like it.

"Sit down, sit down, Mr. Van Horn."

"You're sure I'm not . . . ?"

"I was going to stop soon anyway."

"I feel like a fool," said the big man, lowering himself into the big chair. "Telling everybody to let you alone, and then—" He stopped. Then he said abruptly, "See here, Mr. Queen, there's something I've got to talk to you about."

Here it comes.

"I left for the office this morning before you were up. I'd have spoken to you before I left if . . . Later I did phone, but Eileen told me you and Sally and Howard had gone off on a picnic. Then this evening I didn't want to disturb you." He took out a handkerchief and passed it over his face. "But I couldn't go to bed without talking to you."

"What's the trouble, Mr. Van Horn?"

"About three months ago we had a burglary . . ."

Ellery yearned for West Eighty-seventh Street, where adultery was only a word in the dictionary and the caged antics of nice people trapped by their relationships were confined to his filing cabinet.

"Burglary?" said Ellery, surprised. At least he hoped it sounded surprised.

"Yes. Some second-story man broke into my wife's bedroom and got away with her jewel box."

Diedrich was sweating—a luxury, Ellery thought enviously, he could afford. *He thinks I don't know a thing about this and it's hard for him to talk about it.*

"Not really. Was the box ever recovered?"

Neatly put, Mr. Q. Now if I can control my own sudoriferous glands . . .

"The box? Oh, the jewels. Yes, Sally's jewels were recovered piecemeal in various pawnshops around the East—the box, of course, wasn't. Probably thrown away. It wasn't valuable—an old thing Sally'd picked up in her school days. It's not that, Mr. Queen." Diedrich swabbed himself again.

"Well!" Ellery lit a cigaret and blew the match out briskly.

"That's the kind of burglary story I enjoy hearing, Mr. Van Horn. No harm done, and—"

"But the thief was never found, Mr. Queen."

"Oh?"

"No." Diedrich clasped his big hands. "They were never able to lay their hands on the fellow, or even get a good idea of what he looked like."

Doesn't matter what he says from now on, Ellery thought joyfully. And he seated himself in the swivel chair, feeling better than he'd felt all day.

"Sometimes works out that way. Three months ago, Mr. Van Horn? I've known thieves to be caught after ten years."

"It's not that, either." The big man unclasped his hands, clasped them again. "Last night . . ."

Last night?

Ellery felt the slightest chill.

"Last night there was another robbery."

Last night there was another robbery.

"There was? But this morning no one said—"

"I didn't mention it to anyone, Mr. Queen."

Refocus. But slowly.

"I'm sorry you didn't tell me about this this morning, Mr. Van Horn. You should have booted me out of bed."

"This morning I wasn't entirely sure I wanted you to know." Diedrich's skin was gray under the bronze. He kept clasping and unclasping his great hands. Suddenly he jumped up. "I'm going about this like a woman! I've faced unpleasant facts before."

Unpleasant facts.

"I was the first one up this morning. Rather earlier than usual. I thought I wouldn't bother Laura about breakfast, that I'd have a bite in town. I went into my study to get some contracts on my desk and . . . there it was."

"There what was?"

"One of the French doors—they lead to the south terrace—was broken. The thief had broken the pane nearest the knob, slipped his hand through, and turned the key."

"The usual technique," Ellery nodded. "What was stolen?"

"My wall safe had been opened."

"I'll have a look at it."

"You won't find any signs of violence," said Diedrich very quietly.

"What do you mean?"

"The safe was opened by someone who knew the combination. I'd never even have looked inside if I hadn't found evidence that someone had broken into the study during the night."

"Combinations can be worked out, Mr. Van Horn — "

"My safe is practically burglarproof," said Van Horn grimly. "After the June robbery I had a new one installed. It's most unlikely that I was burglarized by a Jimmy Valentine, Mr. Queen. I tell you the thief last night knew that combination."

"What was stolen?" Ellery asked again.

"I'm accustomed to keeping a large amount of cash in the safe for business reasons. The cash is missing."

Cash . . .

"Nothing else?"

"Nothing else."

"Is it generally known that you keep a lot of money in your study safe, Mr. Van Horn?"

"Not generally." Diedrich's lips were twisted. "Not even the help. Just my family."

"I see . . . How much was taken?"

"Twenty-five thousand dollars."

∽

ELLERY GOT UP and walked around the desk to stare into the darkness over Wrightsville.

"Who knows the safe combination?"

"Besides myself? My brother. Howard. Sally."

"Well." Ellery turned around. "You learn early in this deplorable business not to jump to conclusions, Mr. Van Horn. What happened to the broken glass?"

"I picked up the pieces and threw them away before anyone came downstairs. The terrace floor was covered with 'em."

The terrace floor.

"The *terrace* floor?"

"The terrace floor."

Something in the way Diedrich repeated the phrase made Ellery feel very sorry for him.

"*Outside* the French door, Mr. Queen. You needn't look blank. I saw the significance of that this morning." The big man's voice rose. "I'm not a fool. That's why I threw away the glass — that's why I didn't phone the police. To be lying outside the door, the pane had to be broken from inside. Inside the study. Inside my home, Mr. Queen. This was an inside job amateurishly made to look like an outside job. I knew that this morning."

Ellery came back around the desk to drop into the swivel chair and teeter, whistling softly a tune which, even had his host been able to hear it, would not have cheered him. But Diedrich was paying no attention. He was striding up and down with the angry energy of a strong man who finds nothing to vent his strength on.

"If one of my family," Diedrich Van Horn cried, "needed twenty-five thousand dollars so desperately, why in God's name didn't he come to me? They all know — they must know — that I'd never refuse them anything. Certainly not *money*. I don't care what they've done, what trouble they're in!"

Ellery drummed in time to his whistle, staring out the window. *You'd care about this, I'm afraid.*

"I can't understand it. I waited tonight, at the dinner table, and afterward, for one of them to give me some sign. Anything. A word, a look."

Then you don't really think it's your brother. Wolfert shares your working day. You must have seen him today at your office. You don't think it's Wolfert.

"But nothing. Oh, there was a strain, I felt that, but they all seemed to share it." Diedrich stopped pacing. "Mr. Queen," he said in a hard voice.

Ellery turned to face him.

"One of them doesn't trust me. I don't know if you can understand how hard that hits me. If it were anything but that . . . I don't know how to say it. I could talk. I could ask. I could even plead. Four times tonight I tried to bring it up. But I found I couldn't. Something tied up my tongue. And then there was something else."

Ellery waited.

"The feeling that . . . whichever one it was wouldn't want anyone else to know. It must be something pretty bad. See here." The ugly face was rock. "My job is to find out which one took that money. Not for the money — I'd gladly forget five times that amount. But I've got to find out which member of my family is in serious trouble. Once I know, it will be easier to find out what the trouble is. Then I'll fix it. I don't want to ask questions now. I don't want . . ." He hesitated, then went on determinedly, "I don't want lies. If I have the truth, I can handle it. Whatever it is. Mr. Queen, will you find out for me — confidentially?"

Ellery said at once, "I'll try, Mr. Van Horn, of course," disliking the game. But Diedrich mustn't know he knew; he simply mustn't know. Hesitation might have made him suspicious.

He could see his host's relief. Diedrich dried his cheeks, his chin, his forehead, with the damp handkerchief. He even smiled a little.

"You don't know how I've dreaded this."

"Naturally. Tell me, Mr. Van Horn: this twenty-five thousand dollars. How was the sum composed? What denominations?"

"They were all five-hundred dollar bills."

Ellery said slowly: "Fifty five-hundreds. And did you happen to keep a record of the serial numbers?"

"The list is in my desk in the study."

"I'd better take it."

ॐ

While DIEDRICH VAN HORN opened the top drawer of his desk, Mr. Queen did his best to impersonate a detective searching for clues. He examined the French door, he looked carefully at the wall safe, he scanned the rug closely on a line between the door and the safe; he even stepped out onto the south terrace. When he returned, Diedrich handed him a piece of paper bearing a *Wrightsville Na-*

tional Bank imprint. Ellery put it in his pocket, behind the envelope containing the twenty-five thousand dollars Howard had given him in the afternoon.

"Anything?" Diedrich asked anxiously.

Ellery shook his head. "I'm afraid normal procedures won't help us in this case, Mr. Van Horn. I could send for my fingerprint kit, or borrow one from Chief Dakin — no, that wouldn't be wise, would it? But frankly, even if your own prints haven't messed up the prints of . . . I mean, finding prints wouldn't necessarily mean anything. Not in an inside job. What's that?"

"What, Mr. Queen?"

Diedrich had not yet shut the desk drawer. The lamplight touched off a glittering object in the drawer.

"Oh, that's mine. I bought it right after the June business."

Ellery picked it up. It was a Smith & Wesson .38 safety hammerless, a snubnosed revolver finished in nickel. Its five chambers were loaded. He laid it back in the drawer.

"Nice gun."

"Yes." Diedrich sounded a bit remote. "It was sold to me as the ideal weapon for 'home defense.'" Ellery regretted his remark. "And speaking of the June robbery —"

"You suspect that wasn't an outside affair, either?"

"What do *you* think, Mr. Queen?"

It was difficult to evade this man.

"Any specific reason for thinking so? Like the glass falling on the wrong side in last night's business?"

"No. At that time, of course, I had no idea . . . Chief Dakin told me there were no clues. If he'd had reason to suspect it was an inside job, I'm sure he'd have told me so."

"Yes," said Ellery, "Dakin is devoted to the great god Fact."

"But now I'm convinced the two incidents are tied up. The jewelry is valuable. It was pawned. Money again." Diedrich smiled. "And I'd always considered myself a pretty freehanded bird. Shows how easy it is to kid yourself, Mr. Queen. Well, I'm going to bed. I have a big day tomorrow."

And so have I, thought Ellery, so have I.

"Good night, Mr. Queen."

"Good night, sir."

"If you should find out anything — "

"Of course."

"Don't tell . . . the one that's involved. Come to me."

"I understand. Oh, Mr. Van Horn."

"Yes, Mr. Queen."

"If you should hear a prowler down here, don't be alarmed. It'll only be your house guest, raiding the icebox."

Diedrich grinned and went out, waving in a wide and friendly gesture.

Ellery felt very sorry for him indeed.

And for himself.

∽

LAURA HAD LEFT him a feast. Under other circumstances, and in view of the fact that he hadn't eaten since early afternoon, Ellery would have blessed her with each mouthful. As it was, he had little appetite. He tormented the roast beef and the salad just long enough to give Van Horn time to fall asleep. Then, with a coffee cup in his hand, he returned quietly to the study.

He seated himself in the chair behind his host's desk and swiveled about so that his back was to the door. Then he took the fat manila envelope from his pocket and quickly flipped through its contents. He saw at once that the bills were in numerical sequence; they had come from the United States Mint by a direct route. He returned the bills to the envelope and the envelope to his pocket. Then he dug out the slip of paper Diedrich had given him.

The bills in his pocket were the bills which had been taken from Van Horn's safe the night before.

There had been no doubt of this in Ellery's mind from the moment his host had broached the burglary. The fact had merely called for certification.

Now there was that other matter to attend to.

"You may come in now, Howard," Ellery said.

Howard came in, blinking.

"Shut the door, will you?" He obeyed in silence. He was in pajamas and dressing gown, and he wore moccasinlike slippers over bare feet. "You know, you're really not very good at this sort of thing, Howard. How much did you hear?"

"The whole thing."

"And you waited for me to come back to the study, to see what I would do."

Howard sat down on the edge of his father's leather armchair, his big hands clenched on his knees. "Ellery —"

"Spare me the explanations, Howard. You stole that money from your father's safe last night, and it's in my pocket right now. Howard," said Ellery, leaning forward, "I wonder if you quite realize the position you've forced me into."

"Ellery, I was frantic." Ellery could scarcely hear him. "I don't have that kind of money. And the money had to be got somewhere."

"Why didn't you tell me you'd taken it from your father's safe?"

"I didn't want Sally to know."

"Oh, Sally doesn't know."

"No. I couldn't tell you up at the lake, or on the drive back. She was with us."

"You could have told me this afternoon or evening, when I was alone in the cottage."

"I didn't want to interrupt your work." Howard suddenly looked up. "No, that's not the reason. I was scared to."

"Afraid I'd renege on tomorrow?"

"It's not just that . . . Ellery, it's the first time in my life I've ever done anything like this. And to have to do it to the old man . . ." Howard rose, heavily. "The money's got to be paid. I don't expect you to believe me, but it really isn't for my sake. Or even for Sally's. I'm not as much of a coward as you think. I could tell father tonight — right now — man to man. I could tell him and say I wanted him to divorce Sally and that I'd marry her, and if he hit me I could pick myself up from the floor and say it again."

I believe you could, Howard. And even get a sort of pleasure from it.

"But it's father who needs the protection in this. He mustn't get those letters. They'd kill him. He can stand the loss of twenty-five thousand measly dollars — he has millions — but the letters would kill him, Ellery. If I could have invented a reason, a phony reason that would stand up, for needing that much cash I'd have asked father for it right out. But I knew I'd have to back it up — he doesn't fool easily — and I couldn't back it up. So I took it from the safe."

"And suppose he finds out that you're the thief?"

"I'll have to cross that one when I come to it. But there's no reason why he should find out."

"He knows now it's you or Sally."

Howard looked baffled. He said angrily: "My own stupidity. I'll just have to figure out something."

Poor Howard.

"Ellery, I've dragged you into a nasty mess and I'm damned sorry. Give me the money and I'll go to the Hollis myself tomorrow. And you can stay here, or leave — whichever you think best — and I won't drag you into this any more."

He came up to the desk and held out his hand.

But Ellery said: "What else don't I know, Howard?"

"Nothing. There's nothing else."

"What about the burglary in June, Howard?"

"I didn't do that!"

Ellery looked up at him for a long time.

Howard glared back.

"Who did, Howard?"

"How should I know? Some crook or other. Father's wrong about that, Ellery. It was an outside thief. The whole thing came about accidentally. The thief lifted some jewelry and found the box had value, too. Ellery, give me the damned envelope and clear out of this!"

Ellery sighed. "Go to bed, Howard. I'll see it through."

∽

ELLERY WALKED BACK to the cottage with dragging feet. He was tired, and the envelope in his pocket weighed a great deal.

He crossed the north terrace, felt his way around the pool.

I can't even afford to fall in and drown, he thought. They'd find the money on me.

And then he bumped into the stone garden seat.

A pain shot through him, not entirely from his kneecap.

The stone seat!

The old woman he had seen sitting here last night.

He had completely forgotten about the old woman.

The Fourth Day

ON SATURDAY AFTERNOONS Wrightsville takes on a mercantile air. The goose of commerce hangs high. High Village shops are full, cash registers jump and cry out hour after hour, the Square and Lower Main are jammed, the Bijou Theater's queue stretches from the box office almost to the doors of Logan's Market at the corner of Slocum and Washington, the parking lot in Jezreel Lane raises its fee to thirty-five cents, and all over town — on Lower Main, on Upper Whistling, on State, in the Square, on Slocum, on Washington — one sees faces usually absent during the week: walnut-skinned farmers in stiff store pants from the back country, kids with stiff shoes on, stout ladies in stiff gingham, wearing hats. Model T's rub fenders with jeeps everywhere; and the public parking area on the rim of the Square, surrounding the statue of Founder Wright, forms a cordon of Detroit steel through which pedestrians find it impossible to squeeze. It is all quite different from Thursday evening, which is Band Concert Night and centers about Memorial Park on State Street, near Town Hall. Band Concert Night brings out principally the Low Village contingent and the youth of all sectors. Staring boys in their big brothers' khaki blouses line the edge of the walks and nervous girls parade before them in pairs, trios, and quartets, while the American Legion Band in silver helmets plays Sousa marches sternly in the concentrated headlights of the cars parked in military formation across the street. Thursday is more a field night for popcorn paladins and hotdog hidalgos than for the merchants dispensing their wares under a leasehold.

But Saturday is solid.

It is on Saturday afternoons that the *haut monde* descend into High Village for those quintessential gatherings at which the cultural, civic, and political health of the community is kept under unflagging observation. (Organizationally speaking, this is not industry's day. Business pursues its less selfish affairs on Mondays, which is logical, Saturday retail business being brisk and Monday retail business being sluggish. That is why you will find the Wrightsville Retail Merchants Ass. meeting for pork chops, julienne potatoes, and the Sales Tax at the Hollis Hotel each Monday at noon. The Chamber of Commerce congregates at the Kelton for baked ham, candied sweets, and the American Way on Thursdays; and Rotary assembles at Upham House for Ma Upham's fried chicken, hot biscuits, boysenberry jam, and the Menace of Communism on Wednesdays.) Each Saturday afternoon the ladies of Hill Drive and Skytop Road and Twin Hill-in-the-Beeches fill the ballrooms of the Hollis and the Kelton with their grim twitterings — that is to say, those ladies who must attend the luncheon meetings of the Civic Forum Committee, the Wrightsville Robert Browning Society, the Wrightsville Ladies' Aid, the Wrightsville Civic Betterment Club, the Wrightsville Interracial Tolerance League and such because they cannot crash the more select gatherings of the D.A.R., the New England Genealogical Society, the Wrightsville Women's Christian Temperance Union, and the Wrightsville Republican Women's Club in the Paul Revere Room and the other Early American banquet halls of Upham House. Not all these functions are held simultaneously, of course; the ladies have worked out an efficient stagger plan which permits the spryer among them to attend two, and even three, luncheons on the same day, which explains why the ballroom menus on Saturdays at all three hostelries are so leafy and the desserts so fruity. Nevertheless, husbands have been known to complain of their Spartan Sunday dinners; and at least two enterprising young lady dieticians have moved to Wrightsville, one from Bangor and the other from Worcester, and made a very good thing out of it.

In all this ferment of commerce, culture, civics, and pure yeasty mass, offenses against man seem as distant as Port Said. In fact, the

last thing you would think of on a Saturday afternoon in Wrightsville is that peculiarly nasty aberration of individual behavior known
as blackmail; which is undoubtedly why the blackmailer, Ellery
glumly reflected, selected today for his rendezvous with twenty-five
thousand of Diedrich Van Horn's dollars.

Ellery parked Howard's proletarian roadster halfway down the
winding hill approach to High Village which is Upper Dade Street.
He got out, touched his breast pocket, and then strolled down the
hill toward the Square. He had purposely selected Upper Dade, for
on Saturday afternoons Upper Dade plays host to the traffic over-
flow from the center of town and a man bent on anonymity can
lose himself there without trying. Still, Ellery was surprised at what
he found. Upper Dade Street was almost unrecognizable. A gigantic
housing development in leprous brick had appeared since his last
visit to Wrightsville, on the very site where gray frame, ivy-grown
houses had stood for seventy-five years and longer. It was flanked by
brisk and glittering new stores. There was a great used-car lot
where the coal yard had sprawled, filled with rank after rank of
gleaming cars which, if they had been truly used, had been driven
by spirits of air over ethereal roads for exactly the wink of a
hummingbird's wing.

Ah, Wrightsville!

Ellery grew glummer. Strolling along under the metal banners
of Upper Dade's invading tradesmen, his face lighted variously by
orange, white, blue, gold, and green neon rays — must they pit their
garish little scene against God Himself in the person of His sun? —
Ellery reflected that this was far from the Wrightsville of his tender-
est memories.

Small wonder, blackmail.

But when he rounded the curve at the bottom of the hill, his step
quickened. He was home again.

Here was the honest old Square, which was round, with the
hub of Founder Jezreel Wright's bronze dripping bird droppings
from his crusty nose into the verdigrised horse trough at his feet;
there the spokes of State Street, Lower Main, Washington, Lincoln,
and Upper Dade, each with its altered Wrightsville character, per-

haps, but nonetheless in some mysterious way beckoning the prodigal home from the sinful cities. Up State Street, that broadest of spokes, might be seen Town Hall, and beyond Town Hall Memorial Park; the Carnegie Library (was Dolores Aikin still there, presiding over the stuffed owl and the fierce eviscerated eagle?); and the "new" County Court House, which was already old. Lower Main: the Bijou, the post office, the *Record* office, the shops. Washington: Logan's, Upham House, the Professional Bldg., Andy Birobatyan's. Lincoln and the feed stores and stables and the Volunteer Fire Department. But it was the Square itself which gave them life, as the mother the chicks.

Here was John F.'s bank, no longer John F.'s but Diedrich Van H.'s; but the building was the same, and there is steadfastness in buildings. And here was the very old Bluefield store, and J. P. Simpson's pawnshop (Loan Office), and Sol Gowdy's Men's Shop, and the Bon Ton Department Store, and Dunc MacLean — Fine Liquors; and the sad land change, alas, of the High Village Pharmacy, now but a link in a chain drug store, and of William Ketcham — Insurance, now the Atomic War Surplus Outlet Store.

And, dominant, the marquee of the Hollis Hotel.

&

ELLERY GLANCED AT his wrist watch: 1:58.

He entered the Hollis lobby unhurriedly.

Civic fervor was in full cry. From the Grand Ballroom came a mighty music of culture and cutlery. The lobby seethed. Bellboys raced. The desk bell clanged. The house phones leaped. At the newsstand and cigar counter Mark Doodle's son, Grover, a portly Grover now, dispensed news and tobacco with furious geniality.

Ellery crossed the lobby at a pace calculated to attract no eye, however idle. He adjusted himself to the tempo of the crowd, moving with it, neither faster nor slower. His manner and expression, a blend of abstracted positiveness and pleasant curiosity, suggested to Wrightsvillians that he was a Wrightsvillian and to strangers that he was a stranger. And he waited for the second of the three elevators, so that he might be pushed in with a large group. In-

side, he refrained from calling out a floor number; he simply
waited, half-turned from the operator. At the sixth floor he remembered: the operator was Wally Planetsky, whom he had
last seen on duty at the admission desk of the County Jail, on
the top floor of the County Court House. Planetsky had been
elderly then, and graying; now he was old, white-haired, and with
his thick shoulders heavily stooped. *O tempus!* Grover Doodles grow
pots and policemen retire to run hotel elevators. Just the same, Ellery
was careful to get out at the tenth floor crab-fashion, back to Wally
Planetsky.

A gentleman carrying a salesman's briefcase, who looked like
J. Edgar Hoover, got out with him.

The gentleman turned left, so Ellery turned right.

He searched among the wrong room numbers long enough for
the gentleman to unlock a door and disappear. Then Ellery went
quickly back, past the elevators, noting that his tenth-floor fellow
traveler had entered 1031, and hurried on. The Turkey red carpet
muffled his footsteps.

He saw 1010 coming up and he looked back briefly without checking his stride. But the corridor behind him was empty and no guilty
head popped back into a room. At 1010 he stopped, looking around
again.

Nothing.

He tried the door then.

It was not locked.

So it wasn't a bluff.

Ellery pushed the door in suddenly. He waited.

When nothing happened, he went in, immediately shutting the
door.

◦↜◦

No ONE WAS there. No one seemed to have been there for weeks.

It was a single, without bath. In one corner stood a white sink
with its plumbing showing; there was a wooden towel bar above
the sink. A walk-in closet lay beyond the sink.

The room contained the irreducible minimum prescribed by

Boniface's profession. It featured a narrow bed covered by a tan bedspread with purple candlewicking, a night table, an overstuffed chair, a standing lamp, a writing table, and a bureau with a starched cotton runner. Above the bureau hung a mirror, and on the wall opposite, above the bed, there was a dust-peppered print labeled *Sunrise Over the Mt.* The single window was covered with a slick and sleazy curtain in grim écru, whose edge came the traditional two inches above a large, flaking radiator. The floor was carpeted wall to wall in a green Axminster, thoroughly faded. On the night table stood a telephone, and on the writing table were grouped a water pitcher, a thick glass, and a square glass tray with fluted edges. A menu inscribed *Hunting Room, The Hollis Hotel, "Fine Food for Discriminating Diners,"* stood on the bureau, leaning against the mirror.

Ellery looked into the closet.

It was empty except for a new paper laundry bag on the hat shelf and a curious piece of crockery on the floor which it took him a moment to identify. He made the identification with pleasure. It was what an older generation had forthrightly termed a "thunder jar." He returned it to its place gently. This was Wrightsville at its best.

Ellery shut the closet door, looking around.

It was clear that the blackmailer had not engaged the room in the customary way: the towel bar was empty, the window was fastened. Yet Sally's anonymous caller had known as early as yesterday morning that Room 1010 would be available for the rendezvous. It would be essential for him to insure the room's accessibility. He had, then, reserved it, paying cash in advance. But he had not taken open, formal possession. To unlock the door, the blackmailer had therefore used an ordinary hardware store skeleton key; the Hollis's rooms had not yet progressed to the stage of cylinder locks.

It all added up, mused Mr. Queen, seating himself comfortably in the overstuffed chair, to a cautious scoundrel. He would not put in a personal appearance. But there must be contact. Therefore there would be a message.

Ellery wondered how long he would have to wait and how the message would come.

He sat in the chair, relaxed, not smoking.

At the end of ten minutes he rose and began to prowl. He glanced into the closet again. He got down on his knees and looked under the bed. He opened the bureau drawers.

The blackmailer might be waiting to make certain there were no police or hidden confederates about. Or he might have recognized Sally's emissary as a gentleman of some experience in these matters and been frightened away.

I'll give him another ten minutes, thought Ellery.

He picked up the menu.

Roast Pork with Apple Fritters à la Henri . . .

The telephone rang.

Ellery had the receiver off the hook before it could ring the second time.

"Yes?"

The voice said: "Put the money in the right-hand top drawer of the bureau. Close the door. Then go over to Upham House, Room 10. Walk right in. You'll find the letters in the right-hand top drawer of the bureau there."

Ellery said: "Upham House, Room—"

"The letters will be in that room for eight minutes, just long enough for you to walk over there if you start right now."

"But how do I know you aren't—"

There was a click.

Ellery hung up, raced to the bureau, opened the right-hand top drawer, dropped the envelope of money in it, slammed the drawer, and ran out of the room, shutting the door behind him. The corridor was empty. He swore and punched the elevator button. The first elevator appeared almost at once. There was no one in it. Ellery pressed a dollar bill into the hand of the operator, a red-haired boy with freckles.

"Take me right down to the lobby. No stops!" This was no time for finesse.

It was a rapid trip.

Ellery plunged into the lobby crowd and came up with a bellhop.

"Want to make ten dollars the easy way?"

"Yes, sir."

Ellery gave him the ten-spot. "Go right up to the tenth floor —
fast as you can get there — and keep an eye on the door of Room
1010. If anybody comes along, pull a knob-polishing act, anything.
Don't do or say anything, just wait there. 1010. I'll be back in fifteen
minutes."

He hurried out into the Square.

Upham House was on Washington Street, a hundred feet from
the Square. Its two-story wooden pillars were visible from the
Hollis entrance. Ellery shoved his way through the crowds circling
the Square. He crossed Lincoln, passed the Bon Ton, the pharmacy
which had been Myron Garback's, the New York Department
Store. He ran across Washington against the signal . . .

The voice was maddening. It kept whispering in his ear. *"Put
the money in the right-hand top drawer . . ."* Even a whisper can
be revealing. But this whisper . . . Tissue paper! That was it. The
speaker had been whispering through tissue paper. It had given the
voice a hoarse, vibrant, fluttery quality, completely deforming, de-
sexing, ageless.

Room 10 at Upham House. Ground floor, that would be. There
were a few rooms in the west wing. West wing . . . As he hurried
along, a tiny hand knocked at a door. For some reason a pleasant
black face kept popping up, a young man in the uniform of the
United States Army, General Issue. Corporal Abraham L. Jackson!
Corporal Jackson and his testimony in the Davy Fox case. How
he had delivered the six bottles of grape juice when he had been
a delivery boy for Logan's Market. Logan's Market . . . It was
still there, beyond Upham House, at the corner of Washington
and Slocum, its entrance on Slocum. Jackson had . . . What had
Jackson done, and why was it so bothersome now, after all these
years? He had carried the carton out to the delivery truck in
the alley behind Logan's . . . yes . . . that's what he'd testified . . .
the alley which the market shared with the fire exits at the rear
of the Bijou Theater and . . . *and the side entrance of Upham
House.* Side entrance! West side of the building! That was it. It was
a way of getting into the hotel without attracting attention. Ellery

glanced at his watch as he strode past the Upham House entrance. Six and a half minutes. There was the alley . . .

He turned into the alley and ran the rest of the way to the side door.

The corridor, carpeted in Revolutionary blue and papered with a flag-red illustration of the Minute Men at Concord Bridge, was deserted. Two doors away stood the door numbered 10.

The door was closed.

Ellery ran over to it and without hesitation turned the knob. The door gave and he darted in and to the bureau and jerked the top right-hand drawer open.

There lay a bundle of letters.

∽

SIX MINUTES AND a few seconds later Ellery emerged from the third elevator onto the tenth floor of the Hollis. He had run all the way.

"Boy!"

The bellhop stuck his head out of the doorway marked FIRE EXIT.

"Here I am, sir."

Ellery ran up to him, puffing. "Well?"

"Not a thing."

"*Nothing?*"

"No, sir."

Ellery looked the boy over carefully. But all he could detect on the face of Mamie Hood's youngest was curiosity.

"No one went into 1010."

"No, sir."

"Of course no one came out."

"No, sir."

"You didn't take your eyes off the door?"

"Not once."

"You're sure, now."

"Cross my heart." The boy lowered his voice. "You a detective?"

"Well . . . in a way."

"Dame, huh?"

Ellery smiled enigmatically. "Think if a five-spot joined that ten, you could forget all about this?"

"Try me!"

Ellery waited until the boy disappeared in the elevator. Then he ran over to 1010.

The envelope containing the money was gone.

∽

WHEN YOUR WITS are your stock-in-trade, to be outwitted is a blow. To be outwitted in Wrightsville is a haymaker.

Ellery walked back to Upper Dade Street slowly.

How had the blackmailer got the money?

He hadn't been hiding in 1010; Ellery had searched the room before and after. The closet was empty. The bureau drawers were empty (logic must take midgets into account). There was no one under the bed. There was no bathroom. There was not even a door to an adjoining room. He could hardly have entered through the window; a human fly would have packed the Square below like Times Square on New Year's Eve.

Yet the fellow had managed to get into 1010 after Ellery's departure and he had managed to get out before Ellery's return. He had managed to get out even earlier than that . . . before the bell-boy took up his post on the tenth floor.

Of course.

Ellery shook his head at his own innocence. Unless the hop was lying, the answer lay in a simple time sequence. The room was under observation for all but one short period: between the time Ellery stepped into the down-elevator until the time the bellboy stepped out.

In that interval the blackmailer had acted.

He had phoned from inside the Hollis, either from another room on the tenth floor, or the ninth, or from one of the house phones in the lobby. He had placed a time limit on the letters. Shrewd! Reflection should have shown that either the letters were not in the bureau of Room 10 of Upham House at all, or, if they were, the blackmailer would scarcely risk appearing there at the expiration of a stipulated number of minutes to retrieve them. But he had given Ellery no time for reflection. And he had had still another advantage. Reflection or no, Sally's representative was hardly in a position to disobey instructions. The whole point of the blackmailing operation, from the victims' standpoint, was to regain possession of the letters. To achieve this, even the risk of losing the money and failing to get the letters back had to be run. The blackmailer could count on this. And he had done so.

He had simply entered Room 1010 after Ellery's departure, he had taken the money, he had come out again before the bellhop reached the tenth floor. Probably he had strolled down the fire stairway to one of the lower floors and taken an elevator down from there.

Ellery considered returning to the Hollis and investigating the reservation for 1010, and going back to Upham House for some clue the blackmailer may have left there. But then he shrugged and got into Howard's car. He might wind up, through a suspicious clerk, in the hands of Chief Dakin or a reporter for Diedrich Van Horn's *Record*. The police and the newspapers must be avoided.

He found himself wondering by what insanity he had come to be mixed up in the whole dreary business.

⟡

ELLERY PARKED HOWARD's roadster outside *The Hot Spot* on Route 16 and went in. It was thronged and noisy. He sauntered over to the second booth from the rear, on the left, and said, "Mind if I join you?"

The beer before Sally was untouched but there were three empty whiskey glasses before Howard.

Sally was pale: her lipstick made her look paler. She was dressed in a mousy sweater and skirt, with an old gabardine coat over her shoulders. Howard wore a dark gray suit.

They both stared up at him.

Ellery said: "Shove over, Sally," and he sat down beside her, turning so that his back was to the room. A white-aproned waiter pounded past, saying, "I'll be right with you folks," and Ellery said, without looking around, "No hurry." He slipped something into Sally's lap with his left hand as with his right he picked up her glass of beer.

Sally looked down.

Her cheeks flamed.

Howard muttered: "Sally, for the love of God."

"*Oh, Howard.*"

"Pass them to me."

"Under the table," said Ellery. "Oh, waiter. Two beers and another whiskey."

The waiter grabbed the empty glasses and began to swab the table off with a dirty rag.

"Never mind the damn rag," said Howard hoarsely.

The waiter stared and hurried away.

Ellery felt a hand in his. The hand was small, soft, and hot. Then it was withdrawn, quickly.

Howard said: "All four of them. All four, Sal. Ellery — "

"You're sure they're all there. And the right ones."

"Yes."

And Sally nodded. Her eyes burned at Howard.

"They're the originals, not copies?"

"Yes," said Howard again.

And Sally nodded again.

"Pass them to me under the table."

"To you?"

"Howard, you'd argue with God," Sally laughed.

"Watch it!"

The waiter slapped down two beers and a whiskey, belligerently. Howard fumbled in his back pocket.

"I've got it," said Ellery. "Oh, keep it, waiter."

"Say! Thanks." Mollified, the waiter went away.

"Now, Howard." And a moment later, Ellery said: "Now pass the ash tray over here."

He put his hand on the ash tray, looked around casually, and when he looked back the ash tray was on the booth seat between him and Sally.

"Both of you drink, talk."

Sally sipped her beer, her elbows on the table, smiling, and she said to Howard, "Ellery, I'll thank God every night on my knees for you and for this till the day I die. Every night and every morning, too. I'll never forget this, Ellery. Never."

"Look down here," he said.

Sally looked. There was a pile of small scraps on the big glass ash tray.

"Can you see it, Howard?"

"I can see it!"

Ellery lit a cigaret and then transferred the burning match to his left hand and dropped it into the ash tray.

"Watch your coat, Sally."

He made the burnt offering four times.

༆

W<small>HEN THEY HAD</small> gone, separately, Ellery brooded over his third beer. Sally had been first to leave, her shoulders back and her step as light as the flying birds over Quetonokis Lake. There's a quality in pure relief, Ellery mused, which puts a velvet lining on the roughest reality.

As for Howard, he had talked loudly and with exultation.

The letters were retrieved, they were burned, the danger was over. This was what Sally's step had said, and Howard's tone.

No point in disillusioning them.

He went over the events of the afternoon.

The blackmailer had risked leaving the originals of the letters to be picked up *before* collecting his blackmail. Would any self-respecting blackmailer have done this? Suppose the envelope in the bureau drawer at the Hollis had contained strips of blank paper? The originals would have been repossessed and he would have had exactly nothing for his pains. So of course he had had photostats of the four letters made beforehand. Then returning the originals cost him an insignificant asset. Photostats would serve almost precisely the same purpose, especially in this case. Howard's handwriting was distinctive: a peculiar, very small, engraving-like script identifiable at a glance.

No point in telling them now.

Walk in the sun today, Sally. Tomorrow cloudy.

And when the blackmailer calls again, Howard, then what? If you were forced to steal the first time, how will you satisfy a second demand?

And there was something else.

Ellery frowned into his beer.

There was something else.

What it was, exactly, he didn't know. But whatever it was, it made him uneasy. That old prickly sensation again in the scalp. The tickle of doom.

Something was wrong. Not the adultery, or the blackmail episode, or anything he had yet run into in the Van Horn household. Those things were "wrong," but this wrong was a different wrongness, it covered everything. It was a great wrong, as distinguished from a number of lesser wrongs, component wrongs. That was it — component wrongs! When he tried to isolate the source of his unease, a vaguely satisfying solution arose from the sheer concept of an *all-over* wrong of which these individual wrongs were mere parts. As if they were portions of a pattern.

Pattern?

Ellery drained the beer.

Whatever it was, it was developing. Whatever it was, it could only end badly. Whatever it was, he'd better stick around.

He left *The Hot Spot* on the double and exceeded the speed limit returning to North Hill Drive. It was almost as if something was happening at the Van Horn house and by getting there quickly he might avert it.

ஏௗ

BUT HE FOUND nothing out of the ordinary, unless relief is out of the ordinary, and the sudden release of tensions.

Sally at dinner was vivacious. Her eyes sparkled, her teeth flashed. She filled her lord's hall with herself, and Ellery thought how right she looked at the end of the table, opposite Diedrich, and what a pity it would be if not Diedrich sat there, but Howard. Diedrich was in seventh heaven and even Wolfert made a remark about Sally's spirits. Wolfert seemed to take it personally; his remark was edged with malice. But Sally simply laughed at him.

Howard was feeling good, too. He talked volubly about the Museum project, to his father's delight.

"I've started sketching. It feels right. It feels great. I think it's going to be something."

"Which reminds me, Howard," said Ellery. "You know, I haven't even seen your studio. Is it sacred ground, or . . . ?"

"Say! That's right, isn't it? You come on upstairs!"

"Let's all go," said Sally. She glanced at her husband significantly and intimately.

But Wolfert snapped: "You promised to work on the Hutchinson deal tonight, Diedrich. I told him I'd go over the papers with him tomorrow."

"But it's Saturday night, Wolf. And tomorrow's Sunday. Can't that crowd wait until Monday morning?"

"They want to get going Monday morning."

"Hell!" Diedrich scowled. "All right. Darling, I'm sorry. I'm afraid you're going to have to be host as well as hostess tonight."

Ellery had expected something vast and grand, with gargantuan draperies in royal swoops and huge blocks of stone sitting about in various stages of nascence, the whole resembling a sculptor's studio on a Hollywood sound stage. He found nothing of the sort. The studio was large, but it was also simple; there were no great blocks of stone ("You don't have the architectural mind, Ellery," Howard laughed. "This floor would hardly support them!") and the draperies were reasonable. The place was a clutter of small armatures, points, modeling stands, and tools — clamps, gouges, vises, scrapers, chisels, mallets and so on, which Howard explained had different uses, in wood and ivory carving as well as in stone. Many small models stood about, and rough sketches.

"I use this place for the preliminary work," Howard explained. "There's a big barn of a building 'way out in back which I'll show you tomorrow if you like, Ellery. I do the finished work there, I mean on the stone. It has a good solid floor and it'll take a lot of weight. It also simplifies carting the blocks in and the finish out. Imagine trying to hoist a three-ton block of marble up here!"

Howard had done a number of sketches for the Museum figures. "These are all very rough," he said. "Just an all-over visualization. I haven't got down to specifics yet. I'll make more detailed sketches and then get to work with the plasticine. I'll be holed up in the attic here for a long, long time before I'm ready to go ahead in the back studio."

"Dieds told me, Howard," said Sally, "that you wanted some changes made in the studio down there."

"Yes. I think the floor will have to be strengthened and I want another window cut into the west wall. I'll need all the light I can get. And a lot more distance. I'm considering having the west wall knocked out and the studio there enlarged by at least half."

"You mean to hold all your sculptures physically?" asked Ellery.

"No, for perspective. The problem of decorative, monumental sculpture is a lot different from portrait sculpture or even the sort of thing Michelangelo did. You have to get up close to his work really to appreciate it—the textures, details of contour, and so on. At a distance that kind of work tends to blur, get shapeless. My problem is different. These figures must be planned to be seen from a distance, in the open air. The technique will have to be sharp and clear—clear silhouettes, profiles. That's why Greek sculpture appears to such remarkable advantage in the open—why, as a matter of fact, I go for the neoclassic. I'm strictly an outdoor chiseler."

Howard was a different man here. His confusion and introspection were gone, his brow was untroubled, and he spoke with authority and even grace. Ellery began to feel a little ashamed of himself. He had thought of Diedrich's "purchase" of a museum as a rather sickening phenomenon of wealth. Now he saw it as possibly giving a talented young artist an opportunity to create something altogether worth-while. It was a new element in his calculations; one he liked very much.

"All these evidences of creative activity," said Ellery with a grin, "recalls me to my own piddling efforts over at the cottage. Would you two consider me very unfriendly if I ducked over there and tormented my typewriter for a while?"

They were properly contrite; and Ellery left them with their heads together over a sketch, Howard talking animatedly and Sally listening with bright eyes and her lips moist and parted.

So it's all over, is it? Ellery thought grimly. Not all evidence takes the form of letters. He was glad that Diedrich was two floors down, in his study.

＊ ࿓

ELLERY WAS THINKING that it would serve the blackmailer right if Diedrich found out simply by using his eyes and thereby rendered the photostats null, void, and of no value . . . when he saw her again.

He was just rounding the bend in the staircase halfway between the top and second floors. It was the shadow of a shadow, but the shadow's shadow was in the half-bent shape of an angry cat, and he knew it was the old woman.

He leaped noiselessly down the few steps to the second floor and flattened himself against the wall.

She was moving slowly down the hall, an old sickle of a creature with a cowling shawl over her head, and as she moved she mumbled something incredible.

"*There the wicked cease from troubling, and there the weary be at rest.*"

She stopped at the very end of the hall, before a door. To Ellery's astonishment she fumbled in her garments and produced a key. This key she inserted into the lock. When she had unlocked the door she pushed it open and Ellery saw nothing beyond it. It was a rectangle of outer space.

Then the door shut and he heard the snick of the key from the invisible ether.

She lived here.

She lived here, and no one had mentioned her in two and a half days. Not Howard, not Sally, not Diedrich, not Wolfert — not Laura or Eileen.

Why? And who was she?

The old woman had a way of slipping in and out of his consciousness like a witch in a dream.

Guest or no guest, Ellery thought wildly, running down the stairs, here's where I find out what the hell gives.

The Fifth Day

ELLERY HAD JUST reached the foot of the stairway when he heard running and he looked up to see Sally swooping down on him like Superman.

"What is it?" he asked quickly.

"I don't know." She caught at his arm to steady herself and he felt her shaking. "I left Howard just after you did and I went to my room. Diedrich called on the intercom to come right down to the study."

"Diedrich?"

She was frightened.

"Do you suppose . . . ?"

Howard came clattering down, white.

"Father just called me on the intercom!"

And there was Wolfert, the skirt of an old-fashioned bathrobe flapping about his skinned legs, his Adam's apple sticking out like an old bone.

"Diedrich woke me up. What's the matter?"

They hurried to the study in a clash of silences.

Diedrich was waiting for them impatiently. The papers on his desk had been brushed to one side. His hair was all exclamation points.

"Howard!" He grabbed Howard, hugged him. "Howard, they said it couldn't be done and, by God, it's *been* done!"

"Dieds, I could strangle you," Sally said with an angry laugh. "You scared us half to death. *What's* been done?"

"Yes! I almost broke my neck getting down those stairs," growled Howard.

Diedrich put his hands on Howard's shoulders, held him off. "Son," he said solemnly, "they've found out who you are."

"*Dieds.*"

"Found out who I am," Howard repeated.

"What are you talking about, Diedrich?" asked Wolfert peevishly.

"Just what I said, Wolf. Oh, we have Mr. Queen at a disadvantage, don't we?"

"Perhaps I'd better be getting on to the cottage, Mr. Van Horn," said Ellery. "I was on my way there when — "

"No, no, I'm sure Howard won't mind. You see, Mr. Queen, Howard's my adopted son. He was left on my doorstep as an infant by . . . well, until now," chuckled Diedrich, "it might just as well have been by the stork. But sit down, sit down, Mr. Queen. Howard, get off those big feet of yours before you fall off 'em. Sally, come sit on my lap. This is something of an occasion! Wolf, smile. That Hutchinson business can wait."

Somehow they were seated and Diedrich went on happily to tell Ellery what he already knew. He managed to convey the proper surprise, while observing Howard out of the corner of his eye. Howard was sitting motionless. His hands were on his knees. The expression on his face was baffling. Was it apprehension that pinched his mouth? Certainly his eyes had a glaze over them; and a little irregular tom-tom was beating his temple.

"I hired a detective agency in 1917," said Diedrich, his hand on Sally's hair, "when Howard was left with me, in an effort to track down his parents. Wasn't really an 'agency' — or rather, it was a one-man agency. Old Ted Fyfield was the man. He'd retired as police chief and gone into business for himself. Well, I practically supported Fyfield for three years with fees for his work — including all the time I was in the Army — you remember, Wolf. And when he couldn't find a trace after all that time I gave up."

It was hard to tell whether Howard was even listening. Sally saw it, too. She was puzzled, worried.

"It's funny how little things sometimes are the most important,"

Diedrich went on heartily. "Couple of months ago I was getting a trim in Joe Lupin's chair at the Hollis barber shop — "

"Tonsorial Parlor," murmured Mr. Queen nostalgically. Joe Lupin had come into the Haight case through his wife Tessie, who worked in the Lower Main Beauty Shop. It was The Hollis Tonsorial Parlor, Luigi Marino, Prop., and now that Ellery thought of it, he'd noticed Marino's salt-and-pepper head that very afternoon, bent over a lathered face, as he had sidled through the Hollis lobby.

" — and I got to talking to J. C. Pettigrew, who was under the sun lamp in the next chair. You know, dear. The real estate fellow . . ."

Ellery could still see J. C.'s Number Twelves up on his desk in the real estate office on Lower Main that day he had hit Wrightsville for the first time; the shoes and the ivory toothpick.

"The conversation got around to old-timers who had passed on and somebody — I think it was Luigi — mentioned old Ted Fyfield, who'd been dead for years. J. C. perked up and said, 'Dead or not dead, that Fyfield was a crook and a skunk,' and he went on to tell about the time he'd paid Ted a small fortune in expense money and fees to track down a fellow who'd run out on a realty deal leaving J. C. holding the bag, only to find out that Ted was giving him completely fictitious reports all the time he was collecting J. C.'s money for 'investigating' — that Ted hadn't even left Wrightsville or lifted a finger to earn that money! J. C. said he threatened to have Fyfield's private detective license revoked and the old scoundrel ponied up fast. Well, it gave me a queer feeling, because I'd paid Fyfield a small fortune myself for three years. Then it turned out that nearly everybody in the barber shop had some discreditable yarn to tell about Ted Fyfield, and by the time they were through I was sick. I hate to be played for a sucker, makes me see red. But more important than that, I'd depended on Fyfield in a matter that . . . well, that was mighty important to all of us."

Sally's frown was deep now. She put her arm around her husband's neck and said lightly: "You should have been a writer, darling. All these *details*. What's the exciting part?"

Wolfert just sat there, in brine.

"Well, sir," Diedrich said grimly, "I played a hunch. I decided to reopen the whole business on the chance that Fyfield had skinned me thirty years ago and not done any real investigating at all. I put the matter in the hands of a reputable agency in Connhaven."

"You never told me." It came out stiff and new, in a strange-sounding voice, not like Howard's at all.

"No, son, because I figured it was the longest kind of shot — after thirty years — and I didn't want to raise your hopes until I had something definite.

"Well, the long shot came through. Fyfield *had* skinned me, the —" Sally put her hand over his mouth. He grinned. "Just a few minutes ago I got a call from Connhaven. It was the head of this agency. They had the whole story, son. They couldn't believe their own luck — they'd taken the case on, telling me I was wasting their time and my money. But I played my hunch — and now we know."

Howard asked: "Who are my parents?" in the same stiff way.

"Son . . ." Diedrich hesitated. Then he said gently: "They're dead, son. I'm sorry."

"Dead," said Howard. You could see him struggling through that intelligence: they were dead, his father and mother were dead, they weren't living, he would never see them, know what they had looked like, and that was bad, or was it good?

Sally said, "Well, I'm not sorry."

She jumped off her husband's lap and perched on his desk, fingering a paper. "I'm not sorry because if they were alive, Howard, it would be the most stupid sort of mess. You'd be a total stranger to them and they to you. It would confuse everybody and do no one concerned the least good. I'm not sorry at all, Howard. And don't you be!"

"No." Howard was staring. Ellery didn't like the way he was staring. The glaze was thickening over his eyes. "All right, they're dead," he said slowly. "But who were they?"

"Your father, Howard, was a farmer," Diedrich replied. "And your mother was a farmer's wife. Poor, poor people, son. They lived in a primitive farmhouse about ten miles from here — between

Wrightsville and Fidelity. You'll remember, Wolf, how desolate that stretch in there was thirty years ago."

Wolfert said: "Farmer, huh?" The way he said it made Ellery want to stuff his dentures down his throat. Sally slew him with a look, and even Diedrich frowned.

But Howard was impervious to tones of voice. He simply sat staring at his foster father.

"They were too poor to hire hands for the farm, according to the information the agency gathered," continued Diedrich. "Your parents had to do it all themselves. They barely managed to scratch a living from the soil. Then your mother had a baby. You."

"And zing, she tosses me on the nearest doorstep." Howard smiled, and Ellery wished he would go back to staring.

"You were born in the middle of the night during a bad summer thunderstorm," Diedrich smiled back, but no longer was his face happy; he was regretful now, uneasy, and a little sharp, as if he were angry with himself for having misjudged Howard's reaction. And he spoke more rapidly. "The Connhaven agency was able to reconstruct the events of that night from the records they found, and the thunderstorm is important.

"Your mother, Howard, was attended by a Wrightsville man, a Dr. Southbridge, and when you'd been born and taken care of and your mother was comfortable, the doctor started back to town in his buggy, at the height of the storm. Well, on the way back his horse must have been frightened by lightning and got out of control, because the horse, Dr. Southbridge, and the buggy were found at the bottom of a ravine, just off the road. The buggy was smashed, the horse had two broken legs, and the doctor a crushed chest — he was dead when they found him. Of course, he'd had no opportunity to record your birth at Town Hall. The agency thinks that's one of the reasons your parents did what they did. Apparently they felt they were too poor to bring you up right — there were no other children — and realizing when they heard about Dr. Southbridge's accident that he couldn't have had time to record your birth, they saw a chance to put you into the care of someone better off who wouldn't be able to trace you back to them.

"Apparently only they and Southbridge knew about your birth, and the doctor was dead.

"Why they left you on our doorstep, of course, no one will ever know. I doubt if it had anything to do with us personally — it was a pretty prosperous-looking house; at least it must have seemed so to a couple of poor farmers."

"That's all on the assumption," smiled Howard, "that they did it all for little Nameless. But how do you know they didn't do it just because they didn't want little Nameless?"

"Oh, Howard, shut up and stop that breast-beating," snapped Sally. She was terribly concerned; concerned and restless and angry with Diedrich.

Diedrich said hastily: "Anyway, the Connhaven detectives found out all this as a result of locating Dr. Southbridge's appointment book. It was a pocket affair, a notebook, and it had been taken from the doctor's clothes by the undertaker and put among the dead man's effects, winding up in the attic of his old house where the investigators located it. The entry in the doctor's handwriting, apparently made as he was leaving the farmhouse, of the birth of a male child to the farmer's wife corresponds exactly in date to your date of birth, Howard, as given in that note that was pinned to your blanket when I found you; and the agency man tells me — I'd of course kept the note all these years and I'd given it to the agency — that the hand-writing on it is absolutely beyond question the handwriting of the farmer — they managed to dig up a sample on an old mortgage. And that, Howard," concluded Diedrich with a sigh of relief, "is the story. So now you can stop wondering about who you were" — his eyes twinkled — "and start being what you are."

"And that's the first *bright* thing I've heard you say tonight, Dieds," cried Sally. "Now how about all of us having some coffee?"

"Wait," said Howard. "Who am I?"

"Who are you?" Diedrich winced. Then he said heartily, "You're my son, Howard Hendrik Van Horn. Who on earth would you be?"

"I mean who was I? What was the name?"

"Didn't I mention it? It was Waye."

"Waye?"

"W-a-y-e."

"Waye." Howard seemed to be tasting it. "Waye . . . " He shook his head, as if it had no flavor for him at all. "Didn't I have a first name?"

"No, son. I guess they hadn't given you one — left that job, and it was sensible, too, to the ones who'd bring you up. At least no Christian name for the child appeared in Dr. Southbridge's notation."

"Christian. Were they Christians?"

"Oh, what difference would that make?" said Sally. "Christian, Jewish, Mohammedan — you're what you were brought up. Let's stop this now!"

"They were Christians, son. What denomination I don't know."

"And you say they're dead, huh?"

"Yes."

"How'd they die?"

"Well . . . Son, I think Sally's right." Diedrich rose suddenly. "We've talked enough about this."

"How'd they die?"

Wolfert's eyes were bright. His glances kept darting from Diedrich to Howard like quick little animals.

"About ten years after they left you with me, a fire broke out on their farm. They were both burned to death." Diedrich rubbed his head in a rather odd gesture of fatigue. "I'm really sorry, son. This was stupid of me."

The glaze fascinated Ellery. It suddenly occurred to him that he might be witnessing the beginning of an amnesia attack. The thought jarred him.

He said quickly: "Howard, this is all pretty unsettling and exciting, but Sally was right before. It's all for the best — "

Howard did not even glance in his direction. "Didn't they leave anything, Father? An old photo or something?"

"Son . . . "

"Answer me, damn it!"

Howard was on his feet, swaying. Diedrich looked shocked. Sally gripped his arm reassuringly, without taking her eyes off Howard.

"Why . . . why, after the fire, son, some relative of your mother's saw to the funeral and took away the few things that weren't destroyed in the fire. The farm itself was mortgaged to the hilt —"

"What relative? Who is it? Where can I find him?"

"There's no trace of him, Howard. He moved from here shortly afterward. The agency had no information about his whereabouts."

"I see," said Howard. And then he asked, in a slow thick voice, "And where are they buried?"

"I can tell you that, son," said Diedrich quickly. "They're in adjoining graves in the Fidelity cemetery. Now how about some of that coffee, Sally?" he boomed. "I know I can use some, and Howard —"

But Howard was on his way out of the study. He was walking wide-eyed, hands raised a little, and he kept stumbling.

They heard his uneven steps going upstairs.

And in a little while they heard the slam of a door from the top of the house.

ᖆᕵ

SALLY WAS so incensed that Ellery thought she was going to be indiscreet.

"Dieds, this was terribly ill-advised! You know how the least emotional upset sends Howard off!"

"But, dearest," said Diedrich miserably, "I thought it would do him good to know. He's always wanted to so badly."

"You might at least have discussed it with me beforehand!"

"I'm sorry, darling."

"Sorry! Did you see his face?"

He looked at his wife in a puzzled way. "Sally, I don't understand you. You've always thought it would be a good thing if Howard learned about . . . "

Sally. This is a clever man you're married to.

"I'm completely out of order," said Ellery cheerfully, "and nobody's asked me to put my two pennies in, but, Sally, I think Mr. Van Horn's done the only possible thing. Of course it's a shock to Howard. It would be to a stable personality. But Howard's ignorance of his origin has been one of the mainstays of his unhappiness. When the shock wears off — "

She caught it. He knew it by the way her lids came down and her hands fluttered down to rest. But she was still angry, woman-wise; perhaps angrier.

All she actually said was, "Well, I can be wrong. Forgive me, dearest."

And then Wolfert Van Horn said a really shocking thing. He had been sitting forward with his skeletal knees drawn up and his torso bent far forward. Now, like Jack-in-the-Box, he sprang to the perpendicular, his bathrobe falling open to reveal his furred and brittle chest.

"Diedrich, how does this affect your will?"

His brother stared at him. "My what?"

"You never did have a head for technicalities." Now Wolfert's voice was more metallic than acidulous; it had something of the whine of a band saw. "Your will, your will. Wills can be mighty important instruments. In a situation like this they can cause a lot of trouble — "

"Situation? I wasn't aware, Wolf, of any 'situation.'"

"What would you call it — normal?" Wolfert smiled his sucked-in smile. "You've got three heirs — me, Sally, Howard. Howard's an adopted son. Sally is a pretty recent wife — " and Ellery could actually hear the quotation marks around the last word.

Diedrich was sitting very quietly.

" — and as I understand it, we share and share alike?"

"Wolf, I don't get this at all. What's this all about?"

"One of your heirs now turns out to be a man named Waye," grinned Wolfert. "It could make a difference to a lawyer."

"I think," said Sally, "Mr. Queen and I'll take a walk in the garden, Dieds," and Ellery was half out of his chair when Died-rich said gently, "Don't," and then he got up and went over to his brother and stood looking down at his brother and his brother pushed away a little nervously and showed his gray dentures.

"It doesn't, Wolfert, and it won't. Howard is properly identified in my will. His legal name is Howard Hendrik Van Horn. And that's what it stays unless he himself wants to change it." Diedrich loomed unusually large. "What I don't understand, Wolf, is why you'd bring it up at all. You know I don't like double talk. What's on your mind? What's behind this?"

And there was that hell again in Wolfert's little avian eyes. The brothers stared at each other, one sitting, the other standing. Ellery could hear them breathing, Diedrich deeply and Wolfert in sniffly spurts. It was one of those interminable moments of pure crisis during which whole histories are written; when the flutter of a fly's wing can start an avalanche. Or that was how it felt. For it was impossible to say that Wolfert *knew*. He was so naturally snide that even his ignorance seemed rotten with meaning; he gave off the unpleasant secrets of corpses.

Then the moment passed, and Wolfert creaked to his feet. "Diedrich, you're a damned fool," he said, and he stalked out of the study like the Scarecrow of Oz.

And Diedrich stood there, in the same position, and Sally went up to him and stood on tiptoes to kiss his cheek; and she said good night to Ellery with her eyes and then she walked out, too.

ɔᴎɔ

"Don't go yet, Mr. Queen."

Ellery turned back at the door.

"This hasn't worked out quite as I expected." It sounded plaintive, and Diedrich laughed at his own tone and motioned to a chair. "Life keeps us hopping, doesn't it? Sit down, Mr. Queen."

Ellery found himself wishing Howard and Sally had not gone upstairs.

"I seem to recall defending my brother," Diedrich went on with a grimace, "on the ground that he's unhappy. I forgot to mention that misery likes to have company. By the way, have you got anywhere yet on that twenty-five thousand dollar business?"

Ellery almost jumped.

"Why . . . Mr. Van Horn, it's only been twenty-four hours."

Van Horn nodded. He circled his desk and sat down behind it
and began to fuss with some papers. "Laura told me you were out
this afternoon. I thought . . . "

Damn Laura! thought Mr. Queen.

"Well, yes, but . . . "

"A thing as simple as this," Diedrich said carefully. "I mean, I
thought it would be child's play . . . "

"Sometimes," said Ellery, "the simplest cases are the hardest."

"*Mr. Queen*," Diedrich said slowly, "*you know who took that
money.*"

Ellery blinked. He was annoyed with himself, with Van Horn,
with Sally, Howard, Wrightsville — but chiefly with himself. He
might have known that a man of Diedrich's perspicacity would not
be taken in by mumbo-jumbo, even of the superior Queen brand.

Ellery decided quickly.

He said nothing.

"You know, but you won't tell me."

The big figure swiveled behind the desk, turning his face away
as if he felt the sudden need for withdrawal. But there were long
twists of wrinkle on his shoulder and his very immobility betrayed
the forces at work beneath it.

Ellery said nothing.

"You must have a strong reason for not telling me." He sprang
to his feet. But then his big body settled and there he was, his
hands clasped behind him, looking out into the darkness.

"A very strong reason," he repeated.

But Ellery could only sit there.

Diedrich's powerful shoulders sagged and his hands contracted in
a sort of convulsion; the whole effect was curiously like death. *If an
autopsy were to be held at this moment Van Horn would be found
to have died of doubt. He knows nothing and he suspects everything
— that is, everything but the truth. To a man like Diedrich Van
Horn, this could be very like dying.*

Then he turned back and Ellery could see that, whatever it was
that had died, Diedrich had already anatomized it and flung it away.

"I didn't get to my age," he said with a grim smile, "without learning how to tell when I'm licked. You know, you won't tell me, and that's that. Mr. Queen, drop the whole thing."

And all Ellery could find to say was, "Thank you."

೧೨

THEY TALKED FOR a few minutes about Wrightsville, but it was not a successful conversation; at the first opportunity Ellery rose and they said good night.

But at the door Ellery stopped in mid-step.

"Mr. Van Horn!"

Diedrich looked surprised.

"I almost forgot again. Would you mind telling me," Ellery said, "who in heaven's name that very old woman is? The one I've seen in the gardens and upstairs entering a dark bedroom?"

"You mean to say — "

"Now don't tell me," said Ellery firmly, "that you never heard of her. Because I'll run screaming into the night."

"Good grief, hasn't anyone told you *that?*"

"No, and it's driving me mad."

Diedrich laughed and laughed. Finally, wiping his eyes, he fumbled for Ellery's arm and said: "Come on back and have a brandy. That's my mother."

೧೨

THERE WAS NO mystery. Christina Van Horn was approaching her hundredth year; rather, her hundredth year was approaching Christina Van Horn, for she had no awareness of time and she was today what she had been for forty-odd years — an arrested creature roaming the barrens of her mind.

"I suppose the reason none of us mentioned her," said Diedrich over the brandy, "is that she doesn't 'live' with us in the usual sense. She lives in another world — the world of my father. Mother began to act queer after Father's death, when Wolfert and I were still boys. Far from her bringing us up, we tended more and more to take care of *her*. She'd come from a very strict Dutch Calvinist home, but when she married Father she really lived with hell's fire, and at Father's death she took up his . . . " Diedrich groped, "his *ferocious* piety as a sort of tribute to his memory. Physically, Mama's a wonderful specimen; the doctors marvel at her stamina. She leads an absolutely independent life. She won't mix with us, she won't even eat with us. Half the time she doesn't even bother to put her lights on. She knows the Bible practically by heart."

Diedrich was surprised to hear that Ellery had seen his mother in the gardens.

"She doesn't leave her room for months at a time. She's perfectly capable of caring for herself and she's almost comically insistent on her privacy. She hates Laura and Eileen," Diedrich chuckled, "and she won't let them into her room. They have to leave her meals on a tray outside her door, and fresh linen, and so on. You ought to see that room of hers, Mr. Queen — she keeps it clean herself. You could eat off the floor."

"I'd like very much to meet her, Mr. Van Horn."

"You would?" Diedrich was pleased. "Well, come on."

"At this hour?"

"Mother's a night owl. Up half the night, does most of her sleeping during the day. She's marvelous. Anyway, as I told you, time doesn't mean a thing to her."

On their way upstairs, Diedrich asked: "Did you see her very clearly?"

"No."

"Well, don't be surprised at what you find. Mama got out of step with the world the day Papa died. She just dropped out of the ranks and there she's stayed, at the turn of the century, while everybody else has gone on."

"Forgive me, but she sounds like a character in a novel."

"She's a character in five novels," chuckled Diedrich. "She's never ridden in an automobile or seen a movie, she won't touch a telephone, she denies the existence of the airplane, and she considers the radio sheer witchcraft. In fact, I often think Mama believes she's living in a literal purgatory — presided over by the Devil in person."

"What will she say about television?"

"I hate to think about it!"

They found the old woman in her room, an unopened Bible in her lap.

Whistler's great-grandmother, was Ellery's first thought. Her face was a mummified, shrunken version of Diedrich's, with a still formidable jaw and proud cheekbones covered loosely with pale leather. Her eyes, like Diedrich's, were the essence of her; they must once, like her elder son's, have been of extraordinary beauty. She was dressed in black bombazine and her head, which Ellery surmised was nearly bald, was concealed under a black shawl. Her hands had a feeble sort of independent life; the thick stiff blue knobby fingers moved ever so slightly, but continuously, over the Bible in her lap.

A tray lay on a table beside her, barely touched.

It was like walking into a different house, in another world, at a distant time. The room bore no relationship to the rest of the mansion. It was poor and old, with battered, very crude handmade furniture, its papered walls yellow with age, and hooked rugs on the floor from which the colors had all but disappeared. There was almost no decoration. The fireplace was of blackened brick, with a handhewn mantelpiece. A Dutch cupboard with chipped and undistinguished delftware stood incongruously beyond the wide and swaybacked bedstead.

There was no beauty in it anywhere.

"It's the room my father died in," explained Diedrich. "I simply took it along with me when I built this house. Mama could never be happy in anything else . . . Mama?"

The ancient woman seemed glad to see them. She peered up at her son and then at Ellery and her withered lips parted in a grin. But then Ellery realized that her pleasure was the pleasure of a disciplinarian about to employ the switch.

"You're late again, Diedrich!" Her voice was remarkably strong and deep, but it had a curious flickering quality, like a radio signal that keeps fading out and in again. "Remember what your father says. *Wash ye, make you clean.* Let me see your hands!"

Diedrich dutifully held out his great paws and the old lady seized them, peered at them, turned them over. During her inspection she seemed to notice the massiveness of the hands she held in her claws, for her expression softened and she looked up at Diedrich and said: "Soon now, my son. Soon now."

"Soon what, Mama?"

"You'll be a man!" she snapped, and then she cackled at her own wit. Suddenly her glance darted to Ellery. "He doesn't come to see me often, Diedrich. Nor the girl."

"She thinks you're Howard," whispered Van Horn. "Incidentally, she doesn't seem to be able to remember that Sally's my wife. Half the time she calls her Howard's wife — Mama, this isn't Howard. This gentleman is a friend."

"Not Howard?" The news seemed to distress her. "Friend?" She kept peering up at Ellery like an animated little question mark. Suddenly she popped back in her rocker and began rocking violently.

"What is it, Mama?" asked Diedrich.

She refused to answer.

"Friend," said Diedrich again. "His name is — "

"Yea!" said his mother; and Ellery quailed, her glance was so fierce. "*Yea, mine own familiar friend, in whom I trusted, which did eat of my bread, hath lifted up his heel against me!*"

He recognized the Forty-first Psalm with uneasiness. She had mistaken him for Howard; and the word "friend" had sent her untethered mind skittering back to what seemed to Ellery a wonderfully relevant cross reference.

She stopped rocking, snapped, "Judas!" with pure venom, and set herself in motion once more.

"She seems to have taken a dislike to you," said Van Horn sheepishly.

"Yes," muttered Ellery. "I'd better go. No point in upsetting her."

Diedrich stooped over the little centenarian, kissed her gently, and they turned to leave.

But Christina Van Horn had not finished.

Rocking with an energy Ellery found slightly distasteful, she shrieked: "*We have made a covenant with death!*"

The last thing Ellery saw as his host closed the door was the little creature's fierce eyes, still glaring at him.

"Dislike is right," Ellery said with a laugh. "What did she mean by that parting shot, Mr. Van Horn? It sounded rather lethal to me."

"She's old," Diedrich said. "She feels her death is near. She wasn't talking about you, Mr. Queen."

But as Ellery picked his way across the dark gardens to the guest house, he wondered if the old lady might not have meant someone else entirely. That Parthian glare had had a point.

Just as he reached the cottage, a delicate rain began to fall.

The Sixth Day

AND THERE WAS no sleep in him.

Ellery moved restlessly about the cottage. Beyond the picture window Wrightsville frolicked. The bars would be swarming in Low Village; there would be the Saturday night dance at the Country Club in summer formals; Pine Grove would be jumping with bebop; he could actually see the pearly shimmer of *The Hot Spot* and Gus Olesen's *Roadside Tavern* on the silver chain of Route 16; and the decorous blaze above Hill Drive told him that the Granjons, the F. Henry Minikins, the Dr. Emil Poffenbergers, the Livingstons, and the Wrights were "entertaining."

The Wrights . . . All that seemed so long ago, so tenderly pure. And that was laughable, because when it happened it had been neither tender nor pure. Ellery supposed that his memories had undergone the usual metamorphosis through the witchcraft of time.

Or was it that what had been neither tender nor pure appeared so sheerly by contrast with the present reality?

Good sense challenged this theory. The crimes of adultery and blackmail were surely not more heinous than cunning murder.

Then what was it that made him sense a special quality of evil. in the Van Horn case? Evil, that was it. *We have made a covenant with death, and with hell are we at agreement . . . for we have made lies our refuge, and under falsehood have we hid ourselves . . . For the bed is shorter than that a man can stretch himself on it; and the covering narrower than that he can wrap himself in it.*

Ellery scowled. It was God with whom Isaiah had threatened

Ephraim. Old Christina had misquoted Scripture. *For the Lord shall rise up as in mount Perazim, he shall be wroth as in the valley of Gibeon, that he may do his work, his strange work; and bring to pass his act, his strange act.*

He had the most irritating feeling that he was trying to grab at something as impalpable as it was slick. Nothing made sense.

He was as bad as the mummified crone in her tomb over there.

Ellery put away the Bible he had found on the bookshelf and turned to his reproachful typewriter.

ᕯ

TWO HOURS LATER he examined what he had milled. It was a stony grist. Two pages and eleven lines of a third, with numerous X-marks and triple word changes, and nothing sang. In one place, where he had intended to write *Sanborn*, he had actually written *Vanhorn*. His heroine, who had been reasonably emancipated for two hundred and six pages, had suddenly turned into an elderly Girl Guide.

He tore up two hours' work, covered the typewriter, filled his pipe, poured himself a Scotch, and strolled out onto the porch.

It was raining hard now. The pool looked like the moon and the garden was a black sponge. But the porch was dry, and he sat down in a cane-bottomed bamboo easy chair to watch the attack.

He could see the watery bombardment on the north terrace of the main house and for a long time he gave himself over to simple observation, with no purpose but distraction from his restlessness. The house was as dark as his thoughts; if the old woman was still up, she had turned out her lights. He wondered if she might not be sitting in the dark, as he was, and what she might be thinking . . .

ᕯ

HOW LONG ELLERY sat there he could not have said. But when it happened he found himself on his feet, the pipe in scattered ashes on the floor beside the empty glass.

He had fallen asleep, and something had aroused him.

It was still raining; the garden was a swamp. He had a faraway recollection of thunder.

But then he heard it again, above the rain.

It was not thunder.

It was a racing automobile engine.

A car was coming around the main house, from the south, from the direction of the Van Horn garage.

There it was.

It was Howard's roadster.

Someone was trying to warm up a cold motor, riding the clutch and pumping the accelerator in short bursts. Whoever it was couldn't know much about cars, Ellery thought.

Whoever it was.

Of course, it must be Howard.

Howard.

As the car got halfway under the porte-cochère, the engine stalled.

Howard.

Ellery could hear the sullen whines of the starter. The engine did not turn over, and after a moment the starter stopped whining. He heard the roadster door open and the sound of someone jumping onto the gravel of the driveway. A dark figure came quickly around and raised the hood. An instant later a slender beam appeared, groping in the motor.

It was Howard, all right. There was no mistaking the long trench coat, the wide-brimmed Stetson Howard affected.

Where was he going? There was a frantic quality in the swift movements of the figure behind the headlights' glare. Where was Howard going in the late night, in a heavy rainstorm, frantically?

And suddenly Ellery remembered Howard's face as it had been in the study a few hours before: the pinchiness about the mouth, the glaze over the staring eyes, the tom-tom in his temple, as his father related the findings of the Connhaven detective agency. His stumbling from the study, his erratic steps mounting to the studio. *Might be witnessing the beginning of an amnesia episode . . .*

᷍

ELLERY DASHED INTO the cottage, not stopping to switch on the lights. It took him no more than fifteen seconds to find his topcoat

and run out again, struggling into his coat as he ran. But already
the motor was roaring, the hood was down, the car was in motion.

As he splashed across the gardens Ellery opened his mouth to
yell. But he didn't; it was useless; Howard wouldn't hear him
above the motor and the storm and the headlights were already
swinging away toward the open drive.

Ellery flew.

He could only hope one of the cars in the garage had keys in it.
The first car. . . Key in the ignition!

He blessed Sally as he sent her convertible hurtling out of the
garage.

He was already damp from the run around; within ten seconds
at the wheel he was soaked from head to foot. The top was down
and he made an attempt to find the switch that controlled it. Not
finding it quickly, he gave up; it didn't matter now, he couldn't
get any wetter; and the condition of the corkscrew driveway called
for concentration.

There was no sign of Howard's roadster anywhere along the
drive. Ellery skidded to a stop just outside the entrance to the
estate, on North Hill Drive, prepared to turn either way instantly.

Nothing was to be seen to the right, toward Hill Drive.

But to the left, going north, there was a dwindling taillight.

Ellery swung Sally's convertible hard left and stepped on the
accelerator.

ᖰᕙ

AT FIRST HE thought Howard was heading for the Mahoganies, perhaps Quetonokis Lake, which was atonement, or Lake Pharisee,
which was original sin. In the grip of amnesia Howard might be
moved by some obscure urging to return to the scene of an emotional crisis. All this, of course, if it was Howard's taillight. If it
was not, if Howard had turned south on North Hill Drive and
headed for town, he was lost for good.

Ellery pressed harder.

At sixty-five he began to gain.

Serve me right, he thought, if I find out it's some upstate drunk's car just as I skid off the road and bring my career as a wet nurse to a messy conclusion.

The rain spouted off his nose. His shoes were so wet that his right foot kept slipping off the accelerator.

But he continued to gain, suddenly with great rapidity, and then he saw the brake light of the car he was following and he jammed on his own brake. Why was the car slowing?

The blinker of an intersection answered him just as the car ahead turned sharply left. But for an instant it was fixed in the convertible's headlights and Ellery saw that the roadster was Howard's. Then it disappeared.

He missed the road sign in the darkness and rain. But left was west, which meant they were flanking Wrightsville. He kept the red light at a constant distance. Howard had decelerated to a mere twenty-five miles an hour, another puzzle; but it enabled Ellery to turn off his brights and become less conspicuous.

So it wasn't either of the lakes.

What was it?

Or didn't Howard himself know?

It occurred to Ellery that for the first time he was justifying his trip to Wrightsville.

All at once he knew why Howard had slowed down.

He was looking for something.

Then the roadster's taillight disappeared for the second time.

So he'd found it.

And Ellery found it a few moments later.

It was a fork in the road. At the fork there was a small local sign, and the sign said:

FIDELITY

2 Miles

∞

THE FORK HAD been a dirt road; now it was deep and affectionate glue. It not only clung to the wheels; it twisted and dipped and soared and doubled back like a fox on the run. Within thirty seconds Ellery had lost Howard.

Mr. Queen began to curse, bubbling like a whale as he wrestled with the convertible.

His speedometer sank to 18, then to 14, and finally to 9 miles an hour.

He clung to the wheel doggedly, not caring whether he caught up with Howard or not. He was seated in a small lake and he squished every time he shifted. He could feel cold rivulets coursing down his naked back. He had long since turned his brights on again, but all he could see was the interminable striped wall of the rain and drenched trees to either side. He passed a few miserable houses, cowering by the roadside.

He also passed Howard's roadster before he realized what it was. There had been no town. It was less than two miles from the fork. Why had Howard stopped here, in the very center of nowhere?

Maybe amnesiacs have their own logic. Ha-ha.

Howard had not merely stopped; he had turned the roadster around, so that now it was facing south.

Accordingly, Ellery straddled the narrow road and persuaded the convertible backward and forward until he, too, could face south. He coaxed the sliding car to a position some twenty-five yards from the roadster, turned off his ignition and headlights, and crawled out of the convertible.

Immediately he sank into mud to the tops of his Oxfords.

ᏯᎧ

THE ROADSTER WAS unoccupied.

Ellery sat down on Howard's running board and wearily rubbed his streaming face with his streaming hand.

Where the hell was Howard?

Not that it mattered. Nothing mattered now except the deliciously unattainable, which was a hot bath and dry clothes afterward. But as a question of simple scientific interest, where had Howard gone?

Ah, for footprints.

But this mud would be as trackless as the sea.

Anyway, he didn't have a flash.

Well, thought Ellery, I'll wait a few minutes. Then if he doesn't show up, the hell with it. Seeing was impossible. No moon . . .

Out of stern habit he got to his feet, although reluctantly, opened the roadster door, and felt around on the dashboard.

Just as he discovered that Howard had taken the keys, he saw the light.

It was a coy light, bobbing and curtseying and for brief moments disappearing altogether. But it kept reappearing. It would fix itself for a moment, then it would bob and curtsey again and disappear again and reappear a few feet away.

The light was performing these antics a good distance off, not up or down the muddy road, but off to the side, beyond the roadster.

Was it a field over there?

Sometimes the light was close to the ground. Sometimes it was waist-high to a man.

Then it steadied for a longer moment and Ellery caught a glimpse of a dark mass surmounted by a broad hat.

Howard using a flashlight!

Ellery slogged around the roadster with his hands before him. There was probably a flashlight in the convertible's glove compartment but to go for it might mean missing something. And there was always the possibility that another light might frighten Howard away.

Ellery's hands encountered a wet stone wall beyond the roadster. The wall came up to his waist.

He swung himself up and over, landing neatly in a thorny bush.

At this point Mr. Queen included Heaven itself in his imprecations.

Then, because part of him was pure leech, he wrenched himself from the embrace of the brambles and set a stumbling, groping course toward the light.

∽

IT WAS THE most baffling place. He found himself going up little rises and sliding down on the other side. He encountered cold hard wet objects. Once he fell over one and found that it was lying flat on the weedy ground. And occasionally there was a tree, usually encountered first by his nose.

It was the most puzzling terrain he had ever tried to cross in the dark, full of traps for the feet. What made it especially difficult was the necessity for keeping the light continuously in view. If only the damned thing would stay in one place! But it kept moving jerkily, in a sort of dance.

And Ellery made the exasperating discovery that he was not gaining on it.

It danced in the distance like *ignis fatuus*, a snare for the unfortunate traveler, never seeming to come nearer.

The traveler's toe caught on something and he fell for the second time. But this time, as he fell, something happened to his head. It flew right off his shoulders, exploding in a burst of flame, and surely he died, because everything stopped, the rain and the chill and Howard and the dancing light and everything.

Perhaps it was the Providence he had cursed, shaming him with Its beneficence, but when Ellery opened his eyes the light was no more than twenty feet from where he was lying. And, sure enough, there was the trench-coated, Stetson-surmounted mass that was Howard, before the light, which was now steady. It gave enough illumination for Ellery to make out what he was lying on, what he had stumbled over, and what had struck him on the side of the head.

He had stumbled over a weed-choked little mound of earth of rectangular shape, at the head of which stood a column of marble supporting a stone dove.

It was the dove which had struck his temple, and while he lay unconscious Howard had made a rough circle and had found, only a few yards from where Ellery was lying, the graves he had been hunting.

They were in the Fidelity cemetery.

ᖇ

ELLERY GOT TO his knees. The marble monument stood between him and Howard. Even if he had knelt exposed, there would have been small danger of Howard's seeing him — his back was to

Ellery and he was utterly absorbed in the sight revealed by his flashlight.

Ellery clung to the unknown's monument; he could only stare.

Suddenly Howard lunged. The light made a crazy half circle. Then it focussed again and Ellery saw that Howard had stopped for a handful of mud, mud from one of the graves.

This mud he now hurled with satanic energy full in the face of the broad headstone.

He stooped again, again the light pinwheeled, again it focussed, again he hurled mud.

It seemed to Ellery that this was the strictly logical denouement of the whole nightmare: that a man should drive miles in a pelting downpour in the dead of night to throw mud at a broad headstone. And when the flashlight swooped to the ground and its beam trained itself on the mud-splattered monument and Howard took from one of the pockets of his trench coat a chisel and a mallet and darted forward to strike great blows upon the stone, blows that sent commas, periods, and exclamation points flying through the italic rain into the darkness beyond . . . this too seemed the proper employment for a sculptor groping toward the final shape of the Unknown.

∞

ELLERY CAME TO himself in the dark cemetery.

Howard was gone.

All that was left of him was the light going slowly away in the direction of the dirt road.

And even as Ellery got to his feet the light vanished.

A moment later he heard the faint roar of the roadster. Then that too was gone.

He was surprised to discover that the rain had stopped.

Ellery leaned against the dove-topped column in the darkness. Too late to follow Howard.

But even if there had been time, he would not have followed Howard. The ghost of every soul lying beneath his soaked feet could not have dragged him from the burying ground.

There was something to be done, and to do it he would stand here until dawn, if necessary.

Maybe the moon would show up.

Mechanically he unbuttoned his gluey topcoat and fumbled with muddy fingers in his jacket pockets for his cigaret case. It was a silver case and its contents would be dry. He found it and opened it and took out a dry cigaret and stuck it between his lips and returned the case to his pocket and fumbled for his lighter . . .

Lighter!

He had the lighter out and open and a flame cupped between his palms even as he hurdled three mounds to the place where Howard had exorcised his demon.

Ellery stooped, shielding the little flame.

It was necessary to stoop. For this was surely the poorest of the poor, pale soft crumbly stone, a pitiful affair no taller than the crowding weeds but wide as two graves, rounded at the top and cleft between, like the twin tablets of Moses. Weather and its own infirmities had pocked it honorably; but the sculptor's chisel had dealt the final foul blows, and it tottered above the twin graves now, a murdered thing.

Some of the lettering had fallen victim to the furious chisel; what remained was hard to read. He could make out figures, dates of birth and date of death, but these were all but illegible; and there was a motto, which after patient scrutiny Ellery decided had originally read: WHOM GOD HATH JOINED. But there was no question about the names. Across the top of the gravestone, in crabbed clear capitals, ran the legend:

AARON AND MATTIE WAYE

ELLERY DROVE THE convertible into the Van Horn garage and parked it beside Howard's roadster with no surprise. Nevertheless, he was relieved. He decided that Howard could wait, and he hurried around the main house to the cottage.

He left his mud-stiffened outer garments on the porch, discarded the rest on the way to the bathroom, and scalded his hide under the shower until the chill seeped out of his bones and his muscles unknotted. He rubbed himself down quickly, got into clean dry clothing, paused in the sitting room only long enough to take a flashlight and a pull from the bottle of Scotch, and then he strode over in the lifting darkness to the other house.

Quietly he went upstairs, past sleeping doors. There were no lights anywhere; he stepped cautiously, feeling his way, not using his flash. On the top floor landing, however, he turned it on. A faint trail of muddy prints on the taupe carpeting led from the stairs to Howard's bedroom. And the bedroom door was half open.

Ellery paused in the doorway.

The mud marks wandered to the bed. On the bed, fully clothed, lay Howard, asleep.

He had not even bothered to take off his trench coat.

His soaked hat gaped in a puddle on the pillow.

Ellery shut the door and bolted it.

He drew the Venetian blinds.

Then he switched on the lights.

"Howard."

He prodded the sleeping man.

"Howard."

Howard groaned something unintelligible and turned over, his head thrown back, snoring. He was in a sort of stupor. Ellery stopped prodding him.

I'd better get him out of these clothes first, Ellery thought, or he'll come down with pneumonia.

He unbuttoned the sodden coat. The material was rainproofed and the lining was dry. He tugged until he got one sleeve off, and then he managed to lift Howard's heavy body sufficiently to pull the coat free and strip it off the other arm. He removed Howard's shoes and socks, and his trousers, which were caked and wet to the knee, and, using the blanket as a towel, he rubbed Howard's legs and feet dry; the bed was a mess, anyway.

Then he went to work on Howard's head.

Under the massage, Howard stirred.

"Howard?"

He thrashed about as if he were fighting something off. He moaned. But he did not awaken. And when Ellery had him all dry, he lapsed into the same semicomatose sleep.

Ellery straightened with a frown. Then he saw what he was looking for on the bureau and he went for the whiskey bottle.

ॐ

HOWARD OPENED HIS eyes.

"Ellery."

They were bloodshot and stary.

They took in the bed, himself half undressed, the wet muddy clothing on the floor.

"Ellery?"

He was bewildered.

And then, suddenly, frightened.

He clutched at Ellery.

"What happened!" His tongue was thick; he mouthed it.

"You tell me, Howard."

"It happened, didn't it? Didn't it!"

Ellery shrugged. "Well, something happened, Howard. What's the last thing you remember?"

"Coming upstairs from the study. Pottering around a while."

"Yes, I know. But after that."

Howard squeezed his eyelids shut. Then he shook his head. "I don't remember."

"You came upstairs from the study, you pottered around a while — "

"Where?"

"Where?"

"Oh, you're asking the questions." Howard laughed shakily. "What's the matter with me? I pottered around in the studio there."

"In the studio. And then — nothing?"

"Not a blamed thing. It's a blank, Ellery. Just like . . ." He stopped.

Ellery nodded. "The other times, eh?"

Howard swung his naked legs off the bed. He began to shiver and Ellery pulled the underblanket free and tossed it over his thighs.

"It's still dark." Howard's voice rose. "Or is it another night?"

"No, it's the same night. What's left of it."

"Another attack. What did I do?" Ellery studied him. "I went somewhere. Where did I go? Did you see? Did you follow me? But you're dry!"

"I followed you, Howard. I've changed."

"What did I *do?*"

"Whoa. Wrap that blanket around your feet and I'll tell you — you're sure you don't remember a thing?"

"Nothing! What did I do?"

Ellery told him.

ᴄᴠᴏ

AT THE END, Howard shook his head as if to clear it. He scratched his scalp, rubbed the back of his neck, pulled his nose, stared at the muddy clothing on the floor.

"And you don't remember any of that?"

"Nope."

Howard looked up at Ellery.

"It's hard to believe." Then he looked away. "Especially that part about where I . . ."

Ellery picked up the trench coat, fished in one of the pockets. When Howard saw the chisel and mallet he went very pale.

He got off the bed and began to blunder about the bedroom in his bare feet.

"If I could do that, I could do anything," he mumbled excitedly. "God knows what I've done those other times. I've got no right running around loose!"

"Howard." Ellery dropped into the armchair by the bed. "You harmed nobody."

"But why? Why did I desecrate their graves?"

"The shock of learning who you are, after a lifetime of dreading the moment of discovery, sent you off again. In the amnesic state you expressed the deep resentment and fear and hatred you've

apparently always felt toward the parents who rejected you . . .
I'm speaking psychologically, of course."

"I'm not aware of any hatred!"

"Of course not."

"I'm not aware of ever having felt any!"

"Not consciously."

Howard had paused in the doorway to the adjoining studio. Now
he stared into the gloomy room for several seconds. Then he strode
through and into the studio and Ellery heard him moving about.
The sounds stopped and the lights came on.

"Ellery, come in here."

"Don't you think you ought to get something on your feet?"
Ellery struggled out of the armchair.

"The hell with my feet! Come in here!"

Howard was standing beside a modeling stand. A plasticine figure
of a little bearded Jupiter occupied the stand.

Ellery said curiously: "What's up?"

"I told you I pottered around in here last night after I came
up from the study. This is one of the things I did."

"The Jupiter?"

"No, no. I mean this." Howard pointed to the base of the model.
In the plasticine a sharp tool had scratched:

H. H. WAYE

"You remember doing that?"

"Certainly! I even remember why." Howard laughed stridently.
"I wanted to see what my real name looked like. I've always
signed my work *H. H. Van Horn.* I had to use the *H. H.* — they
didn't give me a first or middle name. But *Waye* was mine. And
do you know?"

"What, Howard?"

"*I liked it.*"

"You liked it?"

"I liked it. I still do. Downstairs, when father first told me, it
didn't mean anything. But later, when I came up . . . it sort of
grew on me. Look." Howard ran over to the wall, indicated a series
of sketches pinned on a board. "I liked it so much I signed *H. H.*

Waye to every sketch I've made for the Museum project so far. I'd damned near made up my mind to make it my professional signature. Ellery, would I have liked it so much if I hated *them?*"

"Consciously? It's quite possible. To conceal your hatred from yourself, Howard."

"I fall in love with my parents' name and then I black out and drive ten miles in a rainstorm to spit on their graves?" Howard dropped into a chair, looking gray. "Then it gets down to this," he said slowly. "When I'm in a normal state, I'm one thing. But when I black out I become another. Consciously I'm a pretty good guy. In amnesia I'm some sort of maniac, or devil. Dr. Jekyll and Mr. Hyde!"

"You're dramatizing again."

"Am I? To hack your parents' gravestone to pieces is hardly a 'reasonable' act! It's vile. You know perfectly well that no matter how much cultures may differ, they meet on the common ground of respect for parents. Whether it's called ancestor worship or honoring your father and your mother!"

"Howard, you'd better go to bed."

"If I'd defile my parents' graves, why wouldn't I commit murder? Rape? Arson?"

"Howard, you're running off at the mouth. Go to bed."

But Howard had Ellery's hand in a convulsive grip. "Help me. Watch me. Don't leave me."

His eyes were terrified.

He's transferred his attachment from Diedrich to me. I'm his father now.

৵৯

SOMEHOW, ELLERY GOT Howard to bed. He remained by the bedside until Howard fell into an exhausted sleep.

Then he trudged downstairs and out of the house and spent a ghastly hour in the garage removing the mud from the convertible and the roadster.

Sunday morning was peering through the cottage windows as Ellery fell into bed.

The Seventh Day

AND HE RESTED on the seventh day from all the work he had not made, specifically his novel; and he tried not to think of a certain publisher, and of how same would brandish a contract, displeased. But labor he had in the cause of letters, if not precisely the letters demanded by his bondage; and he basked in the surcease thereof, delinquently.

There was Church.

Of how pertinent this was to become Ellery had no inkling; sufficient unto the day was Reverend Chichering of St. Paul's-in-the-Dingle, whose voice rolled as the prophet's — a modified thunder, to be sure, since this was High Church; but the spirit was Jeremiah's, judging and exhorting and complaining: "*My bowels, my bowels! I am pained at my very heart; my heart maketh a noise in me;*" which was audible to the last pew; "*I cannot hold my peace, O my soul . . . The whole land shall be desolate . . . Woe is me now! for my soul is wearied because of murderers,*" at which Howard all but disappeared and Wolfert grinned and Sally shut her eyes while Diedrich sat quietly grim. At the peroration of his sermon, however, Reverend Chichering without warning abandoned Jeremiah to enter Luke — VI, 38 — for a new text: "*Give, and it shall be given unto you; good measure, pressed down, and shaken together, and running over, shall men give into your bosom. For with the same measure that ye mete withal, it shall be measured to you again,*" for it shortly appeared that a certain vestryman had donated a new sanctuary for the chancel, the rector having used the present sanctuary hardly; and it further appeared that this outgiving servant of the Lord bore a well-known name — "I say well-known," Father Chichering thundered musically, "not in the temporal sense, although it is that also, but in the eyes of Our Father, for this God-fearing Christian soul has performed his good works not by laying up for himself treasures upon earth . . . or rather, he *has* laid up for himself treasures upon earth, but how else could he have done what he has done, which is to lay up for himself treasures in heaven, where neither moth nor rust doth corrupt, in accordance with the Sermon on the Mount? And I think the good Lord will forgive me if I sound a trumpet and tell you that our beneficent brother in Christ is Diedrich Van Horn!" — at which the congregation hummed, craning and beaming at the servant of the Lord as he shrank deeper into the Van Horn pew and glared at his rector with no humility whatsoever. However, this incident served to disperse the gloom cast by the rector's preceding jeremiad; the closing hymn was roared; and the service ended with everyone feeling mightily spiritual.

Even Ellery left St. Paul's-in-the-Dingle exalted.

The rest of the day was given over to good works also, such as roast turkey with chestnut-and-giblet stuffing *à la Laura,* candied yams, lemon sherbet *soufflé,* and so forth; postprandially, Mendelssohn's *Elijah,* which left Sally solemn and Diedrich excited. Howard had bought a new recording of it weeks before and Ellery thought it clever of him to have saved its first performance for today when each, for his secret reason, had need of soul-searching. And then a social evening in the finest Wrightsville tradition — laughing ladies and gracious gentlemen who had mastered the cliché and occasionally even said something interesting, and none of whom Ellery had ever met before, for which he was — obscurely — grateful.

The day even ended agreeably. Sunday evenings are early evenings in Wrightsville. Everyone was gone by eleven-thirty, and Ellery was in bed by midnight.

He lay in the dark thinking how beautifully everyone had behaved all day, even Howard, even Wolfert; how much duplicity there is in humankind, and how necessary for tolerable existence so much of it is; and finally he prayed the Lord his soul not to take until he had finished the damned novel, which he now sternly commanded himself to sail into with unswervable purpose the very first thing in the morning; and then he was diving into Quetonokis Lake in an old bathrobe trying to reach four furry letters gleaming on the loamy bottom at the foot of a pale nude sculpture of Sally, who, reasonably enough, had Diedrich's face.

∽

THE TYPEWRITER WAS spitting out hot good words at a furious clip at 10:51 Monday morning when the cottage door burst open and Ellery, jumping a foot, whirled to see Sally and Howard huddled in the doorway.

"He called again."

At once Sunday was as if it had never been and this was Saturday again, at the Hollis Hotel.

Nevertheless, he asked: "Who called again, Sally?"

"The blackmailer."

"The damned porker," said Howard thickly. "The swilling greedy swine."

"The call came just now?"

Sally was shaking. "Yes. I couldn't believe my ears. I thought it was all over."

"The same whispery, sexless voice?"

"Yes."

"Tell me what he said."

"Laura answered the phone. He asked for Mrs. Van Horn. I got on and he said, 'Thanks for the money. Now there's the second installment due.' I didn't understand at first. I said, 'Didn't you get *all* of it?' and he answered, 'I got twenty-five thousand. Now I want more.' I said, 'What are you talking about? I got back what you sold me —' (I didn't want to say 'letters' because Laura or Eileen might have been listening) '— they're gone,' I said. 'Destroyed.' He said, 'I have copies.'"

"Copies," Howard snarled. "What can he do with copies? I'd have told him where to go, Sal!"

"Ever hear of photostatic copies, Howard?" asked Ellery.

Howard looked stunned.

" 'I have copies,' he said," Sally continued in a breathless voice, " 'and they're just as good as the originals. Now I'm putting the copies up for sale.' "

"Yes?"

"I said I had no more money. I said a lot of things. Or tried to. But he wouldn't listen."

"How much does he ask for this time, Sally?" Ellery wished people would avoid having to look frightened afterward simply by taking good advice beforehand.

"Twenty-five thousand dollars. Again!"

"Another twenty-five!" roared Howard. "Where the devil are we going to get another twenty-five? Does he think we're made of money?"

"Shut up, Howard. Sally, let's have the rest of it."

"He said to leave twenty-five thousand dollars in the Wrightsville railroad station waiting room, in one of those self-service parcel lockers they just installed."

"Which locker?"

"Number 10. He said the key would be in the first mail this morning, and it was. I just ran down to the road for it."

"Addressed to you, Sally?"

"Yes."

"Have you handled the key?"

"Why, I took it out of the envelope, looked it over. Howard did, too. Shouldn't we have?"

"I suppose it doesn't matter. This bird's too cagey to leave his fingerprints around. Did you save the envelope?"

"I did!" Howard looked around furtively before he took an envelope from his pocket and handed it to Ellery.

It was a cheap slick envelope, perfectly plain — standard stock of the stationery counters of every five-and-dime in America. The address was typewritten. There was nothing on the flap. Ellery tucked the envelope away without comment.

"And, and here's the key," said Sally.

Ellery looked at her.

She flushed.

"He said it's to be put on top of the tier of lockers, above 10. To push it back out of sight, against the wall." She still offered the key.

Ellery did not take it.

After a moment, timidly, she placed it on the desk before him.

"Did he put any time limit on this second payment?" asked Ellery, as if nothing had happened.

She was looking blindly out at Wrightsville through the picture window. "The money must be in the locker at the station by five o'clock this afternoon or he said he'd send the evidence to Diedrich tonight. To Diedrich's office, he said. Where I couldn't intercept it."

"Five o'clock. That means he intends to pick it up during the rush hour, when the station's jammed," ruminated Ellery. "The Slocum, Bannock, and Connhaven traffic . . . He rather rushes things, doesn't he?"

"You'd think he'd give a person a chance," said Sally.

"What did you expect from a blackmailer — sportsmanship?"

"I know. You warned us." Sally was still not looking at him.

"I'm not rubbing it in, Sally. I simply want to indicate the probabilities for the future."

"Future!" Howard loomed. Ellery tipped back in the chair and looked up at him curiously. "What future? What are you talking about?"

Now Sally *was* looking at him.

"You don't think he's through, do you?"

"But — !"

"Sally, he didn't say anything about *giving* you the photostats, did he?"

"No."

"Even if he had. He could have made ten photostatic sets of the four letters. Or a hundred. Or a thousand."

The woman and the man looked at each other, dumbly.

It was not pretty and Ellery swiveled to the sky. He felt sorry suddenly for both of them. So sorry he forgave them their stupidities and foibles and contemplated a few of his own. As it turned out, he would have been better advised to remain objective, unforgiving, and cynical; but Ellery is a hopeless sentimentalist when his emotions are involved, and they were young and in a mess.

He swiveled back. Sally was curled up in the big chair in a foetal position, her hands hiding her face; Howard was pouring himself a drink with an expression of sheer concentration.

"This is just the beginning," Ellery told them gently. "He'll demand more. And more. And, again, more. He'll take what you have, he'll take what you can steal, and in the end he'll sell the evidence to Diedrich. Don't pay. Go to Diedrich this morning, together. And tell him. Everything.

"Could you do that, both of you? Or one of you?"

Sally burrowed deeper into her hands. Howard stared into the glass of Scotch.

Ellery sighed.

"I know, it's like contemplating a firing squad. But it's much worse than the actuality. One blast —"

"You think I'm afraid." Sally had dropped her hands; she had been crying; but she was angry now, angry as she had been angry Saturday night, although this morning for a different reason. "I tell you it's Dieds I'm thinking of. He'd *die*." She sprang from the chair. "I don't care about myself any more," she said in a passionate undertone. "All I want is to forget all this. Start over again. Make it up to him. I can, too. If it became necessary, I'd see that Howard went away. I'd be *ruthless,* Ellery — you don't know how ruthless I could be. But I've got to have that chance." She turned away. "Maybe," she said in a muffled voice, "he'll let a long time go by till the next time. If there is a next time . . . "

"This envelope, Sally," Ellery tapped his pocket, "went through the Wrightsville post office stamping machine at 5:30 P.M. Saturday. *Only a couple of hours after I'd paid him the first twenty-five thousand.* That means he must have mailed it immediately after picking up the envelope in Upham House. Does that look as if he'll let 'a long time go by' before he makes his third demand?"

"Maybe he'll stop altogether," Sally flared. "Maybe when he realizes there isn't any more, he'll *stop*. Maybe he'll . . . maybe he'll *die* in the meantime!"

Ellery said: "And you, Howard?"

"He mustn't find out." Howard tossed off the Scotch.

"Then you'll pay."

"Yes!"

Sally said: "We must."

Ellery laced his fingers across his stomach and asked: "With what?"

Howard threw the whisky glass into the fireplace with all his strength. It broke against the firebrick in a splash, like a spray of diamonds.

"Like diamonds," muttered Howard. "I wish they were."

"Sally." Ellery sat forward, alarmed. "What is it?"

Sally said, in the queerest way: "I'll be right back."

In the gardens, she began to run. They watched her run around the pool and across the terrace and into the house.

Howard shook his head. "Nothing seems to connect this morning," he said apologetically. "I'm sorry about the glass, Ellery. Boyish, aren't I?" He took another glass and poured another drink. "Here's to crime."

Ellery watched him toss it off.

Howard turned blindly away.

Three minutes later Sally appeared on the terrace. Her hand was rammed into the right pocket of her suit jacket. She crossed the terrace and the gardens sedately. But on the cottage porch she hurried, and when she came in she slammed the door.

Howard gawped at her.

She held out her right hand to him.

Dangling from it was a diamond necklace.

⌇

"I took it out of the safe."

"Your *necklace*, Sally?"

"It's mine."

"But you can't give up your necklace!"

"I'm sure twenty-five thousand can be raised on this. It must have cost Dieds a hundred." She turned to Ellery. "Would you like to see it?"

"It's magnificent, Sally." Ellery made no move to take it.

"Yes, so beautiful." Her voice was steady. "Dieds gave it to me on our last anniversary."

"No," said Howard. "No, it's too risky."

"Howard."

"It's bound to be missed, Sal. How would you explain to Father?"

"You took a risk to raise the first twenty-five thousand."

"Why, no, I . . ."

"Wherever you got it, there's some record of it. A note, or something. Of course you took a risk. Now it's my turn. Howard — take it."

Howard flushed.

But he took it.

The sun streaming in through the picture window caught its facets and tossed them about. His hand seemed on fire.

"But . . . it's got to be turned into cash," Howard muttered. "I . . . wouldn't know how to go about it."

Howard the ineffectual. Howard the dependent.

"You know," remarked Ellery from the swivel chair, "this is sheer imbecility."

Howard turned to him hungrily.

"Ellery, I'll never ask you to do anything — "

"You mean you want me to pawn this necklace, Howard."

"You know about these things," stammered Howard. "I don't."

"Yes, and that's why I characterize this entire business as lunacy."

"But we've got to raise that money," said Sally in a hard tone.

Ellery shrugged.

"Ellery." She was begging now, fiercely. "Do it for me. A favor. It's my necklace. I take the responsibility. Howard's right — we won't ever ask you to get mixed up in this again. No matter what happens. But won't you do just this one thing?"

"Let me ask you, Sally," said Ellery clearly. "*Why don't you do it yourself?*"

"I might be seen in town. By Dieds, or Wolfert, or one of their employees. Going into or coming out of the pawnshop. You don't know what a small town's like. It would be all over Wrightsville in no time. Dieds would be bound to hear about it — somebody'd make good and sure he heard about it! Don't you see?"

And Howard jumped in: "Yes, and the same thing goes for me, Ellery." *He hadn't thought of it till Sally brought it up. Now he's grabbing for it.*

"Or the pawnbroker might mention it, or — "

Ellery raised his brows. "Let me get this straight. You want me to pawn this necklace without identifying it as yours, Sally?"

"That's the whole point. That way Dieds couldn't find out — "

"I don't get this. At all." Ellery's face was bleak. "A necklace like this — it must be famous in Wrightsville. Even if the pawnbroker doesn't know it, the minute someone else saw it — "

"But Dieds bought it in New York," said Sally eagerly. "And I've never worn it. Even at home, Ellery, when we've entertained. I've had it only a few months. I've been saving it for an occasion. It's *not* known in town — "

"Or you could pawn it somewhere else," put in Helpful Howard.

"No time to go outside Wrightsville, Howard. You two seem to think a stranger can walk into a pawnshop, plunk down a hundred-thousand-dollar necklace, and walk out with twenty-five thousand of the broker's dollars and no questions asked. There's only one broker in town, old Simpson in the Square, so I can't even shop around. Simpson would want proof of ownership. Or authorization from the owner. He'd have to raise the cash. And at once." Ellery shook his head. "It's not just stupid. It's almost impossible."

But now they were both at him, collaborating their arguments, with a determination he found a little sickening.

"Why, you told me yourself you knew J. P. Simpson," Sally was saying. "From the time you were in Wrightsville visiting the Wrights. The Haight case —"

"I didn't know Simpson, Sally. We met briefly during Jim Haight's trial; he was a witness for the prosecution."

"But he'd remember you," cried Howard. "You're somebody, Ellery. They've never forgotten you in this town!"

"Maybe so, but do you expect Simpson to have twenty-five thousand dollars in his till?"

"He's one of the richest men in town," countered Sally triumphantly. "Has one of the largest accounts at the Wrightsville National. And he does occasionally make big loans. Only last year Sidonie Glannis got herself in an awful mess with some smoothie who swept her off her feet — that was a letter business, too — and he blackmailed her for I don't know how much. Sidonie had a lot of jewels left to her by her mother, and she pawned them at Simpson's to pay this man off before he turned the letters over to Claude — that was Claude Glannis, Sidonie's husband. I don't know how much Simpson gave her, but I've heard it was well over fifteen thousand dollars. They caught the man and the story came out and Claude Glannis blew his brains out, but even before the blackmailer was arrested — he's in prison now — everybody in town knew about it and —"

"Then what makes you think everyone in town won't know about this?"

"Because you're Ellery Queen," she retorted. "All you'd have to do would be to tell Simpson you were in Wrightsville on a very hush-hush case — staying with the Van Horns as a blind — that you couldn't disclose the name of your client but that you had to pawn her necklace, or something like that. You see? I'm even writing your dialogue, Ellery. Oh, do it!"

Every reasonable cell in Ellery's body bade him rise, pack his bag, and flee to the first train out of Wrightsville bound for any destination whatever.

Instead, Ellery said: "Whichever way this turns out, I warn you both now, in advance, that I'll have nothing further to do with this childish, dangerous nonsense. Don't ask me to connive at anything but the truth from now on. I'll refuse. — Now let me have the locker key and the necklace, please."

∾

ELLERY RETURNED FROM town shortly after one o'clock.

They were watching for him, because he had scarcely got his hat off when they appeared in the cottage doorway.

He said, "It's done," and stood there, his silence inviting them to leave.

But Sally came in and dropped into the armchair.

"Tell us about it," she begged. "How did it go?"

"You called the turn, Sally."

"Didn't I tell you? What did Simpson say?"

"He remembered me." Ellery laughed. "It's depressing how gullible people are. Especially the shrewd ones. I keep forgetting it, and every time I do I go wrong . . . Why, Simpson did it all by himself, with hardly a suggestion from me. Assumed I was working on something very big, very secret, and very important. Fell all over himself co-operating." He laughed again.

Sally slowly got out of the chair.

"But the money," Howard demanded. "Did you have any trouble about the money?"

"Not the slightest. Simpson locked his store and went over to the bank in person. Came back with a bagful." Ellery turned to Wrightsville. "He was so very impressed. With the necklace, with me, with his part in what he obviously suspects has international ramifications . . .

"The money's in Locker 10 at the station. The key is on top of the tier of lockers, at the back, against the wall. It's too high to be noticed accidentally; he had it all figured out." And Ellery said, "Do you two have any idea what I feel like?"

He turned around.

"Do you?"

They stood before him, just looking at him and not at each other and after a moment not looking at him, either.

Then Sally's lips parted.

"No thanks are necessary," Ellery said. "Now would you mind very much letting me get on with my work?"

He did not join the household at dinner Monday evening. Laura brought a tray over to him, which he emptied dutifully before her eyes; then she took the tray away.

He worked through half the night.

❧

ELLERY WAS PUTTING his shaving things away Tuesday morning when a voice called from the sitting room: "Queen? You up?"

He could not have been more astounded if the voice had been Professor Moriarty's.

He went to the doorway in his undershirt, razor still in hand.

"Not intruding, I hope." Wolfert Van Horn was all friendliness this morning, eager-beaverish, with a vast dental smile and his hands plunged in his pockets boyishly.

"No, indeed. How are you this morning?"

"Fine, just fine. Saw your door open and wondered if you'd be up. Weren't your lights on most of the night?"

"I worked until almost 3:30."

"That's exactly what I thought." Wolfert beamed at the littered desk; he's the only man I ever saw, Ellery thought, who can look sly with his eyes wide open. "So this is what an author's desk looks like. Wonderful, wonderful. Then you didn't get much sleep, Queen."

So we're going to play games.

"Hardly any," Ellery smiled. "You work yourself into a thing, Mr. Van Horn — everything tight, everything wound up — it sometimes takes a long time to unwind."

"And I've always thought writers live the life of Riley. Just the same, I'm glad you're up."

Here it comes.

"Haven't seen you since Sunday. How'd you like Chichering?"
Not yet.

"Earnest, in an earnest sort of way."

"Yes, ha-ha! Very spiritual man. Reminds me a little of my

father," Wolfert laughed deprecatingly, "although Pa was a fundamentalist, of course. He used to scare Diedrich and me so our knees shook. But here, I'm rattling along as if neither of us had a lick to do." Wolfert lowered his voice, cocked his ax of a head, and struck. "You weren't thinking of having breakfast with the family this morning, were you, Mr. Queen? You didn't have dinner with us last night and I thought . . ."

Ellery smiled back. "Something special on the menu this morning, Mr. Van Horn?"

To his horror, Wolfert winked.

"Extra-special!"

"Eggs benedictine?"

Wolfert howled and slapped himself. "Very good! No, it's something a whole lot better'n that."

"Then I'll certainly come over."

"I'd better tip you off first. My brother's a funny coot. Hates formality. To get him to make a speech you practically have to call out the State Militia. Get it?"

"No."

"You hurry up and get dressed, Queen. This is going to be a circus!"

Nevertheless, Mr. Queen was not elated.

ᐁᔭ

WOLFERT VAN HORN nursed and nuzzled his mystery all through breakfast, chuckling and making obscure remarks to his brother and behaving so remarkably unlike his unwholesome self that even Howard, bogged down in his problems, noticed and said, surprised: "What's happened to *him?*"

"Now, son," said Diedrich dryly, "let's not look a gift horse in the mouth."

They all laughed, Wolfert the most loudly.

"Don't be mean, Wolf," said Sally with a smile. "Give out."

"Give out what?" said Wolfert innocently. "Ha-ha!"

"Don't rush him, dear," said her husband. "Wolf so seldom allows himself to laugh . . ."

"All right, that did it," said Wolfert, winking at Ellery. "I'll put you out of your misery, Diedrich."

"Me? Oh, I'm the joke."

"Get set, now."

"All set."

So was Sally. So was Howard. Suddenly. *The wicked flee when no man pursueth.*

"Where d'ye think you're going tonight, Diedrich?"

"Going? Not a darned place but home."

"Incorrect. Sally," said Wolfert with a flourish of his cup, "more coffee."

Sally poured with an ever-so-unsteady hand.

"Oh, come on," growled Howard. "What's all the mystery about?"

"Why, Howard. You're in it, too. Ha-ha-ha!"

"All right, son," said Diedrich quietly. "Well, well, Wolf? And where am I going tonight?"

His brother set bony elbows on the table, took a slup of his coffee, set the cup down, and brandished a forefinger coyly. "I'm not supposed to tell you this, now — "

"Then don't." Diedrich promptly pushed his chair back.

"But it's too good to keep," said Wolfert hastily. "And you'll know, anyway, this morning at the office. They're sending a delegation to invite you."

"Invite me? Where, Wolf? To what? What delegation?"

"All the old girls of the Art Museum Committee — Clarice Martin, Hermy Wright, Mrs. Donald Mackenzie, Emmy DuPré and the rest of that crew."

"But why? Invite me to what?"

"Tonight's shindig."

"What shindig?" demanded Diedrich, with a note of alarm.

"Brother," said Wolfert triumphantly, "you told me you hoped the Committee didn't make a fuss about your donation. Well, sir, tonight you're going to be guest of honor at a grand banquet in the Grand Ballroom of the Hollis — testimonial dinner to that patron of the arts, that benefactor of culture or whatever it is, the Man Who Made the Art Museum Possible — Diedrich Van Horn! Hip-hip! Yayyyyy!"

"Testimonial dinner," said Diedrich feebly.

"Yes, sir. Soup-and-fish, speeches, the works. Tonight the Van Horns become Public Property! The great man in the middle, his beautiful wife at his right, his talented son at his left — everybody all togged out!" — Wolfert laughed again, and it sounded like a snarl " — try getting out of this one, Diedrich. Matter of fact, I'll tell you a secret." There went that wink again. "I was the one put 'em up to it!"

It was fortunate, Ellery thought, that Diedrich reacted in character. His dismay and Wolfert's enjoyment of it enabled Sally to fight the cornered animal in her eyes, and Howard sat slack-jawed, trying to close his mouth.

Ellery felt a little sickish himself.

As Diedrich bellowed and stormed — he'd be damned if he'd do it, they couldn't make him — and Wolfert baited him — banquet's set, dinner's ordered, invitations sent out — Sally and Howard managed to take hold of themselves.

So that when it was all over and Diedrich threw up his hands and said to Sally, "I guess we're stuck, darling. Well, there's one saving grace — it'll give you a chance to doll up. Wear that diamond necklace I gave you, Sally," Sally was able to smile and say, "Naturally, dear," and tilt her face to be kissed — exactly as if wearing the necklace which lay in J. P. Simpson's safe was the most delightful prospect in the world.

⁂

DIEDRICH AND WOLFERT left. The three conspirators sat. Laura came in and began to clear the breakfast dishes. Sally shook her head and Laura went out, banging the door.

"I think," said Ellery at last, "we'd better go somewhere else."

"The studio." Howard rose, stiffly.

Upstairs Sally collapsed. Her body shook and shook. Neither man said anything. Howard stood wide-legged, only the semblance of a man. Ellery strolled back and forth before little Jupiter.

"I'm sorry." Sally blew her nose. "I seem to have a genius for doing the wrong thing. Howard, what are we going to do?"

"I wish I knew."

"It's like a sort of punishment." Sally held on to the arms of the chair and addressed the rafters tiredly. "No sooner do you get out of one corner than you're trapped in another. It's almost humorous. I'm sure I'd laugh if it were happening to somebody else. We're a couple of frantic bugs trying to get out of a matchbox. *How am I going to explain about that necklace?*"

Ellery did not say that that was a question she should have considered when she decided to pawn the diamonds.

"I thought I had time." She sighed. "I thought, I'll figure out a way when the time comes. And here it is. So soon . . ."

Yes, thought Ellery, that's the remarkable thing about this problem. The pressure. The pressure of events crowding one another. They're piled up now in a space too small to contain them. Something has to give . . . The unusual factor of pressure. Unusual factor . . . The phrase kept repeating itself until his conscious mind took note of its insistence. Unusual . . .

Howard was saying something over and over, too, and not brightly.

"What was that, Howard?"

"It doesn't matter," said Sally. "Howard said maybe I could say the necklace was in my japanned box and was stolen with the other jewels in June."

"And never recovered, Sal! That's the point!"

"Howard, you're not being helpful. I gave Dieds a full list of the contents of the jewel box at the time. The necklace wasn't on the list because the necklace hadn't been in the box. What do you want me to say—that I *forgot* it? Anyway, it's been in his safe downstairs all this time. I told you I went to the study to get it. Dieds *must* have seen it there; he goes to the safe frequently. For all I know, so does Wolfert."

"Wolfert." Howard grabbed at that, black-angry. "If not for that—that corpse, none of this would be necessary!"

"Oh, stop it, How."

"*Wait.*"

"For what?"

"No, wait, wait." Howard's voice was soft, almost unpleasant. "There is a way out of this, Sal. I don't like it, but . . ."

"What way?"

Howard looked at her.

"What way, Howard?" She was really puzzled.

He said very carefully, "Stage a . . . robbery."

"A robbery?" She sat up straight. "A *robbery*?" She was horrified.

"Yes! Last night. Or during the night. Father and Wolfert didn't go into the study this morning, I'm sure of it. We can say . . . We'll open the safe. *Leave* the safe door open. Break a pane in the French door. Then, Sal, you can call father at the office . . ."

"Howard, what are you talking about?"

He's forgotten she doesn't know about the other robbery. Now she's beginning to wonder. Now he sees it. Now he covers up.

"Then you suggest something," he said shortly.

Sally glanced at Ellery but then — quickly — she glanced away.

"Ellery." Howard sounded very reasonable. "What do you think?"

"Lots of things, Howard. None of them pleasant."

"Yes, I know, but I mean —"

"It won't work."

"But what else can we do?"

"You can tell the truth."

"Thanks!"

"You asked me, I'm telling you. This thing is now so involved, so hopeless, that there's no other way." Ellery added with a shrug, "There never was, really."

"No. I can't tell him. I won't. I can't hurt him that much!"

Ellery looked at him.

Howard's glance shifted. "All right, have it your way. I don't want to hurt myself, either."

"But that's not my reason," moaned Sally. "I'm not thinking of myself. I'm not, I'm not."

"We seem," said Ellery in the silence, "to have come to some sort of ending."

Howard said abruptly, "There's nothing you can suggest?"

"Howard, I told you. That pawnshop deal was my last. I'm utterly, immovably against all of this. If I can't stop you from acting the fool, I can at least stop compounding your folly. I'm sorry."

Howard nodded, curtly. "Sally?"

She got out of the chair.

ᘒ

ELLERY TRAILED THEM to Diedrich's study compelled by a psychology he tried wearily to analyze. The sensible course was to pack up and leave. And yet he persisted in following them in their awkward gyrations as if he were a part of the problem. Maybe it was just curiosity. Or curiosity and a perverted sort of loyalty, or a compulsion of conscience, as if, having agreed to one bargain, he had to stick to the end, even though it had long since been superseded by other bargains to which he was not a party.

They went in and Sally put her back against the study door and Ellery stood in a corner.

None of them said a word.

Howard wadded a handkerchief. It was like watching a pantomime. With it he opened Diedrich's safe. He wrapped the handkerchief around his hand and made violent gestures inside, tumbling things about. His hand came out with a velvet box. He opened it. It was empty.

"This is it, isn't it?"

"Yes."

Howard dropped the box, open, on the floor just below the safe. He left the safe open.

Now what? The scene had a certain academic interest.

Howard strode to the French door. On the way he snatched a cast-iron paperweight from his father's desk.

"Howard," said Ellery.

"What?"

"If you're manufacturing evidence to indicate that the thief was an outsider, don't you think it might be wiser to break the pane from the terrace side?"

Howard looked startled. Then he reddened. And then he opened the French door with his handkerchief-wrapped hand, stepped through, shut the door, struck the pane nearest the handle with the paperweight. Glass showered onto the study floor.

Howard came back in. This time he left the door open. He stood looking around.

"Have I forgotten anything? All right, Sally. That's it."

"What, Howard?" Sally looked at him blindly.

"It's up to you now. Phone him."

Sally swallowed.

She went around her husband's desk, avoiding the glass, sat down in the big chair, pulled the telephone to her, dialed a number.

Neither man said anything.

"Mr. Van Horn, please. No, *Diedrich* Van Horn. Yes, this is Mrs. Van Horn calling."

She waited.

Ellery moved closer to the desk.

"Sally?" He heard the big voice, reduced.

"Dieds, my necklace is gone!"

Howard turned away, fumbling for a cigaret.

"Necklace? Gone? What do you mean, darling?"

Sally burst into tears.

Nor all your Tears wash out a Word of it.

"I just went to take the necklace out of the safe for tonight's affair and . . . "

"It's not in the safe?"

"No!"

Weep, Sally, weep.

"Maybe you took it out and forgot, dear."

"The safe's been opened. The door to the terrace . . . "

"Oh."

And a very queer oh that was, Mrs. Van Horn. You don't know what he knows and what he suspects. Careful now.

"Dieds, what am I going to do?"

Weep, Sally, weep.

"Sally. Dearest. Now stop. Ask Mr. Queen to—Is he there?"

"Yes!"

"Put him on. And stop crying, Sally." *Still odd*. "It's just **a** necklace."

Sally held the telephone out, mutely.

A mere hundred thousand dollars' worth.

Ellery took it.

"Yes, Mr. Van Horn."

"Have you looked over the — "

"The French door has been broken through. The wall safe is open."

Van Horn did not ask the question about the glass. He waited. But Ellery waited, too.

"You'd better tell my wife not to touch anything. I'll be right home. Meanwhile, Mr. Queen, would you keep an eye on things?"

"Of course."

"Thanks."

Diedrich hung up.

Ellery hung up.

"Well?" Howard's face was all out of shape. Sally just sat there.

"He asked me to keep an eye on things. No one is to touch anything. He's coming right home."

"No one's to touch anything!" Sally got up.

"I think," said Ellery slowly, "he intends to notify the police."

⁓

CHIEF OF POLICE Dakin had grown old. Where he had been lean, he was fragile; his hide was crumbling; his hair was ashes. His big nose seemed even bigger.

But his eyes were still two panes of frosted glass.

Dakin came in between the brothers and it was characteristic that, even though he must have known Ellery would be there, his glances went first to the broken pane, next to the open safe, and only thirdly to Ellery. But then it turned warm; and he came over to pump Ellery's hand.

"We never seem to meet excepting there's trouble," he exclaimed. "Why didn't you let me know you were back among us?"

"I've been more or less in hiding, Chief. And the Van Horns have been covering me up. I'm writing a book."

"Seems to me you could have kept your eye on things better for these folks between paragraphs," said Dakin, grinning.

"I'm humiliated, believe me."

Wrightsville's chief of police stood rubbing his lean jaw.

"Diamond necklace, huh? Oh, hello, Mrs. Van Horn." He nodded to Howard, too.

Sally said, "Oh, Dieds," and Diedrich put his arm around her.

In the doorway, Wolfert said nothing. He kept looking around peckishly. Searching for worms, Ellery thought.

Chief Dakin strolled over to the French door, glanced at the glass on the floor, at the jagged hole in the pane.

"Second robbery since June," he remarked. "Seems like somebody's got it in for you, Mrs. Van Horn."

"I hope I'm as lucky this time, Mr. Dakin."

Dakin drifted over toward the safe.

"Did *you* find anything, Mr. Queen?" Diedrich asked. His jaw was jutting.

"It's a pretty clear case, Mr. Van Horn, as Chief Dakin will tell you. Incidentally, you don't need me with Dakin around. I have a great deal of respect for the chief's talents."

"Say, thanks," said Dakin, picking up the velvet box.

Diedrich nodded rather grimly, as if to say, *So have I.*

Mad clear through, Ellery thought. First the twenty-five thousand, now the diamond necklace. Can hardly be blamed.

Dakin took his time. Dakin always took his time. He had the exasperating deliberateness of a rising tide. You could hardly see it move, and yet you knew it would engulf everything in its own time and that nothing could stop it.

He was fascinating Sally and Howard.

"Mrs. Van Horn."

Sally jumped. "Oh! Everybody's been so quiet. What, Mr. Dakin?"

"When's the last time you saw the necklace?"

"Over a month ago," said Sally quickly.

Too quickly.

"Why, no, dear," said Diedrich, frowning. "It was two weeks ago, don't you remember? You took it out of the safe to show — "

"Millie Burnett. Of course." Sally was crimson. "I'd forgotten, Dieds. Stupid of me."

"Two weeks." Dakin stood digesting the fact. "Anybody see it after that?"

"Did you," said Diedrich, "Howard?"

The ugly face was stone.

"Me?" Howard laughed, nervously. "Me, father?"

"Yes."

"How could I have seen it? I never have any reason to go to the safe."

Diedrich said in a thick voice, "I just thought you might have seen it, son."

He suspects. He doesn't know. He suspects, and it's killing him. It's killing him to suspect and not know. Howard? Impossible. Sally? Unthinkable. But . . .

Diedrich turned away.

"It was in the safe Monday morning," said his brother.

"Yesterday?" Diedrich eyed Wolfert sharply. "You're sure?"

"Sure I'm sure." Wolfert smiled his meager smile. "I had to get at those Hutchinson papers and I opened the safe. The necklace was there."

Dakin asked, "In this box, Mr. Van Horn?"

"That's right."

"Box open?"

"No . . . but — "

"Then how'd you know the necklace was in it?" said Dakin mildly. "Have to be careful about these things, Mr. Van Horn. In gettin' the facts, I mean. Or did you happen to, now, open the box, Mr. Van Horn?"

"As a matter of fact, I did." The tips of Wolfert's furry ears were turning fuchsia.

"You did?"

"Just looked at it, that's all." Wolfert was furious. "Or do you think I'm lying?"

Diedrich roared, "What difference does it make? The burglary occurred during the night, that pane of glass was all right late last night. What difference does it make when the necklace was last seen?"

He's sorry already. Sorry he's called Dakin in on this. That was bitterness. This is bitter regret.

The police chief said, "You'll be hearin' from me about this, Mr. Van Horn," and before they grasped that he had said something definite and threatening, Dakin was gone.

∾

DIEDRICH DID NOT return to town. Wolfert did, but Diedrich remained in his study most of the day behind a closed door. Once, seeking a reference book, Ellery approached the door; but hearing the footsteps of his host blundering about aimlessly, Ellery went back to the cottage. Howard had shut himself up in his studio. Sally was in her room.

Ellery worked.

At five o'clock Diedrich appeared in the cottage doorway.

"Oh, hello."

He had fought his battle and won it. The lines were deeper, but controlled.

"See that deputation of old hens?"

"The Committee? No, I didn't. Working . . ."

"Mountain coming to Mohamet. What could I say? I felt like a fool. Of course, we have to go."

"*To each his suff'ring,*" said Ellery with a laugh.

"What's that in Job?" Diedrich responded with a slight smile. "Pa used to quote it. Oh, yes. *Man is born unto trouble, as the sparks fly upward.* Some of us look as if we were being attacked by acetylene torches . . . See here, I don't want to disturb you, Mr. Queen, but it occurred to me we hadn't said a word about your coming with us tonight to that blamed testimonial dinner. Of course we want you to—"

"I'm afraid I'll have to beg off," said Ellery quickly, "although it's very kind of you to include me in the family."

"No, no. We'd love having you."

"I have no evening clothes with me —"

"You can wear an extra tuxedo of mine."

"I'd swim in it. Anyway, Mr. Van Horn, this is your show."

"You mean you want to stay here and punish that typewriter."

"It hasn't taken half enough abuse. Frankly, yes."

"I wish we could change places!"

They laughed at that, companionably and after a while Diedrich waved and went away.

A strong man.

❧

ELLERY WATCHED THE Van Horns leave. Diedrich, magnificent in tails and a silk topper, held the door open for Sally, who wore a mountainous mink wrap with a gardenia corsage, a white gown sweeping the steps, and a gossamer something over her head; and, behind them, Wolfert, looking like an undertaker's assistant. The Cadillac limousine rolled up with Howard at the wheel, Diedrich and Sally got into the tonneau, Wolfert slipped in beside Howard. The *bon ton* of Wrightsville rarely employed chauffeurs.

The big car roared down the drive and around a bend and disappeared.

And it seemed to Ellery that none of them had uttered a word through the whole thing.

He returned to his typewriter.

At seven-thirty Laura appeared. "Mrs. Van Horn told me you'd be home for supper, Mr. Queen."

"Oh, Laura. You don't have to bother."

"No *bother*," said Laura. "Will you be having it in the dining room, Mr. Queen, or would you like me to bring you a tray?"

"Tray, tray. Don't go to any trouble, Laura. Anything'll do."

"Yes, sir." But Laura lingered.

"Yes? What is it, Laura?" That heroine was an increasing pain in the neck.

"Mr. Queen, is . . . somethin' wrong? I mean —"

"Wrong, Laura?"

Laura plucked at her apron. "Mrs. Van Horn in her room cryin' all day, and Mr. Diedrich bein' so . . . And then, him comin' back with the chief of police this morning and all."

"Well, if something's wrong, Laura, it's really none of our affair, is it?"

"Oh. No, Mr. Queen."

When Laura returned with the tray, her mouth was set in a very thin line indeed.

Ellery gathered that she had just discovered the clay in her idol's feet.

∾

HE REALLY MADE progress. The pages flipped off and he heard nothing but the typewriter's chatter.

"Ellery."

He was surprised to find Howard beside him. He hadn't even heard the door open.

"Back already, Howard? Why, what time is it?"

Howard was hatless; his evening topcoat was open and the tails of his white scarf dangled. His eyes made Ellery remember everything.

Ellery pushed back.

"Come over to the house."

"Howard, what's the matter?"

"We just got back from the dinner. We found Dakin waiting for us."

"Dakin. Is *Dakin* here? I've been so absorbed — "

"Dakin sent me over here for you."

"For me."

"Yes."

"Didn't he say why he . . . ?"

"No. He just said to get you."

Ellery buttoned the collar of his shirt, reached for his jacket.

"Ellery."

"What?"

"He's got Simpson with him."

Simpson.

"The pawnbroker?"

"The pawnbroker."

Ellery clamped his mind shut instantly.

∽

J. P. SIMPSON WAS A balding, grape-eyed little countryman who always looked as if he were sniffing something. His stained topcoat was buttoned and he clutched his hat tightly. He was seated on the rim of Diedrich's big chair. When Ellery and Howard strode in, he jumped up and scuttled behind it.

Sally was in a shadow near the French door, still in her fur coat. Her white gloves crumpled a menu.

The old baffled look was on Diedrich's face. He had dropped his coat and top hat on the floor; his scarf, like Howard's, was still around his neck; his hair was disorderly. And he was extremely quiet.

Wolfert hovered behind his brother.

Chief Dakin leaned against a bookcase.

"Dakin."

Dakin pushed away from the case, reaching into his pocket.

"I thought we'd better have you in on this, Mr. Queen."

"In on what?"

As if I didn't know.

"Well, here he is," said Diedrich roughly. "Now what's this, Dakin?"

Dakin's hand emerged from his pocket with the diamond necklace.

"This your necklace, Mrs. Van Horn?"

The souvenir menu fell to the floor.

Sally stooped but Dakin was quicker. He had it, and he handed it to her politely, and Ellery thought how beautifully this man worked. The way he had got to her side without making a point of his approach. He was really wasted in Wrightsville.

"Thank you," said Sally.

"Is it, Mrs. Van Horn?"

Sally let it drip, glittering, over her gloved hands.

"Yes," she said faintly. "Yes. It is."

"Why, Dakin," said Diedrich, "where'd you find it?"

"I'll let Mr. Simpson tell you that, Mr. Van Horn."

The pawnbroker said in an excited voice: "I made a loan on that! Yesterday. Yesterday afternoon."

"Take a look around, Mr. Simpson," drawled the chief of police. "Recognize anybody here as the person who pawned it?"

Simpson shook an indignant finger at Ellery.

Even Wolfert was surprised. But Diedrich was stunned.

"This gentleman here?" he asked incredulously.

"Queen. Ellery Queen. That's him!"

Ellery grimaced. He had told them it wouldn't work. Now they were in for it. He glanced sadly at Sally and Howard. Sally was clutching the necklace and staring at it. Howard was trying to look surprised.

How silly this all is.

"Mr. Queen pawned this necklace?" Diedrich was saying. "Mr. Queen?"

"Made me think it was for a client or some such tittle-tootle," cried the little pawnbroker. "Led me by the nose! Took me in! Well, I always said you never can tell about these New Yorkers. Bigger they are, foxier they are. Stolen article all the time — why didn't ye tell me that, Mr. Queen? Why didn't ye tell it was stole from Mrs. Van Horn?" He was dancing behind the armchair.

Diedrich laughed. "Why, I frankly don't know what to say, what to think. Mr. Queen . . . ?" He stopped, helplessly.

Your turn, boys and girls . . . Ellery looked at Howard again. And a strange thing happened.

Howard looked away.

Howard looked away . . .

But he must have caught that glance.

Ellery succeeded in catching Howard's eye again.

Howard looked away again.

Quickly, Ellery glanced at Sally.

But Sally seemed to be counting the diamonds.

Can't be. They can't be this perfidious. Howard! Sally!

This time Ellery compelled her to look up.

Sally looked through him.

And suddenly Ellery felt a tightness around his throat. When he felt it he knew it for what it was. He found himself angry. Angrier than he had ever been in his life. So angry that he did not trust himself to speak.

Diedrich was looking him over now, no longer helplessly; more questioningly now, and with a certain joy that lit up the question and sharpened its outline swiftly.

He's glad. He's going to hang onto this. He's been floundering; and here's a life preserver flung from nowhere and he's grabbing for it.

Ellery lit a cigaret, deliberately.

"Mr. Queen." Dakin was being respectful. "I don't have to remind you this all looks pretty queer. I'm dead certain you can explain it, but — "

"Yah! Let him explain it!" shouted Simpson.

"Would you please explain it, Mr. Queen?" So respectfully.

Ellery blew out the match. He smoked, he waited.

Dakin's eyes became opaque.

"Well? Mr. Queen!" This was Diedrich. And harsh.

He's grabbed it.

"Writing a book, did he say?" Wolfert Van Horn exploded. He rocked and hawked with the miserable joy of it.

"Mr. Queen." Diedrich again. *Now we're going to be fair. Chance to talk before pronouncing execution. Well, I'll be damned if I . . .* "Mr. Queen, won't you please say something!"

"What can I say?" Ellery smiled. "That I'm humiliated? Insulted? Furious? Astounded?"

Diedrich considered this. Then he said quietly: "This could be very clever."

"Could it, Mr. Van Horn?"

"Because now that I think of it, there are certain facts. Other facts."

"Such as?"

"That other robbery. Friday morning."

Dakin said quickly: "What's this, Mr. Van Horn?"

"My safe was burglarized some time during the early hours of Friday morning, Dakin. Twenty-five thousand dollars in cash were taken."

Jump, Sally. Yes, look at him. Oh, but away. So fast.

"You didn't report that, Mr. Van Horn," said Dakin, blinking.

"Diedrich, you didn't even tell me," said Wolfert. "Why . . . ?"

"You were here then, too, Mr. Queen," said Diedrich.

Ellery nodded thoughtfully.

"That pane in the French door was broken then, too, Dakin. I had a glazier fix it over the week end. But that first time the pane'd been broken from inside the study here. I must admit . . . at the time I thought it was an inside job—I mean . . . one of the help."

Unworthy of you, Diedrich. One of the help? Well, what else can you say?

"But now . . . The job done on that first pane could have been a smart dodge. A trick."

"To make it look like an amateur job?" Dakin nodded slowly. "It could at that, Mr. Van Horn."

"What are you just looking at him for?" shrilled Simpson. "What is he, God or somebody? He buncoed me! He's a crook!"

Diedrich frowned, rubbing his jaw. "Simpson, you *sure* Mr. Queen was the one who pawned that necklace?"

"Am I sure? Van Horn, my business is remembering faces. You bet your sweet life I'm sure. I'm *sure.* I shelled out good American money and lots of it. Ask him. Go ahead!"

"You're quite right, Simpson." Ellery shrugged. "I pawned Mrs. Van Horn's necklace . . . yes."

Sally said, "Excuse me," in a faint voice. She started from the room.

Diedrich said, "Sally," and she stopped in mid-step and turned around a moment later and Ellery saw the oddest expression on her pretty face. Sally stood on the brink of a decision. He wondered grimly whether she would jump or run. "We've got to get to the bottom of this," said Diedrich harshly. "I just can't believe it. Queen, you're no fly-by-night. You're somebody. You'd have to have a tremendous reason to do a thing like this. Won't you tell me what's behind it? Please."

"No," said Ellery.

"No?" Diedrich's jaw settled.

"No, Mr. Van Horn. I'm going to let Howard answer for me."

Not Sally. Sally has to do it by herself. That's important. I'm a fool but that's important.

"Howard?" said Diedrich.

"Howard, I'm waiting," said Ellery.

"Howard?" said Diedrich again.

"Haven't you anything to say, Howard?" Ellery asked gently.

"Say?" Howard licked his lips. "What would I have to say? I mean . . . I don't get this. At all."

Committed, Howard?

"Queen." Diedrich seized Ellery's arm. Ellery almost cried out. "Queen, what's my son got to do with this?"

"Last chance, Howard."

Howard glared at Ellery.

Ellery shrugged. "Mr. Van Horn, Howard handed me that necklace. Howard asked me to raise money on it."

Howard began to shake. "That's a damned lie," he said hoarsely. "I don't know what he's talking about."

Committed. Over.

And Sally?

Sally just stood there.

She's standing there but she's jumped. She would be ruthless, she'd said. And Howard said he'd do anything. To keep Diedrich from learning the truth they'd lie, steal, betray. You weren't kidding, either of you.

There was no reason whatever for keeping Sally out of this. And yet an obscure something checked Ellery's tongue. Pure sentiment, he decided. What's more, she knew it. He could read the little, wicked, triumphant woman's knowledge in her eyes. And yet Sally was neither wicked nor small. Perhaps she was better than any of them, and bigger. He was almost happy to be able to keep her out of it. Unless Howard mucked to the very bottom and dragged

her down with him. But Ellery didn't think he would. Not to
spare her. To spare himself.

Ellery stopped thinking altogether. But then he pulled himself in.
Diedrich was watching him, watching Howard. And then Diedrich did a strange thing. He strode over to Sally and took the necklace from her fingers and ran to the safe and hurled the necklace
in and slammed the safe door and twirled the dial.

When he turned to Chief Dakin his face was composed.

"Dakin, the matter's closed."

"No charges?"

"No charges."

Dakin's clouded eyes shifted ever so slightly. "Mr. Van Horn, it's
your property."

"Wait a minute!" screamed J. P. Simpson. "The matter's closed,
is it? And what about that money I loaned him on the necklace?
Think I'm goin' to be done out of my money?"

"How much was it, Simpson?" asked Diedrich courteously.

"Twenty-five thousand dollars!"

"Twenty-five thousand dollars." Diedrich's lips tightened. "Rem-
iniscent, Mr. Queen, isn't it? By the way, is that right — that
figure?"

"Quite right."

Diedrich went to his desk and in the intolerable silence wrote out
a check.

⚬⚬⚬

WHEN DAKIN AND Simpson had gone, Wolfert seeing them out,
Diedrich got up from his desk and put his hand on Sally's arm.

She quivered, but she said, "Yes, Dieds."

He steered her to the doorway. Howard moved, too, but somehow his father's bulk managed to get in the way.

The door closed in Howard's face.

Neat.

Howard shouted, "Why'd you come out with it? Damn you, why
did you?"

His hands were fists and he was pale and flushed alternately and he seemed about to throw himself at Ellery in a perfect frenzy of outrage.

"Why did I come out with it, Howard?" asked Ellery incredulously.

"Yes! Why didn't you stick by us!"

"You mean why didn't I confess to a crime I didn't commit?"

"You didn't have to say a damned thing! All you had to do was keep your big mouth shut!"

I've got to get hold of myself.

"In the face of Simpson's identification?"

"Father would never have pressed charges!"

He's insane.

"Instead of which you welshed on us! You've made him suspicious! You forced me to lie. And he knows I lied. And if he doesn't get it out of me, one of these days he'll worm it out of Sally!"

Just hold on.

"I rather think, Howard, that Sally will take care of her end very capably. He doesn't suspect she's involved in any way. The only one he suspects is you."

Forced him to lie. Howard believes it.

"Well, that's true." As suddenly as it had begun, the tantrum ended. "I'll give you that much. You kept Sally out of it."

"Yes," said Ellery. "Big-hearted Queen. So now all your father can think is that you're a thief, Howard; he has no reason to learn that you cuckolded him, too. As I said, big-hearted Queen."

Howard went very pale.

He dropped into the armchair and began to bite his nails.

"This whole thing, Howard," said Ellery, "is so completely incredible that frankly, for the first time in my life, I don't know what to say. I ought to knock your head right off your shoulders. If I thought you were normal, I would."

Ellery reached for the telephone.

"What are you going to do?" Howard mumbled.

Ellery sat down on the desk. "If I stay on here, Howard, I can only continue to muddy the existing mess. That's one thing. Another is that I've had a bellyful — I wash my hands of the whole stupid, unbelievable business. You and Sally work it out as you see fit — you never took my advice, anyway. This adultery thing wasn't what brought me up here; had I known about it in advance, I shouldn't have come in the first place. As for your amnesia, my advice — which undoubtedly you won't take — is what it was back in New York: See a really top man or woman in psychiatry and open up.

"The third thing, Howard," said Ellery with a slight smile, "is that I've learned an important lesson, to wit: Never reach a conclusion about a man's character on the basis of a few weeks in Paris, and never, *never* reach a conclusion about a woman on any basis whatsoever."

He dialed Operator.

"You're leaving?"

"Tonight. Immediately. Operator — "

"Wait a minute. You calling for a cab?"

"Just a moment, Operator. Yes, Howard. Why?"

"No more trains out tonight."

"Oh — never mind, Operator." Ellery hung up, slowly. "Then I'll have to stay over in one of the hotels."

"That's silly."

"And dangerous? Because it might get around that Howard Van Horn's house guest spent his last night in Wrightsville at the Hollis?"

Howard reddened.

Ellery laughed. "What do you suggest?"

"Take my car. If you insist on leaving tonight, drive back. You can garage the car in town and I'll pick it up on my next trip in. I've got to run into New York the end of the week anyway to buy some stuff for the Museum project. I'll tell father you suddenly decided to leave tonight — which is true — and that I lent you my car — which is also true."

"But look at the risk I'm running, Howard."

"Risk? What risk?"

"Of finding Dakin on my trail," said Ellery, "with a warrant charging me with automobile theft."

Howard muttered: "You're very funny."

Ellery shrugged.

"All right, Howard. I'll chance it."

∞

ELLERY DROVE STEADILY. It was very late, there was almost no traffic on the main highway, Howard's roadster hummed the song of escape, there were honest stars to look at, the tank was full, and he felt happy and at peace.

It had been wrong from the start. He'd had no business meddling in Howard's amnesia. But there had been a mystery then, and the human element of liking and curiosity. Later, however, when he learned about the erotic explosion at Lake Pharisee, he should have run rapidly for the nearest exit. Or, if he had stayed, he should have refused firmly and finally to act in any capacity whatever in the negotiations with the blackmailer. At any step along the way he might have spared himself the sickening eventuality of Howard's perfidy simply by being sensible. So, really, he had no one to blame but himself.

But it was a comfortable castigation. Peace perched on his suit-case, a therapeutic companion.

It was possible to see Wrightsville now in the perspective of his receding tracks, a sore spot rapidly vanishing. It was possible to see Diedrich Van Horn and his great trouble, and Sally Van Horn and hers. It was even possible to see Howard for what he was — the disturbed and degenerating prisoner of a cruel personal history, an object of sympathy rather than a subject for anger. And Wolfert was simply a little nastiness, to be flicked off. As for Christina Van Horn, she was less than a phantom — the ancient shadow of a phantom, toothlessly mouthing in the darkness of her crypt a few dry morsels of the Bible.

The Bible.

The Bible!

∞

ELLERY FOUND HIMSELF parked on the side of the road, crouched over the dead wheel, gripping it while his heart labored to right itself and his head filled with the unthinkable.

❧

IT TOOK HIM some time to work out. There was the wonder to fight clear of, and the deadwood to pick out and throw away. An orderly process had to be set up so that the thing might be seen in its unbelievable image. He had to stand far enough off to be able to encompass its sheer magnitude.

But was it possible? Really possible?

Yes. He couldn't be mistaken. He could not.

Each piece had the terrifying color of the whole, the congruent edges of which, fitted together, revealed the tremendous — the simply tremendous and the tremendously simple — pattern.

Pattern . . . Ellery recalled his uneasy thoughts about a pattern, how he had tried to decipher its hieroglyphs. But this was the Rosetta Stone. There was no possibility of a mistake.

One piece was missing.

Which?

Slowly. One . . . four . . . seven . . .

A pale horse: and his name that sat on him was Death.

❧

FRANTICALLY, HE STARTED the roadster, shot the car around.

His foot kicked the accelerator to the floor, held it struggling there.

That all-night diner a few miles back.

❧

THE HOLLOW-EYED NIGHT man in the diner stared.

Ellery's hand shook as he dropped the coins into the slots.

"Hello?"

Quickly!

"Hello! Mr. Van Horn?"

"Yes?"

Safe.

"Diedrich Van Horn?"

"Yes! Hello? Who is this?"

"Ellery Queen."

"Queen?"

"Yes. Mr. Van Horn —"

"Howard told me before he went to bed that you —"

"Never mind! You're safe, that's the important thing."

"Safe? Of course I'm safe. Safe from what? What are you talking about?"

"Where are you?"

"Where am I? Queen, what's the matter?"

"Tell me! Which room are you in?"

"My study. I couldn't sleep, decided to come down and do some paper work I've neglected —"

"Everyone in the house?"

"Everyone but Wolfert. He went back to town with Dakin and Simpson, left me a note saying he'd forgotten some contracts on a deal we've been negotiating, that he'd probably work through the night, and —"

"Mr. Van Horn, listen to me."

"Queen, I can't take much more tonight." Diedrich sounded exhausted. "Can't whatever it is wait? I don't *understand*," he said bitterly. "You pack up and leave —"

Ellery said rapidly: "Listen to me carefully. Are you listening?"

"Yes!"

"Follow these instructions to the letter —"

"*What* instructions?"

"*Lock yourself in the study.*"

"What?"

"Lock yourself in. Not only the door. The windows. The French door, too. Don't open to anyone, Mr. Van Horn, do you understand? *To anyone but me.* Do you understand?"

Diedrich was silent.

"Mr. Van Horn! Are you still there?"

"Yes, I'm still here," said Diedrich very slowly. "I'm here, Mr. Queen. I'll do as you say. Just where are you?"

"Wait a minute. You there!"

The counterman said: "Somebody in trouble, bud?"

"How far am I from Wrightsville?"

"Wrightsville? About forty-four miles."

"Mr. Van Horn!"

"Yes, Mr. Queen."

"I'm about forty-four miles from Wrightsville. I'll drive back as fast as I can. Figure forty to forty-five minutes for the trip. I'll come to the French door on the south terrace. When I knock, you'll ask who it is. I'll tell you. Then, and then only, open — and only when you're completely satisfied that it's really me. Is that perfectly clear? There must be no exceptions. You must let no one into the study either from outside the house or from inside. Is that clear?"

"I heard you."

"Even that may not do it. Is that .38 Smith & Wesson still in your desk drawer? If it isn't, don't leave the study to get it!"

"It's still here."

"Take it out. Now. Hold it. All right, I'm going to hang up now and start. As soon as I do, lock up and keep away from the windows afterward. I'll see you in — "

"Mr. Queen."

"Yes? What?"

"What's the point of all this? From the way you're talking anyone would think my life's in danger."

"It is."

The Eighth Day

FORTY-THREE MINUTES LATER Ellery knocked on the French door.

The study was in darkness.

"Who is it?"

It was hard to say just where Diedrich might be beyond the glass.

"Queen."

"Who? Say it again."

"Queen. Ellery Queen."

A key turned. He opened the French door, stepped through, shut the door swiftly, turned the key. He felt around in the dark until he found the pull of the hanging.

Only then did he say, "You may turn the lights on now, Mr. Van Horn."

The desk lamp.

Diedrich was standing on the other side of the desk, the .38 brilliant. The desk top was a confusion of account books, papers. He was in pajamas and robe; bare feet in leather mules. His face was quite pale, a study in planes.

"Good idea turning the lights out," said Ellery. "I should have thought of that myself. Never mind the gun now."

Diedrich laid the weapon on the desk.

"Anything?" Ellery asked.

"No."

Ellery grinned. "That was quite a drive; I'll dream about it. Mind if I take the load off my feet?"

He dropped into Diedrich's swivel chair and stretched his legs.

A muscle at the corner of the big man's mouth was jumping. "I'm pretty much at the end of my patience, Mr. Queen. I want the whole story, and I want it now."

"Yes," said Ellery.

"What's this about my life being in danger? I haven't an enemy in the world. Not that kind of enemy."

"You have, Mr. Van Horn."

"Who?" His laborer's fists took his full weight as he leaned over the desk.

But Ellery slumped until the back of his neck rested on the top of the chair.

"Who!"

"Mr. Van Horn." Ellery rolled his head. "I've just made a discovery so . . . sidereal that it brought me back here when I'd have said an hour and a half ago an Act of Congress couldn't have pulled the trick.

"A great many things have happened since I stepped off that train last Thursday. At first they seemed disconnected. Then the outlines of connections appeared, but only of obvious and ordinary ones. Through it all I was bothered by the feeling that they had, oh, a greater connection, an all-over something . . . a pattern. I had no idea what the pattern was. It was just a feeling—call it an intuition; you develop a special sense when you've poked around the darker holes of what's laughingly called the human soul as long as I have."

Diedrich's eyes remained glacial.

"I put it down to imagination; I didn't pursue it. But just now, driving away from Wrightsville, the flash came.

"The lightning image is a cliché," murmured Ellery, "but there's no substitute for it as an adequate expression of how it happened. It just struck me. 'The bolt from the blue.' By its light I made out the pattern," Ellery said slowly, "the whole, hideous, magnificent pattern. I say 'magnificent' because there's grandeur in it, Mr. Van Horn—the grandeur, say, of Satan who was, after all, Lucifer. There's beauty in the Dark Angel, of a sort; and the Devil can

quote Scripture to his purpose. I know. This is gibberish to you.
But I'm still not over the," Ellery paused for the word, "the apocalyp-
tic awfulness of it."

"Who?" growled Diedrich. "What did you find out, or figure
out, or whatever it was?"

But Ellery said: "The diabolical feature of this pattern is its in-
evitability. Once it's laid down on the cloth, so to speak, and the
scissors taken up, it must cut to the last selvage. It's the perfect thing;
it must be perfect, or it's nothing. That's why I knew. That's why
I called you. That's why I very nearly broke my neck getting back
to you. There's no stopping it. It's got to fulfill itself. Got to."

"Fulfill itself?"

"Go on to the end."

"*What* end!"

"I told you, Mr. Van Horn. Murder."

Diedrich looked at him a moment longer. Then he pushed away
from the desk and lumbered over to his armchair. He sat down,
put his head back.

*With this man only doubt and uncertainty are defeating. He can
face anything if he knows. But he must know.*

"All right," said Diedrich in a rumble. "There's going to be a
murder. And I take it I'm the murderee. Is that it, Mr. Queen?"

"It's as perfectly sure as — as gravitation. The pattern is incomplete at this point. There's only one thing which can complete it, the
crime of murder. And once I identified the pattern and its designer,
I knew that you were the only possible victim."

Diedrich nodded.

"Now tell me, Mr. Queen. Who's planning to kill me?"

Their glances locked across the room.

Ellery said: "Howard."

∽

DIEDRICH ROSE AND came back to the desk. He opened a humidor.

"Cigar?"

"Thanks."

He held the desk lighter over to Ellery's cigar. The flame was untroubled.

"You know," said Diedrich, puffing, "I was prepared for anything but this murder business. Not that I necessarily accept your conclusion, Mr. Queen. I have a lot of respect for you as a craftsman, as I think I made clear when you first came. But I'd be a fool to take your word for anything like this."

"I don't expect you to take my word for it."

Diedrich looked at him through the blue smoke. "You'll prove it?" he exclaimed.

"It proves itself. I told you, it's perfect."

Diedrich was silent.

Then he said. "This Howard thing. Mr. Queen . . . he's my son. It doesn't matter that I didn't actually conceive him. I've read enough detective fiction to get a laugh out of the writers who avoid a blood relationship between a parent and a child when the child, say, is to be the murderer in the story; they do it by making the child a foster child. As if that made any difference! The . . . the emotional tie between people is a result of a lifetime of living together and has practically nothing to do with genetics. I've brought Howard up from infancy. What he is I've made him. I'm in his cells. And he's in mine.

"I admit I haven't done a very good job, though God knows I've tried my best. But murder? Howard a murderer, with me his intended victim? It's too . . . too storyish, Mr. Queen. Too unbelievable. We've shared a life for over thirty years. I can't accept it."

"I know how you feel," said Ellery irritably. "I'm sorry. But if my conclusion is wrong, Mr. Van Horn, I'll never make another. I'll . . . I'll quit thinking."

"Big words."

"I mean every one of them."

Diedrich began to walk up and down, the cigar jutting from his mouth at an angry angle.

"But why?" he said harshly. "What's behind it? It can't possibly be for the usual reasons. I've given Howard everything—"

"Everything but one thing. And, unfortunately, that thing is what he wants most. Or thinks he does, which comes to the same thing. Also," murmured Ellery, "Howard loves you. He loves you so self-centeredly, Mr. Van Horn, that, granting certain premises, killing you becomes absolutely logical."

"I don't know what you're talking about," shouted Diedrich. "I'm a plain man and I'm used to plain talk. What's this pattern you claim is going to wind up in my murder? By Howard, of all people!"

"I'd rather explain with Howard here — "

Diedrich started for the door.

"No!" Ellery leaped. "You're not going up there alone!"

"Don't be a fool, man."

"Mr. Van Horn, I don't know how he's going to do it, or when — for all I know, it may be planned for tonight. That's why I . . . What's the matter?"

"Planned for tonight." Van Horn glanced ceilingward, very quickly, but shaking his head almost as he did so.

"What's the matter?"

"No. It's too silly. You've got me as jumpy as . . ." Diedrich laughed shortly. "I'm getting Howard."

Ellery had him by the arm before he could unlock the door.

After a moment Diedrich said: "You're really convinced."

"Yes."

"All right. Sally and I occupy separate bedrooms. But it's so damned far-fetched!"

"It can't be a hundredth as far-fetched as what I've got to tell you, Mr. Van Horn. Go on!"

Diedrich scowled. "After that business tonight, after you left, Sally was terribly nervous. More nervous than I've ever seen her. She told me upstairs there was something important she wanted me to know. Something, she said, that she'd kept from me and couldn't keep from me any longer."

Too late, Sally.

"Yes?"

Diedrich glared at him. "Don't tell me you know . . . whatever it is . . . too!"

"Then she didn't tell you after all?"

"I'm afraid I was still upset by the necklace business. Frankly, I couldn't take any more just then. I told her it would have to wait."

"But that's not it, Mr. Van Horn! What was it that worried you just now?"

"What's the matter, Queen? Damn it, what's the matter?"

"*What worried you?*"

Diedrich flung the stub of his cigar into the fireplace with all his strength. "She begged me to listen," he cried, "and I said I had this work to finish tonight and whatever it was could wait. She said, All right—then I'll wait up, I've got to tell you tonight. She said she'd wait up for me in my bedroom. That if I worked very late I might find her asleep in my bed, but that I was to wake her up and—"

"In your bed. *In your bed?*"

∼

DIEDRICH'S BEDROOM DOOR stood open.

Diedrich jabbed the light button and the room leaped at them and Sally, who was part of the room, leaped more strongly than the bed in which she was lying or any of the other dead things around her.

And this was queer, because Sally was dead, too.

Sally was ugly-dead, distorted-dead, she did not look like Sally at all. The only thing of Sally's that lingered on this wrenched and congested gargoyle of a face was the faint smile which had irritated Ellery so at their first meeting. Now, because it alone remained of all the remembered Sally, it comforted him. He put his fingers in her hair and pulled gently to get her head back so that he might look at what he knew was to be seen, the Van Gogh fingerstrokes on the canvas of her throat painting the story of her death in powerful tones.

She lay twisted in a matrix of violence. Her legs and arms had done this to the bedclothes in her last creative moments.

The flesh of her torn neck was very cold.

Ellery stepped away and jostled Diedrich and Diedrich lost his balance and sat down, hard, on the bed, on one of Sally's legs. He sat there, unconscious with his eyes open.

Ellery got a hand mirror from Diedrich's bureau and returned to the bed to put the mirror to the dead mouth, knowing it was dead but performing the act through habit. It was hard to breathe for the congestion at the base of his own throat, but he was unaware of the pain. Inside, somewhere, a voice was charging him with responsibility for this great crime; but he was unconscious of that, too. It was only later, when he put the mirror with its red print of Sally's lips back on her husband's bureau, that he became aware of what the voice was saying, over and over; but then he went quickly out of Diedrich's bedroom.

ᕦᕤ

HOWARD WAS LYING on his own bed upstairs, in the bedroom adjoining the big studio.

He was fully clothed and he was in the same stupid trance in which Ellery had found him after that wild night in the Fidelity cemetery.

You were your own best diagnostician, Howard. You hypothecated Mr. Hyde and you foresaw murder most foul.

There was something about his hands.

Ellery raised one of them. Four long soft hairs were caught between two of the powerful sculptor's fingers and under the nails of all the fingers except the thumb were little bloody particles of Sally's throat.

The Ninth Day

CHIEF DAKIN WAS in and out all night and that was a touch of home, for the others were all new. Where was Prosecutor Phil Hendrix of the dove-bill mouth who had replaced young Cart Bradford who was now in the second renewal of his lease on the gubernatorial mansion in the state capital? Where was nervous Coroner Salemson of the asthma and the gooseberry wine? Where old palsied Dunc, of the Duncan Funeral Parlors? Alas. Hendrix was hunting witches in Washington, Salemson slept gratefully in Twin Hills Cemetery, and the elder Mr. Duncan, who had placed two generations of Wrightsvillians into the waiting earth, was one with the air and the wind and the dust, for he had left imploring orders in his will to be cremated.

There was a saturnine young man who persisted in giving Ellery long exploratory looks; his name was Chalanski, and it turned out that he it was who now played Nemesis to the felons of Wright County; the coroner was a brisk lean surgical fellow named Grupp, with a long nose and scalpel eyes; and the mortician (for Wrightsville was still lacking an official morgue) was the chubby junior Mr. Duncan who, to judge from the shiny-lipped relish with which he discussed the post-mortem problems with the coroner, County Prosecutor Chalanski, and Chief of Police Dakin, had been conceived on a slab, cradled in a casket, weaned on embalming fluid, and had expended the first yearnings of his puberty on some weekend visitor to his father's establishment. Ellery didn't like the way rotund Mr. Duncan looked at Sally; he didn't like it at all.

Some time during Wednesday morning, a stout flat-footed individual with a neck like bark, ploughed in, giving off powerful odors; and this was County Sheriff Mothless, successor to Gilfant. No improvement! Fortunately, Sheriff Mothless lingered only long enough to make sure that the newspaper people outside spelled his name correctly.

And there were others — state troopers, Wrightsville radio patrolmen, civilian-looking people with black bags, and just people — among the latter, Ellery suspected, being some of the more elastic-necked townsfolk who were exercising the traditional American prerogative of tramping around the squire's manse airing a long-smothered curiosity.

Well, he thought, there's no reason why murder in Wrightsville should be sweeter-smelling than murder anywhere else.

Mr. Queen was feeling strangely at peace. In one part of him only, of course; most of him was occupied by fatigues and unpleasantnesses. He had had no sleep; he had unfortunately been compelled to witness the Ayesha-like transformation of Diedrich Van Horn from prime to senescence; he had had to sustain himself through two hours of Wolfert Van Horn, who had trapped him in a corner of the living room and assaulted him with reminiscences of Howard's evil tendencies from earliest boyhood: how Howard had hunted garter snakes and chopped them into little pieces, and pulled wings off flies, and once, at the age of nine, had filled his, Wolfert's, bed with thistles and how he, Wolfert, had always warned his brother that no good would come of suckling the brat of the devil knew what parents, and so on. And, of course, there was always Howard himself, his eyes bright red and his hair a tangle and his air of absolute bewilderment, his only activity being frequent visits to the bathroom accompanied by a Wrightsville policeman Dakin called "Jeep," whom Ellery did not know. This officer reported that on these excursions Howard merely scrubbed his hands, so that as hour after hour dragged by Howard's hands became paler and more water-wrinkled, finally looking like something washed up on a beach. Howard was the real trial Wednesday morning, because he could answer no questions; he could only ask them. The chief neurologist of Connhaven State Hospital spent two hours with him on the scene of the crime and emerged looking thoughtful. Ellery talked to this medical gentleman, giving Howard's amnesic history; and the doctor, who was also Psychiatric Consultant to the State Penal Board, nodded frequently, and with that mysterious about-to-pounce-but-never-doing-so air which Ellery found so trying in so many medical men.

Nevertheless, there was that small portion of peace; and this was because something which had been darkness was now light and The End was within reach.

He had informed Dakin and Chalanski that he had something vital to contribute to the case and he asked that before Howard was removed from the premises he, Ellery Queen, be given the opportunity to divulge it in the interests of truth, if not justice, as the case against Howard would be distorted, baffling, and incomplete otherwise; if, indeed, it would make sense at all. And he further requested that the neurologist remain, at which the neurologist looked annoyed, but remained.

At two-thirty o'clock Wednesday afternoon Chief Dakin came into the kitchen, where Ellery was devouring the half-eaten corpse of a roast duck (Laura and Eileen had locked themselves in their rooms and had not been seen all day), and Dakin said: "Well, Mr. Queen, if you're ready, we are."

Ellery gulped one more mouthful of brandied peaches, wiped his lips, and rose.

∽

"I NOTE," SAID Ellery in the living room, "that Christina Van Horn isn't with us. No," he said quickly, as Chief Dakin stirred, "don't bother. The old lady wouldn't have anything to contribute but quotations from the Bible, which might get in the way. She doesn't know much, if anything, about any of this. Let her stay upstairs.

"Diedrich." It was the first time he had addressed Van Horn so, and his Christian name now roused Diedrich a little, so that he looked up almost with interest. "I'm going to have to say some things that are going to hurt you, I'm afraid."

Diedrich's hand flapped. "I just want to know what this is all about," he said courteously. Then he added, "There isn't much else left," but that was more to himself.

Howard was all shoulders and knees in his chair, needing a shave, needing sleep, needing solace — an isolated lump already out of touch with reality. Only his eyes kept in touch; and they were hard to look at. In fact, he was rather painfully ignored by everyone but the neurologist and Wolfert, and they looked nowhere else.

"To make this . . ." Ellery hesitated, "this thing intelligible, to make it clear to you at each of its specific and numbered steps, I've got to go back to the beginning. To what happened from the time Howard walked into my apartment in New York over a week ago. I'll recap as briefly as I can."

And Ellery went over all the events of the past eight days: Howard's awakening in the Bowery flophouse, his coming to Ellery, the story of his amnesic attacks, his fears, his appeal to Ellery to come to Wrightsville and keep watching him; Ellery's first night in the Van Horn house, when at dinner Wolfert brought the news that the Art Museum Committee had accepted Diedrich's condition that Howard be the official sculptor of the classical gods who were to decorate the face of the proposed Museum building, and of how Howard had fired to the assignment, making sketches and in the succeeding days even beginning work in plasticine for small models; the second day, when Sally, Howard, and Ellery had driven up to Quetonokis Lake, and how Howard and Sally had told Ellery of their debts to Diedrich — Howard, the foundling who owed Diedrich everything, Sally, who had been Sara Mason of Polly Street, destined to poverty and the life of an ignorant drab, but for Diedrich — and then how they had confessed to him the crime of their passion in the Lake Pharisee lodge and its consummation there (and as Ellery told of this he tried not to look at Diedrich Van Horn out of shame for all the sinned-against, for Diedrich shrank into himself like a paper being consumed into ash); and Ellery told of the four indiscreet, revealing letters Howard had written to Sally afterward, and the story of Sally's japanned box with its false bottom and the box's theft in June; and of the sudden telephone call from the blackmailer on the day preceding Ellery's arrival, and of the second call, and of Ellery's part in the negotiations; of his conversation with Diedrich the same night of the excursion to Quetonokis Lake, when Diedrich had told him not only of the June robbery of Sally's jewel box but also of the robbery of the night before, the theft of twenty-five thousand dollars in five-hundred-dollar bills from the wall safe in the study — the very sum in the very bills which Howard had handed to Ellery at the lake in an envelope for payment over to the blackmailer; of the third day, when Ellery had been outwitted by the blackmailer, and of Diedrich's revelation that night that he had finally discovered Howard's origin as the son of two poor farm people named Waye, who were long since dead; of Howard's reaction, and of the Fidelity Cemetery episode in the early hours of Sunday morning, when Howard had attacked the gravestones of his parents with mud and a chisel and mallet during an amnesic seizure, and of how Ellery had brought him back to himself afterward, and of how Howard had shown him the plasticine model of Jupiter on which he had scratched his sculptor's signature, not *H. H. Van Horn* as he had always signed himself, but *H. H. Waye;* and of all the events thereafter, including the third call from the blackmailer, Ellery's pawning of Sally's necklace at Howard's request, and Howard's incredible denial of the truth when Ellery was faced with a charge of grand theft.

And through it all Diedrich wrestled with the arms of his chair and Howard sat sculpturally.

"That's the story to date," continued Ellery. "It may strike you as a series of random incidents, and you may be wondering why I take your time up with a recital of them. The reason is that they're not random at all, but connected — connected so rigidly that no one incident is less important to the whole than another, even though some seem actually trivial.

"Last night," said Ellery, "I was on my way back to New York. I was disgusted with Howard, disappointed in Sally — fed up. A long way from Wrightsville a thought struck me. It was a simple thought, so simple it changed everything. And I saw this case for what it really was. For the first time."

He paused to clear his throat and Prosecutor Chalanski said, "Queen, do you know what you're talking about? Because, frankly, *I* don't."

But Chief Dakin said, "Mr. Chalanski, I've heard this man talk before. Give him a chance."

"It's irregular, anyway. There's no legal ground for this 'hearing' — if that's what it is; I don't know *what* it is — and in any event Van Horn ought to be represented by counsel."

"This is all more a part of the coroner's inquest," said Coronor Grupp. "Maybe it's a trick to lay the ground for some future claim of illegal process or something, Chalanski."

"Let him talk," said Dakin. "He'll say something."

"What?" jeered the Prosecutor.

"I don't know. But he always does."

Ellery said, "Thanks, Dakin," and he waited; and when Chalanski and Grupp shrugged, he went on.

"I drew up to the side of the road and went over the case piece by piece. I re-examined everything, but this time I had a frame of reference."

"What frame of reference?" demanded Chalanski.

"The Bible."

"The what?"

"The Bible, Mr. Chalanski."

"I'm beginning to think," said the prosecutor, looking around with a grin, "that you've got a lot more need for Dr. Cornbranch's services, Queen, than this fellow here."

"Let him go on, Chalanski, will you?" said the neurologist; but even then he did not take his eyes from Howard.

"It became clear very quickly," said Ellery, "that Howard had been responsible for six acts, and that these six acts encompassed nine different crimes."

At this Chalanski lost his grin and the coroner unfolded his long insolent legs.

"*Nine* different crimes?" repeated Chalanski. "You know what they are, Grupp?"

"Hell, no."

"Let him talk," said Dakin.

"*What* nine crimes, Queen?"

But Ellery said: "The nine crimes were different crimes, and yet in a larger sense they were the same crime. I mean by that that they had continuity, congruity, a pattern — they had an integral relationship; they were parts of a whole.

"Once I understood the nature of that relationship," Ellery continued, "once *you* understand it, gentlemen, you'll see, as I did, that it was possible to predict one crime still to come. It had to be. It was an inescapable conclusion. Nine crimes, and they made the tenth inevitable. Not only that. Once you understand the nature of the pattern, you could predict — as I did to Diedrich Van Horn — precisely what the tenth crime would be, against whom it would be aimed, and by whom it would be committed. I've never run into anything so perfect in all my experience, which has been considerable. Without meaning to be presumptuous, I doubt if any of you ever have, either. I'm tempted to say, I doubt if anyone, anywhere, ever will again."

And now there was nothing to be heard but the breathing of many men and, outside, a state trooper's voice raised in anger.

"The only unpredictable factor was time. I couldn't tell when the tenth crime would take place." Ellery said briskly: "Since it could conceivably have occurred even as I sat in the car almost fifty miles from Wrightsville thinking the thing through, I drove for the nearest phone, ordered Mr. Van Horn to take immediate precautions, and returned here as fast as I could.

"I couldn't have known that Mrs. Van Horn would choose tonight to drop off to sleep in her husband's bed, in her husband's bedroom. Howard's hands felt for his father's throat in the dark and choked the life out of the woman he loved instead. If he hadn't been in the amnesic state his sense of touch would probably have told him of his mistake and he might have stopped in time; as it was, he was simply a killing machine, and the machinery, once set in motion, did its job as machines do."

And Ellery said: "That's the story in general.

"Now let's consider Howard's six acts, the six acts embracing the nine crimes I mentioned, revealing the plan behind them and making the tenth crime predictable.

"One." Ellery paused. And then he took the plunge. "*Howard was engaged in sculpturing figures of the ancient gods.*"

And he paused. It was too much to ask of any practical mind that it accept such an extraordinary statement out of context as the utterance of sanity. He could only wait.

"Ancient gods," said the Prosecutor, looking dazed. "What kind of—"

"What d'ye mean, Mr. Queen?" asked Chief Dakin, looking anxious. "Is that a crime?"

"Yes, Dakin," said Ellery, "and not one crime. It's really two crimes."

Chalanski sank back, openmouthed.

"Two. Howard had actually reached the point of signing his sculptures—or his sketches and preliminary models—with the curiously significant signature *H. H. Waye.*"

Chalanski shook his head.

"*H. H. Waye.*" It was the coroner who said that, not even resentfully; he merely said it, as if he wanted to hear how it might sound in a familiar voice.

"Is that a crime, too?" demanded the prosecutor with an exasperated grin.

"Yes, Mr. Chalanski," said Ellery, "and a particularly blasphemous one.

"Third. Howard stole twenty-five thousand dollars from Diedrich."

They all relaxed at that, gratefully, as if in the midst of a lecture in Urdu the lecturer had inserted a sentence in English.

"Well, I'll agree *that's* a crime!" Chalanski laughed, looking around. But no one responded.

"You'll agree, Mr. Chalanski, when you grasp the overlying design, that *all* of Howard's acts were crimes, although not all were necessarily penological crimes.

"Four. Howard abused the graves of Aaron and Mattie Waye."

"We're getting on solider ground," said Coroner Grupp. "Now

that's a crime, Chalanski — vandalism, or something, isn't it?"

"Not exactly. There's a statute that — "

"The two crimes Howard committed in desecrating his parents' graves, Mr. Chalanski," said Ellery, "will not be found in your statutes. May I go on?

"Five. Howard fell in love with Sally Van Horn. And that constitutes two crimes, also.

"And finally, six. Howard's outrageous lie when he denied that he'd given me Sally's diamond necklace to pawn.

"Six acts, nine crimes," said Ellery. "Nine of the ten worst crimes a man can commit, according to an authority a great deal older than your statutes, Mr. Chalanski."

"What authority would that be?"

"An authority who's usually spelled with a capital G."

Chalanski jumped up. "I've had just about — "

"God."

"*What?*"

"Well, God as we know Him from the Old Testament, Mr. Chalanski — Who, after all, in that form, is still professed by Greek and Roman Catholics and most Protestants, as well as by the ancient Jews who first memorialized Him in the Book. Yes, Mr. Chalanski, God — or *Yahweh,* which is a transliteration of the Hebrew tetragrammaton translated as *Jehovah* in the Christian exegesis; the 'ineffable' or 'incommunicable name' of the Supreme Being, Mr. Chalanski . . . the Lord, Mr. Chalanski, Who in whichever nominal form called Moses into the midst of the cloud on the mount of Sinai and kept him there for forty days and forty nights, *and he gave unto Moses, when he had made an end of communing with him upon Mount Sinai, two tables of testimony, tables of stone, written with the finger of God.*

"*IN THOSE SIX ACTS,*" said Ellery, "*HOWARD BROKE NINE OF THE TEN COMMANDMENTS.*"

∽

AND NOW IT was the neurologist who stirred; he stirred uneasily, as if he were himself having a significant dream. But all the others sat still, including Howard, who seemed outside the world of real things and in a world uniquely his own. And into this terrifying land no one intruded, not even Ellery.

"By sculpturing the gods of the Roman pantheon," said Ellery, "Howard broke two Commandments: *Thou shalt not make unto thee any graven image* and *Thou shalt have no other gods before me.*"

And Ellery said: "By signing his sculpture *H. H. Waye,* Howard broke the Commandment: *Thou shalt not take the name of the Lord thy God in vain;* and this is an especially fascinating example of how Howard's mind worked in his criminal illness. Here he dabbles in the cabala and emulates the occult theosophists of medieval times who believed, among other things, that each letter, word, number, and accent of Scripture contains a hidden sense. The greatest mystery of the Old Testament is the name of the Lord, which He Himself revealed to Moses; and that name is hidden in the tetragrammaton I mentioned, the four consonants which were variously written — actually in five ways, from *IHVH* to *YHWH,* and from which the supposed original form of God's name has been variously reconstructed; and of these reconstructions the most commonly accepted in the modern world is *Yahweh.* And if you'll take the letters which form the name *H. H. Waye,* you'll find that they constitute an anagram for *Yahweh.*"

Chalanski opened his mouth.

But Ellery said, "Yes. Quite mad, Mr. Chalanski."

And Ellery said: "By appropriating twenty-five thousand dollars from Diedrich Van Horn's safe, Howard broke the Commandment: *Thou shalt not steal.*"

And Ellery said: "By desecrating the graves of Aaron and Mattie Waye in Fidelity Cemetery during the early hours of Sunday morning last, Howard broke two other Commandments: *Remember the sabbath day, to keep it holy* and *Honor thy father and thy mother.*" He smiled faintly. "I should have asked Father Chichering of St. Paul's-in-the-Dingle to sit in on this, because on one of these points I feel the need for expert advice. I mean about the Sabbath. The 'sabbath day' referred to in the Fourth Command-

ment — it's the Third to Roman Catholics and Lutherans, I believe,
but the Fourth to Jews, Greek Catholics, and most Protestants — is
the Sabbath of Israel, which is of course Saturday and which I think
the earliest Christians kept observing sabbatically as distinguished
from the weekly celebration of the Resurrection, 'the Lord's day,'
which was Sunday; I seem to recall now that this double observ-
ance was practiced for several centuries after the Resurrection, even
though Paul from the start laid down the dictum that the Jewish
Sabbath was not binding on Christians. Well, it doesn't matter. To
Howard, a Christian, *sabbath* means Sunday; and it was in the
early hours of Sunday morning that he dishonored his father and
mother."

And Ellery said: "By falling in love with Sally and taking her
to bed in the Van Horn lodge at Lake Pharisee, Howard broke
the two Commandments: *Thou shalt not covet thy neighbor's wife*
and *Thou shalt not commit adultery*."

And, quickly, Ellery passed on to the ninth of his citations, and
he said: "By lying when he denied having given me Sally's necklace to pawn, Howard broke the Commandment: *Thou shalt not
bear false witness against thy neighbor*."

༄

AND NOW THEY were under the spell of the gigantic oddity, and
they would not have broken it if they could.

And Ellery resumed: "As I sat there on the road last night,
in Howard's car, piecing these nine fragments together, I asked
myself the natural question: Could all this have been coincidence?
Could it have been chance that led Howard to commit just such
specific acts as to cause him to break nine of the Ten Commandments? And I had to answer myself: No, that isn't possible; the
odds that such a congruency of crimes against the Decalogue might
occur by accident are too unreasonably great; those nine Commandments were therefore broken by design, they were broken pre-
meditatedly and systematically, following the Decalogue as a guide.

"But if Howard broke nine of the Ten Commandments," Ellery
cried, "he would not, he could not, stop. Ten is the whole, and nine

is not ten. The Commandment that was missing, that was still to be broken, was the Commandment above all the others which modern man has held to be the most socially desirable, if not the most morally: *Thou shalt not kill*. Ten is the whole, and nine is not ten, and when the tenth is the moral precept forbidding murder, I knew Howard was holding back murder as the climax of his stupendous rebellion against the world.

"Whom was Howard planning to murder? The answer came out the same whether I considered the outward manifestations of Howard's behavior or its underlying psychological implications. What was it Howard wanted? — or thought he wanted, because it's my admittedly layman's theory, Dr. Cornbranch, that Howard was never really in love with Sally at all, but only thought he was. He wanted, or thought he wanted, Diedrich's wife. Who stood in the way of this? Only Diedrich. By removing Diedrich, then, it would seem to Howard that he achieved Diedrich's wife. The fact that in trying to kill Diedrich he accidentally killed Sally is, logically speaking, of no importance — a tragic irrelevance.

"But you arrive at Diedrich as the intended victim by a psychological route, too. There has never been the least question in my mind — in fact, from the time ten years ago when I got to know Howard in Paris — that the chief propulsive force of Howard's emotional mechanism from early childhood has been Oedipean. His worship of Diedrich Van Horn was naked and unmistakable. The sculptures in Howard's Parisian studio were of Zeus, Adam, Moses — Moses even then — but they were all, in essence, Diedrich; and when, ten years later, I met Diedrich in the flesh, I saw that they had all been Diedrich in feature and physique as well.

"Howard's entire history made his adoration of the father-image almost inevitable: the unknown mother who had rejected him in infancy; the big, powerful, admirable male of males who had taken him in and become his father-protector and served as both father and mother to him. And, as in Oedipus, the seeds of father-murder were there, too. Because love became hatred when the father-image rejected the son and transferred his love, as it seemed to Howard, to a woman, and that woman a stranger. At that moment the seed sprouted: coincidental with the event of Diedrich's marriage to Sally came the first amnesic episode. And then Howard 'fell in love' with the woman who had stolen his father! I stand ready to be corrected, Dr. Cornbranch, but I submit that this was no love at all — it was a double-barreled attempt unconsciously *both to punish the father who had rejected him and to regain the father's love by destroying the father's relationship with the woman who was responsible for the rejection.*

"Now observe this remarkable fact: In plotting the murder of the perfidious father-image, the son employs a technique whereby in the process he murders another father-image!" Dr. Cornbranch looked puzzled. Ellery leaned forward, addressing the neurologist directly. "In this family, where Christina Van Horn, the foster grandmother, in Howard's childhood and thereafter was obsessed with the Word of God — deriving from her marriage to a fundamentalist fanatic who had preached the living Jehovah — how could Howard have escaped being steeped in the concept of the paternalism of God? Whereupon we see how perfect this perfection is: *For in deliberately violating the Ten Commandments of God the Father, Howard breaks the greatest Father-Image of all.*"

Ellery glanced at the unjointed lump that had been Howard with the pity and loathing of all normal men in the presence of the mad, and he said with great gentleness: "And now you know, gentlemen, why I've taken your time with this: The whole concept of Howard's plot is the concept of an unbalanced mind.

"I don't know what name you medical men will give to Howard's madness, Dr. Cornbranch, but it must be apparent even to laymen that to take the Decalogue as the pattern for a series of crimes culminating in the crime of murder, and to follow that pattern with the cunning and the pertinacity which this man, both consciously and unconsciously, has followed in this case, calls for a diagnosis in the consulting room by qualified psychiatrists, not for a trial in a court of law according to the rules of punishment laid down for sane lawbreakers.

"This man has no business being handled or treated as an ordinary murderer. He is, if you please, criminally insane; and I'll tell my story and give my Biblical analysis anywhere you designate, at any time, if by doing so I can help place him where I believe he belongs, which is in a mental institution."

And Ellery looked at Diedrich Van Horn, and then away, because Diedrich was crying.

∽

FOR SOME TIME there was no sound but the sound of Diedrich, and then even that stopped.

Prosecutor Chalanski looked at Dr. Cornbranch.

He cleared his throat.

"Doctor, what's your opinion about . . . about all this?"

The neurologist said: "I'd rather not commit myself on the medico-legal aspects of this case right now, Chalanski. It's going to take some time, and a lot of er- consultation."

"Well!" The prosecutor put his elbows on his knees. "From a prosecution standpoint — aside from what his attorneys may try to get across — we have a case I'm ready to take into court as soon as the inquest is out of the way."

Chief Dakin stirred. "Connhaven Labs?"

"Yes. I got a preliminary report from them by phone just before this started, Dakin. The four hairs found between his fingers have been scientifically identified as coming from Mrs. Van Horn's head. The fragments of flesh and so on under his fingernails, it's the Lab's opinion, came from Mrs. Van Horn's throat. Practically speaking, there's no doubt about it; but I think we can establish it legally, too. And, frankly, I'm not too concerned right now with whether he killed her knowing it was she or mistaking her in the dark for Mr. Van Horn. We've got a motive either way. He wouldn't be the first adulterer who killed his partner-in-sin. In fact," and something like a smile came over the prosecutor's face, "I'd find it a darned sight easier adducing that as a motive than all this fancy stuff about hating the father-image. Well, I guess that's that — "

Chalanski started to rise.

Howard said: "Are you taking me away now?"

If the plasticine image of Jupiter in Howard's studio had suddenly broken into speech they could not have been more startled.

He was looking, not at Chalanski, not at Ellery, but at Chief of Police Dakin.

"Taking you away? Yes, Howard," said Dakin uncomfortably, "I'm afraid that's about the size of it."

"There's something I want to do before they take me."

"You mean go to the toilet?"

"The oldest dodge in the world," smiled Chalanski. "Not that it would do you any good, Van Horn. Or Waye, is it? The house is pretty well covered, inside and out."

"Nutty, is he?" drawled Coroner Grupp.

"I don't want to run away," said Howard. "Where would I run to?"

Grupp and Chalanski laughed.

"Why don't you listen to him!"

It was Diedrich, on his feet, his face convulsed.

Howard said in the same, reasonable, patient way: "I just want to go upstairs to my studio, that's all."

No one said anything for some time.

"For what, Howard?" asked Chief Dakin finally.

"I'll never see it again."

"I don't see any harm in it, Chalanski," said Dakin. "He can't get away and he knows it."

The prosecutor shrugged. "Custody of the prisoner is your responsibility, Dakin. Me, I wouldn't let him."

"What's your opinion, Dr. Cornbranch?" asked the chief of police, frowning.

The neurologist shook his head. "Not without an armed guard." Dakin hesitated.

"Howard, just what is it you want to do in your studio?" asked Ellery.

Howard did not answer.

"Howard . . ." And that was Diedrich, too.

Howard just stood there, looking at the floor.

Dr. Cornbranch said, "Why don't you answer the question, Howard? What is it you want to do?"

And Howard said, "I want to smash my sculptures."

"Now that," said the neurologist, "is a reasonable request. Under the circumstances."

He glanced at Dakin and nodded.

Dakin looked grateful. He said to the tall young policeman who was standing behind Howard: "Go with him, Jeep."

Howard turned on his heel and walked steadily out.

The policeman hitched his belt, his right hand feeling for the black butt of his gun. Then he followed Howard from the room, almost stepping on Howard's heels.

"Don't take too long," called Dakin.

Diedrich sat down heavily. Howard had not glanced at him even in leaving.

Or at me, thought Ellery; and he walked over to one of the big man's big windows and looked out over the gardens where three troopers stood in the late afternoon sunshine smoking and laughing.

∽

No MORE THAN three minutes had passed by the time the first splintery crash brought all their heads around and up.

It was followed by another, and another, and then by many others in a quickening rhythm of destruction. And the sounds of breakage stopped, and there was the pause of a long breath, and then one final furious iconoclasm.

This time the silence remained.

They were all turned toward the doorway now, through which the foot of the staircase was visible, waiting for the breaker of images to descend into their view followed by the policeman; but nothing happened, no destroyer appeared, no policeman. There was the same empty perspective of hall and staircase.

Dakin went into the hall and put his hand on the bleached oak newel post. "Jeep!" he shouted. "Bring him down now!"

Jeep was silent.

"*Jeep!*"

This was a roar, with panic in it.

But Jeep did not reply.

"My God," said Dakin. His face, turned momentarily toward them, was clay-pale.

And then he scrambled up the stairs, and they all scrambled after him.

∽

THE POLICEMAN was sprawled before the closed door to Howard's studio with a purple lump over his left ear, his long legs twitching as he tried to struggle to his feet.

The gun was no longer in his holster.

"Hit me in the belly just as we got to the door," he gasped. "Grabbed my gun. Hit me with it. I went out."

Dakin rattled the door.

"Locked."

Ellery yelled, "Howard!" but Chalanski shouldered him aside and shouted, "Van Horn, you open this door and be damned quick about it!"

The door yielded nothing.

"Got a key, Mr. Van Horn?" panted Dakin.

Diedrich looked at him dumbly. He had not understood the words.

"Have to break it down."

They were gathered a few feet from the door, prepared to lunge in a body, when the shot came.

It was a single shot, followed by the sound of something metallic dropping to a floor.

There was no heavier, duller sound, as of a man's body.

They burst through the door in the first rush.

Howard was hanging from the center beam of his raftered studio. His arms dangled and blood still dripped from his wrists into two pools on the floor; he had slashed himself with a chisel. Then he had climbed onto a chair with a rope taken from a sculptor's block-and-tackle and he had slung the rope over the beam and knotted both ends tightly about his neck and kicked the chair out from under him. Then he had put the muzzle of the policeman's gun into his mouth at an acute angle and pulled the trigger. The .38 slug had torn through the roof of his mouth and emerged, taking a piece of the top of his head with it.

Prosecutor Chalanski, making a face, dug the slug out of the rafter in which it had lodged and wrapped it in his handkerchief.

Coroner Grupp said, "He sure wanted to die in the worst way."

Plasticine, clay, stone fragments littered the studio floor, and Wolfert Van Horn yelped when he stepped on a large chunk of Jupiter and turned his ankle.

కఀౢ

THE NEWSPAPERS did nip-ups.

As Inspector Queen said: "Murder, sex, and God — circulation managers dream about a case like this."

Somehow a full report of Ellery's sermon on the Ten Commandments got to the ears of the first wire service to hook onto the case. Thenceforward it was rugged. *Ellery Queen's Greatest Case, Noted Tec's Ten-Strike, Mosaic Murderer Meets Master, Sleuth Traps Bad Man with Good Book, E. Q. Tops Own Triumphs* — these were merely a few of the original headlines and subheadlines which made the master squirm. Blizzards of clips from newspapers all over the United States and Canada whitened the floor of the Queen apartment as Inspector Queen invested his hard-earned money for the greater glory of his son's scrapbook, which was no idea of his son's but strictly of his son's father's. For three weeks wise men and fools beat a widening path to the Queen door, and the telephone rang uninterruptedly. There were reporters for interviews; ghost writers with already typed sagas of the Van Horn case requiring only the master's nod and a modest cut to the apparition; magazine editors at the end of the wire and photographers on the unsafe side of the door; at least two representatives of advertising agencies who thought Noted Sleuth's Endorsement of, in one case, a cream shampoo, in the other, a new perfume to be known as "Murder," would make a dynamic tie-in with the *cause célèbre;* and radio, not to be worsted, came up with an offer to Mr. Queen to appear on Sunday afternoon with a panel of prominent clergymen, representing the Protestant, Roman Catholic, and Jewish faiths, on a program to be entitled "The Holy Bible Versus Howard Van Horn." These in addition to an army of assorted ax grinders who wanted to whittle Noted Sleuth into even more heroic shape, and at uniformly fabulous rates. Ellery threatened wrathfully to perform a little whittling job of his own on the unknown blabbermouth who had given the Ten Commandments story to the press — he swore for months afterward that it had been Dr. Cornbranch, motivated by some abstruse, higher psychology — but Inspector Queen soothed him; and, to withhold nothing, it must be recorded that, after the ninth day of the wonder, when he could do so without fear of being caught at it, Mr. Queen sneaked a few looks into the Inspector's scrapbook, which was now in the final stage of obesity. Whereupon he experienced, willy-nilly, that fine full glow which suffuses the hearts of the most modest at times; and he even read one piece through to the sweet end, the magazine article which called him "the Wonder Boy of West Eighty-seventh Street in his most spectacular performance."

But in all the journalistic literature of that fevered interlude in Ellery's career, none surpassed the neophrastic genius who, in a Sunday feature article for one of the more elevated journals entitled "The Case of the Schizophrenic Bibliomaniac," coined a phrase which was to become part of the dictionary of criminology.

This Einstein of etymology referred to Mr. Queen as "he who must henceforward and for all time be known as The Deca-Logical Detective."

☙

So ENDETH the book of the dead.

And beginneth the book of the living.

PART TWO

....

TENTH
DAY'S
WONDER

....

That would be ten days' wonder at the least.
That's a day longer than a wonder lasts.
— SHAKESPEARE, *King Henry VI*

The Tenth Day

HIS PREY was man, and he prowled the bottom lands of iniquity with an enchanted weapon, swelling in fame with each bloody chase. Never had evildoers seemed fiercer, or more cunning, or more willing for the bag. For he was Ellery, son of Richard, mighty hunter before the Law; and none might prevail against him.

∾

THE YEAR THAT followed the Van Horn *tour de force* was easily the busiest and most brilliantly successful of Ellery's career. Cases besieged him, winging in from all directions; some crossed oceans. He made two trips to Europe that year, and one to South America, and one to Shanghai. Los Angeles knew him, and Chicago, and Mexico City. Inspector Queen complained that he might just as well have brought Ellery up to be an advance man for the circus, he saw his son so seldom. And Sergeant Velie actually went ten feet past Ellery on the sidewalk skirting Police Headquarters before a vestigial memory made him turn around.

Nor was there dearth of crime business on the master's native heath. The moors of New York City resounded with his exploits. There was the case of the spastic bryologist, in which Ellery made the definitive deduction — from a dried mass of sphagnum no larger than his thumbnail — and reached into the surgery of one of New York's most respectable hospitals to save a life and blast a reputation; there was the case of Adelina Monquieux, his remarkable solution of which cannot be revealed before 1972 by agreement with that curious lady's executors; and these are cited merely in example — the full list is on the Queen agenda and will in time, no doubt, find publication in one form or another.

It was Ellery himself who called the halt. Never heavily fleshed, he had lost so much weight since September of the preceding year that even he became alarmed.

"It's this blasted running around," said Inspector Queen over an early breakfast one morning in August. "Ellery, you've got to put the brakes on."

"I've already done so. Saw Barney Kull yesterday and he said if I wanted to die gloriously of coronary thrombosis I was to keep up my pace of the last eleven months."

"I hope that put some sense into your head! What are you going to do, son?"

"Well . . . I've gathered enough material this year for twenty books and I haven't had time to write, or even plan, one. I'm going to get back to authorship."

"And the Crippler case?"

"I've turned it over to Tony, with my condolences."

"Thank God," said the Inspector piously, for there wasn't room enough on the shelves over his bed for even one more scrapbook. "But why the rush? Why not take a rest first? Go away somewhere."

"I'm sick of going away somewhere."

"No, I don't suppose I can expect you to flop sensibly on your back, where you belong," grumbled the old gentleman, reaching for the coffee pot. "Now, I take it, you'll shut yourself up in that opium den you call a study and I won't see you at all. Say! You've put on that crummy old smoking jacket!"

Ellery grinned. "I told you. I'm starting a book."

"When?"

"Right away. Today. This morning."

"Where you get the energy . . . Why don't you blow yourself to a new jacket? If you *have* to wear one of those sissy jobs."

"Give up this jacket? It's my writing habit."

"When you start punning," snarled his father, hastily pushing away from the table, "it's every man for himself. See you tonight, son."

∽

So ONCE AGAIN Mr. Queen enters his study, shuts the door, and prepares to give his auctorial all.

Mark that the process involved in preparing to conceive a book is technically different from that involved in preparing to bear it. In the latter stage there are typewriters to examine and clean, ribbons to change, pencils to sharpen, clean paper to be arranged at the precise distance from the arm at which the least exertion is called forth, notes or outlines to be propped at the exactly acute angle to the machine, and so forth. The situation at the outset of the conceptual stage is quite deplorably different. Even assuming that the author's head is fully charged with ideas and giving off impatient sparks, he has utterly no need for paraphernalia or their care or placement. He has only a rug and his miserable self.

So observe Mr. Queen in his study on this fine early morning in August of the year following the Van Horn case.

He is fired with energetic intentions. He paces his rug like a general, marshaling his mental forces. His brow is clear. His eyes are intent but calm. His legs are unhurried and untroubled. His hands are quiet.

Now observe him twenty minutes later.

His legs pump. His eyes are wild. His brows work fiercely. His hands are helpless fists. He leans against a wall, seeking the cool plaster. He darts to a chair, perches on its edge with hands clasped, as if imploringly, between his knees. He jumps up, fills his pipe, sets it down, lights a cigaret, puffs twice, it goes out, it remains between his lips. He nibbles his fingernails. He rubs his head. He explores a dental cavity. He pinches his nose. He plunges his hands into his jacket pockets. He kicks a chair. He glances at the headline of the morning newspaper on his desk but glances away heroically. He goes to the window and soon becomes interested in the scientific aspects of a fly crawling up the screen. He fingers the tobacco grains in his right pocket, rolls a grain in a wad of lint, places the wad in a piece of paper which happens to be in the same pocket. He folds the paper around it, takes the paper out, glances at it.

It says:

> *Van Horn*
> *North Hill Drive*
> *Wrightsville*

I

ELLERY SAT DOWN in his desk chair. He placed the scrap of paper on the blotter, leaned forward, put his arms flat on the desk, rested his chin on his hands, and stared at the paper two inches from his nose.

Van Horn. North Hill Drive. Wrightsville.

All that's left of the Van Horn case.

He remembered now that scene of almost a year before.

He had been dressed in this same smoking jacket (*by gosh, last time I had it on*).

He had given Howard some money to get home on and walked him downstairs and Howard hailed a taxi and they were shaking hands on the sidewalk when it had struck Ellery that he didn't know where Howard lived. They had laughed over it, and Howard had taken a black notebook out of the suit of Ellery's he was wearing, and he had ripped out a page and scribbled his address.

This page.

And Ellery had gone back upstairs and thought about Wrightsville, and finally he had thrust the scrap of paper into a pocket of the smoking jacket and there it had remained, for he had hung the jacket in his closet the following day, where it had been hanging, uncalled to duty, ever since.

All that's left.

Studying the tiny, etching script, Howard came back to him,

and Sally, and Diedrich and Wolfert and the old woman; he thought of them all.

A fly dropped onto the "Van" and stood there, insolently. Ellery pursed his lips and blew. The fly soared away and the paper turned over.

There was writing on the other side!

The same small, engraving-like handwriting. But this side was covered with it.

Ellery sat up and reached for the paper curiously.

Howard's handwriting. Black notebook. But these weren't addresses or telephone numbers. A solid page of minute script. Sentence after sentence.

A diary?

It began in the middle of a sentence:

> silly pet names he's invented for S., though he has the grace not to use them except when he thinks they're alone. Why should it annoy me? At his *age,* though. Oh, be honest. You know *why* . . . But the damn silliness of it. Calling her "Lia" before they were married — Lia! ! ! ! ! just that way — in his own handwriting in that sappy gush note I f . . . — and then "Salomina" after the wedding. Where did he *get* them? ? ! ! So *cute* — the great D. Van H. So *coy.* Salomina — Sally — Sal — the stupid progression and what the hell was wrong with her real name in the first place? I *like* Sara. I lo — whoa, got to quit this, oughtn't even to write it. It's his right, hers. *Quit it.* Going to bed, *hope* to sleep.

A diary, yes.

One thing Howard had never mentioned.

Lia. Salomina.

Funny how those names stuck.

Lia. Salomina. Where had Diedrich picked those up? A thought shuttled over and dropped suddenly into place and Ellery was back at Quetonokis Lake, sitting beside Sally in the convertible drawn up at the lake's edge. She had turned around and tucked her legs under her, and excellent legs they had been. Howard was off at the mossy boulder kicking at a stone. Ellery had given her a cigaret.

"*My name was Sara Mason.*"

He could hear her voice and the swish of the birds rising from the log in the lake.

"It's Dieds who started calling me Sally, among other things." Among other things. Lia, and Salomina?

Calling her "Lia" before they were married . . . Before they were married. Not Sara Mason. "Lia Mason." Maybe Diedrich didn't like "Sara." "Sara Mason" conjured up the wrong picture: a tight-lipped school teacher, perhaps; a New England housewife wearing a dustcloth about her stingy hair and going around pulling down parlor blinds. "Lia Mason" was young and soft and even mysterious sounding. It suited Sally better. Also, it told something about Diedrich Van Horn. Something secret, and nice.

Salomina after the wedding. Familiar sounding. No, not really. It's the first two syllables that make it seem familiar. Daughter of Herodias . . . Ellery grinned. Then why not "Salome"? Why "Salomina"? The ending *-ina* was in itself a feminization. No, probably a pure invention of Diedrich's, like "Lia." Certainly musical. Sounded like an invention of Poe's.

He sat back and lit his pipe, puffing enjoyably and holding on to the reins of his reflections; to let go meant having to get back to rug-patrol and desperation.

He picked up a pencil, began doodling on a scrap pad.

Lia Mason?

He wrote the name down. Yes, very nice.

He wrote it again, this time in block capitals:

LIA MASON

O-ho, and what's this? LIA MASON—A SILO MAN!

He wrote down the phrase with the agricultural flavor, and now he had:

LIA MASON
A SILO MAN

He studied the letters of the name for another minute, and then he wrote down:

O ANIMALS

An invocation? He chuckled.

The next variation came quickly:

NAIL AMOS

And then:

SIAM LOAN
MAIL A SON
ALAMO SIN
MONA LISA
SAL

Mona Lisa.

Mona Lisa?

Mona Lisa!

That was it. That was *it*. That *smile*. That wise, sad, enigmatic, haunting, contradictory smile! He'd wondered where he had met Sally before. Why, he'd never met her before at all. Sally had the Mona Lisa smile, as identically as if she, and not La Gioconda, had sat for the da Vinci portrait, and . . .

And Diedrich had seen it?

Undoubtedly Diedrich had seen it. Diedrich had been in love. Had Diedrich identified it? As such?

Ellery's eyes clouded over.

He studied the scratch pad:

MONA LISA
SAL

Almost automatically he finished the unfinished variant:

SALOMINA

Salomina.

Lia Mason, Mona Lisa, Salomina.

Lia Mason, Mona Lisa, Salomina.

A pulse began to tick in his temple.

A man is in love with a woman. She owns a provocative, familiar smile which he identifies as the smile of Mona Lisa. Her name is Mason. The man is passing his prime and the woman is young and she is his first and only love. His passion would be powerful, the appetite of a starved man. There would be, especially in the pre-marital state, a total absorption in the object of his hunger. The woman would be an obsession and everything about her would be magnified and sharpened to his eye. And the man is sensitive and discerning to begin with. The Mona Lisa discovery is delicious. He toys with it; it pleases him. He writes it down: *Mona Lisa.*

And suddenly he notices that the five letters constituting his Sara Mason's surname are duplicated in the name "Mona Lisa." He is no longer merely pleased; this delights him. He steals the *M,* one *A,* the *S,* the *O,* the *N* from "Mona Lisa." Three letters are left: *L, I, A.* Why, that's practically a name in itself! It sounds like "Leah" and it looks worlds better. Lia . . . Lia Mason . . . Mona Lisa, Lia Mason.

Secretly, he rebaptizes his love. Henceforth Sara is Lia in the closet of his thoughts.

And then, one day, he opens the door to her. He says it. Aloud. "Lia." Sheepishly. But she is a woman, and this is adoration. She likes it. They now share his secret. When they are alone together, he calls her that: "Lia."

They marry, go honeymooning.

Now is the time of symbiosis, when organisms join and fuse and there is nothing outside the lovers' conjunction: no friends, no business, no distraction or possibility of distraction. Each is absorbed in the other. A life is laid aside. A match is more important than a house, and a name can be the secret of the universe. She asks how he arrived at the name Lia, or, if he has told her previously, he brings it up again. He is gay, daring, inventive. "Lia Mason" will not serve now. She is no longer Mason. Another name must be found. Seize paper and pencil, Diedrich, and demonstrate your in-finite resources, what a fine headstrong ingenious romantic young-old dog you are, Hotspur and D'Artagnan, and death to obstacles! Fee-faw-fum! Abracadabra! Presto! "Salomina."

And they had laughed together, and doubtless she had said "Salomina" was the loveliest name since "Eve" but wouldn't it be a little awkward to explain? And he gravely agreed and they compromised, for social purposes, on "Sally," which must have seemed to her at the time small price enough to pay in return for the love of this wonderful titan.

Ellery sighed.

Probably it happened altogether differently.

As if any of this made any difference now.

As if it wasn't all a self-made conspiracy to abort the unborn book.

Well . . .

He got up from the desk and paced to his former position on the rug, preparatory to —

Still, it *was* interesting to learn at this late date that poor Diedrich had had the type of mind which played around with anagrams. He recalled now having spotted a book of Double-Crostics on Diedrich's desk one day in —

Anagrams?

Anagrams! Why, yes, that's what they were. Funny it hadn't struck him before in just that way that "Lia Mason," and "Salomina," being formed of the same letters of the alphabet as "Mona Lisa," constituted an *anagram*.

Because an anagram . . .

Because an anagram . . .

"*By signing his sculpture* H. H. Waye, *Howard broke the Commandment:* Thou shalt not take the name of the Lord thy God in vain; *and this is an especially fascinating example . . . Here he dabbles in the cabala . . . occult theosophists . . . who believed that each letter, word, number, and accent of Scripture contains a hidden sense . . . And if you'll take the letters which form the name* H. H. Waye, *you'll find that they constitute an anagram for* Yahweh."

H. H. Waye — Yahweh. Anagram. Point whatever-number-it-was, one of the ten nails in Howard's coffin.

Ellery became conscious of the ticking in his head. That same old maid of a pulse.

What was all the excitement about? he asked his pulse irritably. So Diedrich played around with anagrams. Diedrich got an intellectual satisfaction out of anagrams. And so did Howard, unfortunately for him.

Unfortunately . . .

Ellery was really angry with himself.

Is it possible for two men living in the same house to have the same bent toward anagrams?

Possible hell. It was just as possible as for two men living in the same house to have the same bent toward bourbon. Anyway, it had happened. Anyway, Howard probably caught it from Diedrich. Anyway, what am I beating my brains out for?

He was furious with himself.

The case is over. The solution was impeccable. You damned fool, stop worrying over a case and a set of people dead and buried for a year and get back to work!

☙

BUT EVERY IDEA the Queen brain produced turned out to revolve about an anagram.

☙

TEN MINUTES LATER Ellery was seated at his desk again, worrying his nails.

But if Howard probably caught it from Diedrich, if Howard was an anagram man by association — if Howard was an anagram man *at all* — why had he written about the pet names "Lia" and "Salomina" the sentence: "Where did he *get* them??!!"

The names had bothered Howard. He had worried over them. And yet he had remained *ignorant of their derivation*. Ellery was an anagram man, and he had worked out the derivation in five minutes.

Oh, this is stupid!

☙

HE TRIED AUTHORSHIP again.

And he failed again.

☙

I⊤ WAS A few minutes after ten when he put in the long distance call to Connhaven.

It's just a call, he thought. Then I can get back to work.

"Connhaven Detective Agency," said a man's voice. "Burmer speaking."

"Er, hello," said Ellery. "My name is Ellery Queen, and I—"

"Ellery Queen of New York?"

"That's right," said Ellery. "Er, look, Burmer. Something's been bothering me in connection with an old case and I'm doing a little checking just to satisfy myself that I'm an old lady in need of a rocker and a set of knitting needles."

"Well, sure, Ellery. Whatever I can do." Burmer sounded companionable. "Case I was in on?"

"Well, yes, in a way."

"What case was that?"

"The Van Horn case. Wrightsville. A year ago."

"Van Horn case? Say, that was a dilly, wasn't it? I wish I *had* been in on it. Then I'd have got a little of that newspaper space you grabbed off." Burmer laughed, indicating this was man-to-man, inside stuff.

"But you were in on it," said Ellery. "Oh, not in any of the pay dirt, but you did some investigating for Diedrich Van Horn and—"

"I did some investigating for who?"

"For Diedrich Van Horn. Howard Van Horn's father."

"*I put the matter in the hands of a reputable agency in Connhaven.*"

"Killer's old man? Ellery, who told you that?" Burmer sounded surprised.

"He did."

"Who did?"

"Killer's old man. He said, 'I put the matter in the hands of a reputable agency—'"

"Well, it wasn't mine. I never had anything to do with any of the Van Horns, worse luck. Maybe he meant in Boston."

"No, he said in Connhaven."

"One of us is drunk! What was I supposed to be investigating?"

"Tracing back his foster son's real parents. Howard's, I mean." *Just a few minutes ago I got a call from Connhaven. It was the head of the agency. They had the whole story . . .*"

"I don't get it."

"You're the head of your agency, aren't you?"

"Sure thing."

"Who was head of it last year?"

"I was. It's mine. Been in business up here fifteen years."

"Maybe it was an operative of yours — "

"This is strictly a one-man operation, and I'm him."

Ellery was silent.

Then he said: "Oh, of course. I'm not functioning this morning. What's the name of the other detective agency in Connhaven?"

"There is no other detective agency in Connhaven."

"I mean last year."

"*I* mean last year."

"What do you mean?"

"I mean there's never *been* another detective agency in Connhaven."

Ellery was silent again.

"What's this all about, Ellery?" asked Burmer curiously. "Anything I can, uh . . . ?"

"You never spoke to Diedrich Van Horn?"

"Nope."

"Never did any work for him?"

"Nope."

Ellery was silent a third time.

"You still there?" asked Burmer.

"Yes. Burmer, tell me: Ever hear the name Waye? W-a-y-e? Aaron Waye? Mattie Waye? Buried in Fidelity Cemetery?"

"Nope."

"Or a Dr. Southbridge?"

"Southbridge? No."

"Thanks. Thanks a lot."

Ellery broke the connection. He waited a few seconds, and then he let go and dialed the number of La Guardia Airport.

2

It was still early in the afternoon when Ellery alighted from the plane at Wrightsville Airfield and hurried through the administration building to the taxi stand.

His coat collar was up and he kept tugging at the brim of his hat.

He crept into a cab.

"Library. State Street."

Best to avoid the *Wrightsville Record* offices.

Wrightsville was snoozing in the August sun. A few people drifted along under the elms on State Street. Two policemen were wiping their necks on the steps of the County Court House. One of them was Jeep.

Ellery shivered.

"Public library, Mister," said the taxi driver.

"Wait for me."

Ellery ran up the library steps, but in the vestibule he slowed down. He removed his hat and trudged past the stuffed eagle through the open doorway and into Miss Aikin's domain, trying to look like a citizen seeking any port in the doldrums, only providing it was cool. And hoping that Miss Aikin wasn't there. But she was — the same sharp-featured old Gorgon. She was fining a frightened-looking girl of about eleven six cents for a book overdue three days. Miss Aikin glanced up suspiciously as she opened her cash drawer; but the man in the topcoat was wiping his face with a handkerchief, and he kept wiping it until he was past her desk and in the transverse corridor beyond.

Ellery stuffed the handkerchief in his pocket and leaped to the door marked *Periodical Room.*

The periodical librarian's desk was vacant. Only one person was in the Periodical Room, and that was a young lady snoring cheerfully over a file of old *Saturday Evening Posts*.

Ellery tiptoed to the *Wrightsville Record* file. He lugged the heavy volume marked *1917* with exquisite care past the sleeping beauty to a lectern and opened it softly.

"*Bad summer thunderstorm . . .*"

Nevertheless, he began with the issues of April, in order to cover the spring, too.

The accidental death of a local physician in a runaway en route from a confinement would surely have been front-page news in the leading Wrightsville newspaper in 1917. Still, Ellery glanced through all the pages. Fortunately, the *Record* had been a mere four-pager in those days.

He also ran down the obituary column of each issue *en passant*.

In the middle of December he gave up, restored the file to its place on the shelf, left the cheerful young lady snoring over her magazines, and sneaked out of the Wrightsville Public Library by way of a side door clearly marked NO EXIT.

He felt positively sick.

○∿○

ELLERY SHUFFLED TOWARD Upper Whistling, hands trembling in his pockets.

At the entrance to the Northern State Telephone Building he made an attempt to compose himself; the effort took him several moments.

Then he went in and asked to see the manager.

What story he told that functionary he was unable to remember clearly afterward; but it was not the true story, and it got him what he was after: the Wrightsville telephone directories for the years 1916 and 1917.

It took him exactly twenty-five seconds to ascertain that no one named Southbridge was listed in the telephone book for 1916.

It took him twenty seconds more to discover that no one named Southbridge was listed in the telephone book for 1917.

There was a hunted look in his eye as he called for the directories for 1914, 1915, 1918, 1919, and 1920.

No Southbridge was listed in any of them, physician or otherwise.

He felt positively not well as he reached for his hat.

෴

HE AVOIDED THE Square. Instead, he walked down Upper Whistling past Jezreel Lane, past Lower Main, to Slocum. He turned into Slocum and hurried the one long block to Washington.

Logan's Market was alive with flies, and little else. The intersection of Slocum and Washington was deserted. Gratefully, he crossed Washington and darted into the Professional Building. He had glimpsed Andy Birobatyan's one arm and fine Armenian face in the Wrightsville Florist Shop next door and he was altogether disinclined toward flowers and Armenia on this occasion.

He plodded up the wide wooden stairs of the Professional Building, irritated by the noise his own feet made on the aged boards.

At the head of the stairs he turned to the right, and there was the familiar shingle:

MILO WILLOUGHBY, M.D.

He tried out a smile, breathed, and went in.

The door to Dr. Willoughby's examining room was shut.

A farmer with a yellow face and pain-filled eyes was sitting in a chair.

A pregnant young lady was sitting in another, dreamy-eyed.

Ellery sat down and waited, too. Same ugly green overstuffed furniture, same faded Currier & Ives prints on the walls, same old fan clattering overhead.

The examining room door opened and another pregnant lady, not so young as the lady who was waiting, waddled out, beaming. And there was old Dr. Willoughby, again. Really old. Dried out. Shrunken. The sharp eye was blunted and grown-over; he glanced at Ellery, a peery sort of glance, and said, "I'll be with you in a few minutes, sir," and nodded to the other lady.

The other lady rose, clutching a small something done up in a brown sack, and she went into the examining room and Dr. Willoughby shut the door.

When she emerged, without the sack, Dr. Willoughby motioned to the farmer.

When the farmer came out, Ellery stepped into the examining room.

"You don't remember me, Dr. Willoughby."

The old physician pushed his glasses up on his nose, peering.

"Why, it's Mr. Queen!"

His hand was soft, and moist, and it shook.

"I'd heard you were in town last year," said Dr. Willoughby, pulling over a chair excitedly, "even before the newspapers broke that dreadful story. Why didn't you look us up? Hermy Wright's furious with you. I was insulted myself!"

"I was in town only nine days, Doctor, and they were sort of busy days," said Ellery with a feeble smile. "How's Judge Eli? And Clarice?"

"Getting old. We're all getting old. But what are you doing here now? Oh, it doesn't matter. Here, let me phone Hermione—"

"Er, please, no," said Ellery. "Thanks, Doctor, but I'm in town only for the day."

"Case?" The old man squinted at him.

"Well, yes. Matter of fact," Ellery laughed, "I'd probably have been ungracious enough not to call on you even today, Doctor, if I didn't need some information."

"And probably lost your last chance to see me alive," chuckled the doctor.

"Why, what do you mean?"

"Nothing. Old joke of mine."

"Have you been ill?"

"Every time somebody asks me that," said Dr. Willoughby, "I think of one of the aphorisms of Hippocrates. 'Old people have fewer diseases than the young, but their diseases never leave them.' It's nothing important. Not enough work, that's it! I've had to stop operating . . ." The sallow skin, stretched and mordant; the squeezed-looking tissues, shrunken, sapless; cancer? "What information, Mr. Queen?"

"About a man who died in an accident in the summer of 1917. Man named Southbridge. Do you remember him?"

"Southbridge," frowned the doctor.

"You've probably known more Wrightsvillians, living and dead, than anyone else in town, Doctor. Southbridge."

"There was a family named Sowbridge used to live in Slocum, ran a livery stable there around 1906 — "

"No, this man was named Southbridge, and he was a doctor."

"Medical doctor?" Dr. Willoughby looked surprised.

"Yes."

"In general practice?"

"I believe so."

"Dr. Southbridge . . . He couldn't have practiced in Wrightsville, Mr. Queen. Or anywhere in the county, for that matter, or I'd have heard of him."

"My information is that he practiced in Wrightsville. Confinements and things."

"Somebody's making a mistake." The old man shook his head.

Ellery said slowly, "Somebody's made a mistake, Dr. Willoughby. May I use your telephone?"

"Certainly."

Ellery called Police Headquarters.

"Chief Dakin. . . . Dakin? Ellery Queen . . . That's right, back again . . . No, just for the day. How are you?"

"Just dandy," said Chief Dakin's delighted voice. "Come right on over!"

"Dakin, I can't. Simply haven't the time. Tell me, what do you know about a fellow named Burmer up in Connhaven?"

"Burmer? Runs the detective agency?"

"Yes. What's his reputation, Dakin? Is he straight? Reliable?"

"Well, now, I'll tell you . . ."

"Yes?"

"Burmer's the only private detective in the state I'd trust without a second thought. Known him for fourteen years, Mr. Queen. If you're thinking of working on something with him, he's absolutely A-one. His word's his bond."

"Thanks."

Ellery hung up.

"George Burmer's a patient of mine," said Dr. Willoughby. "Comes all the way from Connhaven for treatment. Hemorrhoids."

"Do you consider him trustworthy?"

"I'd trust George with anything I have."

"I think," said Ellery, rising, "I'll be running along, Doctor."

"I'll never forgive you for this short visit."

"I'll never forgive myself. Doctor, take care of yourself."

"I'm being treated by the greatest Healer of all," smiled Dr. Willoughby, shaking hands.

༄

ELLERY WALKED VERY slowly up Washington Street toward the Square.

Diedrich Van Horn had lied.

Last September Diedrich Van Horn had told a long and involved story, and it had all been a lie.

Incredible. But there it was.

Why? Why invent nonexistent parents for a foster son he had reared in love from infancy?

Wait.

Perhaps Mattie and Aaron Waye were . . . Perhaps there was another explanation.

Ellery climbed quickly into a taxi parked before the Hollis and said: "Fidelity Cemetery."

3

HE HAD THE driver wait.

He scaled the stone wall and made his way among the weed-choked graves swiftly. The sun was low.

He found the adjacent graves after a little search; the low double headstone was almost hidden by the undergrowth.

Ellery knelt, parting the weeds.

AARON AND MATTIE WAYE

There it was, cut into the soft, crumbly stone.

AARON AND MATTIE WAYE

He studied the names.

Somehow, they looked different. But then the whole cemetery looked different. A year ago he had been here during and after a storm, at night. He had examined the headstone by the flame of a cigaret lighter which had flickered, and the legend had wavered and danced.

He leaned forward.

There was something wrong with one of the letters.

That was the difference. It was not an illusion of poor light or a trick of memory at all.

The final letter.

The *E* of *WAYE* was cut differently from the other letters.

It was not so deeply incised. It was less professionally hammered out. On close examination it revealed a clumsiness, an irregularity, not characteristic of the other lettering. The more he studied the final *E,* the more plainly its difference stood out. Even its outlines were sharper. In fact, they were considerably sharper.

Because he was a perfectionist he plucked a long darnel from the grave and, stripping its awns, he used it as a rule to measure the distance from the left edge of the headstone to the *A* of *AARON*. Then, with his thumbnail marking the exact length on the weed, he applied his green rule to the right edge of the headstone.

The distance from the *E* of *WAYE* to the right edge was less than the distance from the left edge to the *A* of *AARON*.

Still unsatisfied, he set his thumb on the right edge of the headstone to determine where the other end of the darnel fell.

It fell exactly on the *Y* of *WAYE*.

Ellery struggled to avoid the conclusion. But the conclusion was unavoidable.

The monument maker's stonecutter had originally chiseled:

AARON AND MATTIE WAY

Another hand, much later, had added an *E*.

This was the fact.

Ellery dropped the weed and glanced about. He saw a cracked stone bench, with weeds growing up through it, nearby.

He walked over to it and sat down and began chewing weeds.

ော

"SAY, MISTER."

Ellery came to with a start. The cemetery was gone and he was sitting in a smother of darkness. Before him the darkness showed a yellow rent, conical and puzzling.

He shivered, contracting himself under his coat.

"Who is it?" he said. "I can't see."

"I *thought* you forgot all about me," said the man's voice. "But you're ponying up, Mister, you're payin'. That clock's been workin' all this time. You told me to wait."

It was night, and he was still in Fidelity Cemetery, on the broken stone bench. And this was the taxi driver, with a flashlight.

"Oh. Yes," said Ellery. He got to his feet and stretched. His joints were stiff and they ached, but there was another ache inside him against which stretching was no remedy. "Yes, certainly. I'll pay the clock."

"I thought you forgot me, Mister," said the taxi driver again, with different emphasis and in a mollified tone. "Watch your step! Here, let me use my flash. I'll walk behind you."

Ellery made his way across the dilapidated graves to the stone wall.

As he went over the wall it occurred to him, wryly, that he never had found the entrance to the cemetery.

This had been the route of . . .

"Where to now, Mister?" asked the taxi driver.

"What?"

"I said where to."

"Oh." Ellery leaned back in the cab. "Hill Drive."

∽

To GET TO Hill Drive from Fidelity it was necessary to take North Hill Drive, and Ellery waited.

As the familiar marble monoliths moved by, he leaned forward.

"What's this estate we're passing, driver?"

"Huh? Oh. That's the Van Horn place."

"Van Horn. Oh, yes. I remember now. Is the house open? Occupied?"

"Sure is."

"Van Horn brothers still living there, eh? Both of them?"

"Yep. And their old lady, too." The driver twisted in his seat. "Place is run down somethin' fierce. Real beat. Ever since Diedrich Van Horn's wife was bumped off. That was last year."

"Is that so?"

"Yep. Old Diedrich took it plenty hard. I hear he's lookin' older than his mother, and his mother's older than God. I guess losin' that son of his didn't help. Name of Howard. He was a sculpture." The man twisted again, lowering his voice. "You know, Howard done it."

"Yes, so I read. In the papers."

The driver turned back to his wheel. "Nobody ever sees Diedrich Van Horn any more and hell, he used to run this town. Now his brother runs everything. Wolfert, his name is. Diedrich just stays home."

"I see."

"Damn nasty business. Well, here's where North Hill Drive becomes Hill Drive. Whereabouts on Hill Drive are you goin', Mister?"

"I think it's that house right there, driver."

"The Wheeler place? Yes, sir."

"Don't bother to drive in. I'll get out at the curb."

"Yes, sir." The taxi stopped and Ellery got out. "Say, this clock looks like the Chinese war debt."

"My own fault. Here you are."

"Say. Thanks!"

"Thank you. For waiting."

The man shifted into gear. "It's all right, Mister. Folks go to cemeteries sort of lose track of time. Say, that's pretty good, ain't it?"

He laughed and the cab ground off down the hill.

Ellery waited until its taillight blinked out around a curve.

Then he began walking up the hill, back toward North Hill Drive.

4

THE MOON WAS up as Ellery turned in between the two pylons and began walking up the private driveway.

There used to be lights here, he thought.

There were no lights now.

But the moon was bright, and that was lucky, because the drive was treacherous to feet. The lovely smoothness he remembered had degenerated into ruts, pits, and rubble. As he made his way past the cypresses and yews, beginning the spiral ascent to the hilltop, he noticed that the rare shrubs which had lined both sides of the road, between the spaced trees, had all but vanished under a crazy tangle of uncontrolled vegetation.

Run down is right, he thought.

Ruined. It's a ruin, the whole place.

∞

THE FRONT OF the main house was dark. So was the side facing north—the north terrace, the formal gardens, the guest house.

Ellery walked around the terrace to the gardens and the pool. The pool was dry; rotting leaves half filled it.

He glanced over at the guest house.

The windows were boarded up; the door was padlocked.

The gardens were unrecognizable — weed-grown, disheveled, untended.

He stood there for a few moments.

Then he went cautiously around to the rear.

Wedges of light drew him. He went over on the tips of his toes and looked into the kitchen.

Christina Van Horn was bent over the sink, washing dishes; that curved and ancient back was unmistakable. But when she turned for a moment with dripping hands he saw that she was not Christina at all, but Laura.

The night was stifling, but Ellery put his hands into his pockets. He felt his pigskin gloves.

He pulled them out and put them on, slowly.

Then he made his way along the rear wall, under the kitchen windows, keeping close to the wall.

He rounded the far corner and paused. A sliver of light stuck out into the darkness on this side, touched the wrought-iron railing of the south terrace.

The light came from the study.

Ellery crept along the wall and up the terrace steps.

He stopped just outside the light's shaft and carefully looked into the room.

The hangings were not quite drawn together.

A segment of the study was visible, long and thin and meaningless. Part of it, at about the height of a seated man, was a fragment of face.

It was a fragment of the face of a very old man, a man with gray loose skin.

Ellery did not recognize the fragment of face as belonging to any face of his acquaintance.

But then the face moved a little, and an eye fixed itself in the crevice of the darkness. And Ellery recognized it. It was a large, deep, brilliant, beautiful eye; and from this he knew that he was looking at Diedrich Van Horn.

He put his gloved knuckles to the nearest pane of the French door and rapped, sharply.

The eye swiveled out of view. The other eye appeared. It was looking directly at him, or so it seemed.

Ellery rapped again.

He stepped aside as he heard a squeaky sound from inside the room, as of little-used wheels.

"Who is that?"

The voice was as strange as the fragment of face, and in exactly the same way: it was an old gray voice.

Ellery put his mouth close to the French door.

"Queen. Ellery Queen."

He grasped the handle, turning and pushing.

The door was locked.

He shook it. "Mr. Van Horn! Open this door."

He heard a key stumble into the lock and he stepped back.

The door opened.

Diedrich sat beyond it in a wheel chair, a yellow blanket about his shoulders, his hands taut on the wheels; he was staring at Ellery, squinting, straining, as if to see better.

Ellery stepped inside, shut the French door, turned the key, drew the hangings together.

"Why have you come back?"

Yes, as old as his mother. Older. The strength was lost. Even the shell had crumbled. The hair was dirty white, sparse; what was there hung lifelessly.

"Because I had to," said Ellery.

The study was much as he remembered it. The desk, the lamp, the books, the armchair. Only now the room seemed bigger. But that was because Diedrich was smaller.

When he shrinks up and dies, Ellery thought, the room will stretch so in every direction that it will plop out of existence, leaving nothing behind, like an overblown soap bubble.

He heard the squeaks and looked around to see Diedrich retreating in his moving chair, retreating to the center of the study, out of range of the light from the desk lamp. Only his legs were illuminated; the rest was shadow.

"Because you had to?" said Diedrich from the shadow. He sounded puzzled.

Ellery sat down in the swivel chair and slumped on his spine, his coat tumbled about him, his hat still on his head, his gloved hands resting on the chair's arms.

"I had to, Mr. Van Horn," he said, "because this morning I found a page of Howard's diary in a pocket of my smoking jacket and for the first time I read what Howard had written on the other side."

"I want you to go away, Mr. Queen," said the ghost of Diedrich's voice.

But Ellery said: "I discovered, Mr. Van Horn, that you're an anagrammatist. I hadn't known about 'Lia Mason' and 'Salomina.' I hadn't known that your mind worked that way."

The wheel chair was still. But the voice was stronger; it held a note of warmth. "I'd kind of forgotten all that. Poor Sally."

"Yes."

"And that 'discovery' brought you all the way back here, Mr. Queen, to see me? That was kind of you."

"No. That discovery, Mr. Van Horn, made me telephone the Connhaven Detective Agency."

The wheel chair squeaked.

But the voice said: "Oh, yes?"

"And after that call I flew up here. Mr. Van Horn," said Ellery, slumping still lower in the swivel chair, "I've been over to Fidelity Cemetery. I've taken a good look at the headstone of Aaron and Mattie Way."

"Their headstone. Is it still standing? We die, stones live. It doesn't seem fair, now, does it, Mr. Queen?"

"Mr. Van Horn, you never engaged the Connhaven Detective Agency to trace Howard's parents. Undoubtedly you made an attempt through the man Fyfield you mentioned, when Howard was an infant, to trace his parents then; but when he turned up nothing, that was the end. *The rest you manufactured.*

"It was not Burmer of Connhaven who found the graves of Aaron and Mattie Way; it was you, Mr. Van Horn. It was not Burmer who told you the story of Howard's birth; you invented it. God knows who Howard's parents were, but they weren't the Ways. There was never a Dr. Southbridge. You concocted the entire fantasy — after you chiseled an extra *E* on the Ways' headstone, making their name read *W–A–Y–E.* You gave Howard false parents, Mr. Van Horn. You gave Howard a false name."

The man in the wheel chair was silent.

"And why did you give Howard a false name, Mr. Van Horn?

"Because, Mr. Van Horn," said Ellery, "that false name — *Waye* with an *e* it never had — combined with the *H. H.* of Howard's signature, *Howard Hendrik,* made possible a 'new' signature, *H. H. Waye,* with an *e,* which, as I so brilliantly showed in my by now world-famous analysis of last year, Mr. Van Horn, is an anagram of *Yahweh.* And this proved that Howard had broken the Commandment which says: *Thou shalt not take the name of the Lord thy God in vain.*"

Diedrich said: "I'm not the man I was, Mr. Queen. You say things to me that sound threatening and bitter and it's all so confusing. What are you talking about?"

"If your memory is failing," said Ellery, "let me try to restore it. You knew, Mr. Van Horn, that if you provided Howard with a surname but not with a given name, Howard would simply have to retain the Christian name you gave him when you adopted him — Howard Hendrik; and you knew, further, that he always signed his work *H. H. Van Horn.* Then if he were to adopt his supposedly genuine surname of Waye, he would accordingly sign himself *H. H. Waye,* with an *e,* Mr. Van Horn. And since Howard was engaged in a heroic sculpturing project, it was very likely that he'd scratch the 'new' name on his models.

"But if Howard didn't do that, *you* could have done it, Mr. Van Horn. Because you had a tremendous advantage in Howard's amnesic lapses. You could have scratched the name *H. H. Waye* — with an *e* — into his models, and it would be assumed that Howard had done it during one of his blackouts — and who, including Howard, could deny it? You couldn't lose, Mr. Van Horn, either way.

"As it turned out, Howard did sign one of his models *H. H. Waye,* and a number of his working sketches."

"I simply don't know what you're talking about," said Diedrich feebly from the wheel chair. His big hand, all loose flesh and ropy veins, was up to his eyes. "Why in Heaven's name would I do a thing like that?"

"You invoke the name of Heaven naturally, Mr. Van Horn," said Ellery. "As you did then. Why did you do it? Because you wanted to impose on Howard an anagram for the name of the Lord."

Diedrich was silent.

But then he said: "I find it hard to believe any of this is really happening. Do you really mean all this — this — I mean, imposing anagrams of the Lord's name on Howard, inventing stories of Howard's birth in order to do it! Most fantastic thing I ever heard."

"Oh, it's fantastic," said Ellery, "but it really did happen. It's the only explanation. There are no alternatives. You lied about Howard's parents, you chiseled an extra *e* on the name in Fidelity Cemetery, and this enabled me to make an anagram out of God's name which in turn enabled me to accuse Howard of having broken one of the Ten Commandments. Fantastic, as you say. Unbelievably farfetched. And yet it happened, Mr. Van Horn, and it happened because you're a man of uncanny insight into human nature and of colossal imagination. You were dealing with a man to whom the fantastic and the farfetched are attractive, Mr. Van Horn. You knew my needs!"

Ellery half rose in an unaccustomed excitement; but then he sank back. And when he resumed, it was in a quiet tone again.

"You had to work toward fantastic ends, Mr. Van Horn, but the means were practical, ordinary, and logical. Your plan called for imposing on Howard an anagram for the Lord's name. In selecting one, you had a choice. Probably you narrowed the choice down to two: Jehovah and Yahweh. But it wasn't easy to work with the name Jehovah. Jehovah, minus the two *H*'s Howard would have to retain, left *j, e, o, v, a,* a discouraging combination of letters to anagrammatize into a credible surname. But Yahweh, minus the two *H*'s, gave you the letters *y, a, w, e,* which could be transposed to form the perfectly acceptable surname of Waye. All that was required then was to find the graves of a couple — or of a woman alone, if you were pressed, but a husband and wife were better — in or around Wrightsville Township, or in Slocum, or Connhaven — anywhere in the County would do, or even in the State — people who had borne the name of Waye and had died after the known birth date of Howard, leaving no family.

"You didn't find *Waye,* but you did find *Way.* The word itself is of Anglo-Saxon origin; the ethnic background of New England is largely English; it would have been remarkable if you hadn't found a *Way,* or a number of *Ways* among whom you could choose. As for Aaron and Mattie Way, it's possible you invented their history, too. Or they may well have been poor farmers, as you said. It didn't really matter; you could shape the facts to your purpose, or your means to the facts; you had a great deal of leeway."

The ache in his abdomen had disappeared; but he still felt cold. He did not look at Van Horn.

The old man in the wheel chair said, "Mr. Queen, what are you attempting to prove with all this — this stuff?"

"That Howard," said Ellery, "did not break all of the Ten Commandments. At this point I was able to say: I now know that at least one of the Commandments whose violation I ascribed to Howard was not Howard's work at all, but was the result of *your* work, Mr. Van Horn.

"So I asked myself as I sat in Fidelity Cemetery in the twilight today, Mr. Van Horn: If Howard didn't break one Commandment, *is it possible he didn't break some of the others?*"

5

Diedrich was seized by a spasm of coughing that made the wheel chair dance. Bent over, his eyes frantic, he made a violent gesture toward the desk.

There was a silver decanter on the desk and Ellery jumped up to pour a glass of water from it and hurry with it to the coughing man. He held the glass to Diedrich's lips.

Finally Diedrich said, "Thank you, Mr. Queen," and Ellery returned the glass to the desk and sat down again.

Diedrich's big chin rested on his breast now; his eyes were closed and he seemed asleep.

But Ellery said: "I asked myself another question. I asked myself which of the ten crimes I'd charged Howard with could I be *sure* he'd committed? Not crimes he was made to appear guilty of, Mr. Van Horn; not crimes he was forced to commit; not crimes imposed on him — but crimes of which he was personally, directly guilty, of his free will. And do you know?" Ellery smiled. "Of the ten crimes I heaped on Howard's head that day a year ago, I could now — a little late, wouldn't you agree? — I could now be *sure* that he'd been unequivocally responsible for only two."

The eyelids flickered.

"I knew beyond possibility of error that Howard had wanted or had thought he wanted Sally; he'd told me that himself. And I knew beyond possibility of error that Howard had slept with Sally; they'd both told me that."

The hands twitched.

"So I *knew* Howard had broken two Commandments: *Thou shalt not covet thy neighbor's wife* and *Thou shalt not commit adultery*.

"But what of the other eight? I'd proved that you were responsible for the Commandment clue involving the name of God, Mr. Van Horn. *Was it possible you were also responsible for the seven remaining unaccounted for?*"

Ellery got up suddenly. Diedrich's eyes flew open.

"I sat on a broken stone bench in Fidelity Cemetery in the darkness this evening, Mr. Van Horn, and I went through a kind of hell. I'm going to take you with me on that tour of hell, Mr. Van Horn! Do you mind?"

Diedrich's mouth opened. He tried again, and this time a croak came out. "I'm an old man," he said. "I'm confused."

But Ellery said: "Last year I began by 'proving' that Howard broke the Commandments: *Thou shalt have no other gods before me* and *Thou shalt not make unto thee any graven image*. And what did my proof consist of, Mr. Van Horn? This: That Howard was in the process of sculpturing the ancient gods. And this was very good proof — as far as it went, Mr. Van Horn. But, Mr. Van Horn, it didn't go far enough. Because who — when you really examine the facts — made Howard's sculpture of the ancient gods possible?

"*You, Mr. Van Horn — you alone.* It was you who came to the rescue of the Wrightsville Art Museum Committee when their fund-raising drive failed of its goal by a wide margin. It was you who promised to make up the enormous deficit providing Howard was commissioned to execute the sculptures for the exterior of the proposed Museum building. *It was you who specified as a condition of your financial assistance that the statues Howard was to execute were to be of the classical gods.*"

6

THE WHEEL CHAIR SLID back and now Diedrich was altogether in shadow. Ellery experienced a shock of recognition, as if this had happened before. But then he knew it was simply the resemblance between the great lump in the wheel chair and the lump of the old woman as he had first glimpsed her seated in the gardens that night so long ago.

"Then I charged Howard with having broken the Commandment: *Thou shalt not steal.* Now there I felt I was on solid ground, Mr. Van Horn. Was there, could there be, any doubt that Howard had stolen the twenty-five thousand dollars which he'd handed me at Quetonokis Lake to pay over to Sally's blackmailer? Not the least bit. The money came from your wall safe here; it was your money; I had your check list of the serial numbers of the fifty stolen five-hundred-dollar bills to compare with the fifty five-hundred-dollar bills Howard had given me — and they checked to the last number. Why am I flogging the point? Howard himself admitted stealing the money from your safe.

"And yet this evening, in the cemetery, Mr. Van Horn, I had to ask myself: But did Howard steal that money because he was naturally a thief, or naturally susceptible to temptation, or did he steal it because something had happened of such an unusual nature, exercising such an unusually strong compulsion, as to *force* Howard to steal it against a nature normally impervious to such temptation? And if events forced Howard to steal your twenty-five thousand dollars, Mr. Van Horn, who created those events?

"And this brings me to the crux of the case."

Diedrich stirred in his cocoon of shadows, almost as if he were preparing to rise.

"Now I knew that Howard had been framed for some of the crimes I'd held him responsible for.

"So I considered the framer.

"I considered the framer, Mr. Van Horn, as a disembodied entity, a factor in a mathematical problem — an unknown. Howard was framed; therefore a framer existed. Immediately I asked myself: What did this ponderable, if unknown, quantity represent? What were his values, this Mr. X?

"Well, out of five Commandments broken, I knew that my X-entity was responsible for three. It began to look bad for Mr. X. It began to look very bad. Because I'd reached an answer last year, and the answer was that Howard had broken the Ten Commandments. Now I knew that had not been true in the important sense. My X had made possible the appearance, the *illusion,* of Howard's violation of the Decalogue, or at least of three of the five parts of it which I'd examined. This, then, seemed to have been X's 'value,' mathematically speaking: *He had manipulated events to make it appear that Howard had set out to break all ten of the Commandments.*

"But if this were so, what did X — Howard's framer — have to know? He had to know this basic fact: That Howard himself, unmanipulated, of his free will, had broken two of the Commandments; or rather that he had committed two crimes against the ethical code which we call the Ten Commandments. I say Framer X had to know this, Mr. Van Horn, because to say otherwise is to say that Framer X arrived at his extraordinary decalogic plan independently of Howard's acts. This is unthinkable. No; it was Howard's breaking of the Commandments against wife-coveting and adultery which gave Framer X the larger, broader, encompassing inspiration of causing Howard to break *all* the Commandments. Or all but one, Mr. Van Horn; but the whole illusion tended to that one and it's the climax of my argument; I'll leave it to its proper place."

Ellery poured a glass of water for himself. He put it to his lips. But after staring at the glass for an instant, he rubbed his gloved finger over the place which his lips had touched and he set the glass down, untasted.

"How could Framer have known that Howard desired Sally and that he subsequently satisfied his desire? In only one way. Two people alone knew in the beginning: Howard and Sally. Neither told anyone but me. And I had told no one. That any of the three of us, but especially Howard and Sally, could have told a fourth was a possibility to be discarded as soon as it was broached. All the trouble they got into was a result of *their refusal to tell*. And I was bound to silence by their wishes.

"How, then, did the Framer know? How could he have known? Did a fact exist which made his knowledge possible?

"Yes! The written record of Howard's feelings and Howard's and Sally's adulterous act; the four letters Howard stupidly wrote after the Lake Pharisee episode.

"Conclusion? *Framer read those letters.*

"But this is remarkable, Mr. Van Horn!" cried Ellery. "Because someone else read those letters . . . the mysterious person whose knowledge of the contents of those letters made it possible for him to blackmail Sally! Did I say someone else? Why should I say someone *else*? Why shouldn't I say . . . Framer X read letters, Blackmailer read letters, *Framer X is therefore Blackmailer?*"

Diedrich was staring at the glass Ellery had set down at the desk. It seemed to fascinate him.

"But now, Mr. Van Horn," said Ellery in a quivering voice, "we can get away from mathematical symbols and back to human quantities. Who was Framer X? I've proved that already: *You, Mr. Van Horn.* But Framer Equals Blackmailer. *Therefore, Mr. Van Horn, you were the one who blackmailed Howard and Sally.*"

Now Diedrich raised his head and Ellery saw his face full. And what Ellery saw in Diedrich's face made him go on more rapidly, as if to falter now was in some baffling way to lose a battle.

"I think this was the low point of my thoughts this evening on that bench, Mr. Van Horn. Because it took me back to last year, to my 'brilliant' analysis, when I was delivering the death blows to Howard with the merciless perfection of my reasoning. And I saw, Mr. Van Horn," said Ellery with a single glance so bitter cold that the great eyes across the room glittered, "that while my reasoning had been merciless, it had been anything but perfect. It had been not only loose, not only superficial, but it concealed a great hole — it had neglected even to bring up the question of the all-important black-mailer's identity! Unconsciously, stupidly, I had absorbed the re-peated suggestion that the blackmailer was John Doe, burglar. But there was no John Doe, Mr. Van Horn; there was no burglar. You were John Doe, Mr. Van Horn; you were the blackmailer."

He paused, but Diedrich said nothing; and he went on.

"How did you become the blackmailer? Very simply, I think. In May of last year, or early in June, you discovered the false bottom to Sally's japanned box. You found the four letters. It could have happened quite accidentally: You were putting in or taking out a piece of Sally's jewelry, the box fell out of your hands, the false bottom popped open, you saw the letters, the fact that they were in a hiding place prompted you — out of curiosity or your total absorption in all matters concerning your wife — to read them. Or perhaps you caught a word, or a phrase, without even intending to read them — there were no envelopes; and if it were a certain word, or a certain phrase, then you would be sure to read them. Quite sure."

Diedrich still said nothing.

"You didn't disclose to your son and your wife that you had learned their secret. Oh, no. They misjudged you ludicrously there. How often they assured me you didn't suspect a thing! How frantic they were, how childishly frantic, to keep you from suspecting what you'd known for months! And how consummately you acted the role of unsuspecting innocence.

"But all the time you knew and all the time you were watching for your opportunity. . . . Sally told me that if you found out you'd give her a divorce without a word, settle a fortune on her.

"Poor Sally," said Ellery with a smile.

And he said: "To maintain yourself in the role of pure and unsuspecting cuckold, and to create the atmosphere essential to your greater plan, you took the jewel box and its contents and manufactured the evidence necessary to give the impression that a professional burglar had entered Sally's bedroom and stolen the box for the jewels in it. You cleverly saw to it that the jewelry got to pawnshops in various cities — no doubt that period of your activities last year, if it were checked, would be found to involve several sudden and important 'business trips.' And, of course, you knew the jewelry would be recovered.

"But the letters you kept, Mr. Van Horn. And when the time was right, you used them blackmail-wise; you became the blackmailer. I blush to recall that every time the 'blackmailer' telephoned, and that during the one time that he made a physical if invisible appearance — to take the money from the bureau drawer of that room at the Hollis — *you were away from this house.*"

Ellery took out a cigaret. The action was automatic. But when he saw the cigaret between his fingers, he carefully put it back in his pocket.

"At the time you laid your blackmail plans, back in last May or early June, when you found the four letters, I doubt if the decalogic idea was in your mind; in fact, I'm sure it wasn't. Your purpose then was more likely to prepare the ground for a campaign of assault on Howard's and Sally's nerves. The inspiration was born later, out of independent developments — like the Museum project — and the information in the letters in your possession; and I don't think it reached its full growth until the day Howard phoned you from my apartment in New York to say that I was coming up to Wrightsville as his house guest. But I'll go into that later."

Ellery stirred restlessly.

"Let's move on to the events surrounding the blackmail operation itself. As the blackmailer, you demanded twenty-five thousand dollars in cash from Sally; your first demand. You knew Sally would tell Howard. You knew that neither Sally nor Howard, or the two of them together, had twenty-five thousand dollars. You knew them so well, their gratitude to you, their obsessive dread of hurting you, that you could be certain they would do anything to keep the 'blackmailer' from making good his 'threat' to turn the letters over to you! You knew that both were aware of the large amount of cash you usually kept in the study safe at home here. You knew that, pushed to the wall, Howard would think of that money and that he would take it from the safe; and you saw to it that in the safe there was exactly enough; or perhaps what was in the safe dictated the amount of blackmail you demanded.

"We conclude then, Mr. Van Horn, that when Howard broke the Commandment against stealing, it was because events forced him to; *and it was you who created those events for precisely that purpose.*"

Diedrich rolled his chair forward into the light and he smiled.

He smiled and showed his teeth and he said with energy, almost with good humor: "I've been listening to this remarkable speech of yours, Mr. Queen, with what amounts to awe. So clever, so complicated!" He laughed. "But it's getting to be too much of a good thing, don't you agree? You're making me out some sort of god. God Himself! I created this, I created that — I was 'sure' Howard would do this, I 'knew' Howard would do that . . . Aren't you giving me far too much credit, Mr. Queen, for . . . what would you call it?"

"Omniscience?"

"Yes. How could I or anyone else be sure of anything?"

"You couldn't always be sure," said Ellery quietly. "Nor was it essential always to *be* sure. Your plan was flexible; you had lots of latitude.

"But throughout this infernal business, Mr. Van Horn, you planned and acted from a profound and detailed understanding of what made Howard and Sally tick. You didn't misjudge their characters as they misjudged yours. You were as familiar with the innermost operation of their minds as with your own. Consistently you could, and you did, predict with great accuracy what they would feel, what they would think, and what they would do. You'd had thirty years or so to study Howard, and you knew Sally from the time she was nine, was it? Through all those years of correspondence when, as Sally said, she told you things about herself most girls would hesitate to tell their mothers; and in Sally's case, your knowledge of her was climaxed by the intimate relationship of marriage. In your own way, Mr. Van Horn, you're a master psychologist. It's a pity you didn't apply your talents more constructively."

"Somehow," said Diedrich with a grim smile, "that doesn't sound like a compliment."

"On the other hand, you didn't have to be right each time. If Howard and Sally didn't jump in quite the direction you intended when you jerked the string, because of a lapse in judgment, or an imponderable you couldn't have been aware of, or because of some accident you couldn't have foreseen, you simply had to set into motion another string, actuate another series of events; and sooner or later, Howard would do what you wanted him to do.

"But as it turned out, you were remarkably accurate in your judgments. You provided exactly the right stimuli, exerted exactly the right pressure at the right places, and Howard and Sally moved exactly as you wanted them to move.

"And, I might add," said Ellery in a very low voice, "not merely Howard and Sally."

7

"Go on," said Diedrich Van Horn, after a while.

Ellery looked up, startled. "I beg your pardon.

"So far, then, in my analysis you've imposed three crimes on Howard and forced him to commit a fourth.

"Which event produced my conclusion that Howard had broken the Commandments enjoining: *Remember the sabbath day, to keep it holy* and *Honor thy father and thy mother?* His trip in the dark hours one Sunday morning to Fidelity Cemetery to desecrate the graves of the two people you had told him were his parents.

"I must confess," said Ellery, "that when I reached this point in my reconstruction earlier this evening I was held up. It was quite impossible, with all your shrewd evaluation of Howard, to have been able to count on Howard's desecrating the Ways' graves — and out of the question that you should have been able to count on Howard's doing so on a Sunday. The whole structure of my argument was in danger of collapsing. But then I saw what the answer must be.

"Since you couldn't count on Howard's making that trip, since you couldn't force Howard to make that trip, *you could make it for him.*

"The more I thought about this, the more convinced I became that that was what happened. Not once had I caught a glimpse of Howard's face, or heard his voice. I saw Howard's car, I saw a man about Howard's size wearing Howard's coat and hat, I saw this man use a sculptor's mallet and chisel . . . In view of the fact that your plan called for Howard to make that trip, and you couldn't possibly have made Howard make it, someone else must have been acting the part of Howard that night; and since it was your plan, and you and Howard are of a size, that someone else must have been you.

"A reconstruction was then simple. Suppose that on that Saturday night, quite late, and after the rest of us had got out of the way, you dropped into Howard's studio, or bedroom, for a nightcap. Father and son stuff, Mr. Van Horn. And suppose you handed Howard a drink containing a drug, a drug in a dose sufficient to make him sleep all night, if he was undisturbed. When Howard dropped off, you put on yourself his distinctive and readily identifiable wide-brimmed Stetson and long trench coat, his socks, his shoes, and his trousers. And you left Howard sleeping in his room or studio and went quietly downstairs and outside and to the garage. You put Sally's keys in the ignition lock of her convertible — for my benefit. You got into Howard's roadster. And you drove around to the front, deliberately racing the engine. That was to attract my attention, of course, from the guest house. To make certain, you just as deliberately stalled the car under the porte-cochere . . . to make certain, and to give me time to dress, if I were undressed. Or perhaps you'd scouted me before taking the car out and had seen me dozing on the porch of the guest house; and the engine stall was to give me time to get a coat. And when you saw me begin to run across the garden, you drove off.

"Mr. Van Horn, you played me that night the way a veteran sportsman plays a tarpon. Your timing throughout was superbly delicate. You didn't make the mistake of making it too easy for me. You gave me just enough line to delude me into thinking I was giving you a run for your money. And, if I'd lost you, you'd have seen to it that I picked up your trail again.

"The rain helped, but even if it hadn't rained you were still safe; it was a dark night, and that you could have known in advance. In any event, you knew I wouldn't come too close or try to stop you. You knew I'd be positive you were Howard and that my function was not to interfere but to observe.

"And at the graves of the Ways you attacked the headstone, using a mallet and chisel you'd taken from Howard's studio.

"What happened after that illustrates the impeccability of your judgment of people and situations — a talent, by the way, that undoubtedly accounts for your success in business.

"You left and drove home. You knew I wouldn't follow you at once. You knew I'd examine the headstone after the attack, to check up on it. You knew that when I returned to North Hill Drive the odds were greatly in favor of my changing my wet clothing before going up to see if Howard was back. Yes, you were taking a chance on that; but the calculated risk is part of every careful plan, and the risk was not great. I'd probably not want to leave a trail of mud in the main house which might require explanations the next day — even if I didn't mind risking pneumonia.

"While I was changing in the guest house, you were putting the finishing touches to your master-illusion on the top floor of the house here. You took off Howard's soaked socks and mud-caked shoes and put them on Howard's feet. You took off Howard's wet, muddy trousers and pulled them over Howard's legs. You took off Howard's trench coat and sat Howard up and put his arms through the sleeves and drew the coat around him and buttoned it. Howard's sopping hat you placed on the pillow beside him. And then, calmly, you went to bed."

Ellery said: "You must have calculated that it was even possible I wouldn't come to Howard's room until morning. But whether immediately or after the lapse of several hours, I was sure to come to Howard's room to check up on him. And so I'd find Howard in what would inevitably seem to me to be one of his typical amnesic stupors, fully dressed in the wet and muddy clothing which had made the nasty trip to the cemetery.

"Yes, Mr. Van Horn, it was you who committed the two crimes of breaking the Sabbath and dishonoring Howard's 'parents,' doing it in such a way as to fool me into believing the Commandment-breaker had been Howard."

8

AND DIEDRICH SAID again, "Go on, Mr. Queen."

"Oh, I will," said Ellery. And he said: "And now I come to perhaps the most spectacular example of your psychological shrewdness.

"I blithely proved last year that Howard had broken the Commandment: *Thou shalt not bear false witness against thy neighbor,* when I pointed out that Howard had denied having given me the necklace to pawn. That was true, of course; he *had* given me the necklace to pawn, and he lied when he said he hadn't.

"But here again it was you who, by manipulating events and accurately estimating Howard, placed Howard in the position where, being what he was, he had to lie!

"In your role of blackmailer, Mr. Van Horn, you demanded a second payment of twenty-five thousand dollars — virtually on the heels of the first demand, which had been paid. Obviously, you did this to exert the maximum pressure at the weakest point. For where could Sally and Howard get another twenty-five thousand dollars? There was no more of your cash lying conveniently around to be stolen. You knew they had nowhere to borrow the money, even if they dared leave such a trail. There was only one thing between them which might yield such a large sum: Sally's necklace. It was virtually a certainty, then, that one or the other of them would think of Sally's necklace as the means of satisfying the blackmailer's second demand.

"More than that. You knew I had acted as Sally's go-between in the first negotiations with the blackmailer, so it was a better-than-fair guess that I'd act in the same capacity in their attempt to raise the second payment. And if I didn't, you were no doubt ready with another scheme in which I'd have to permit myself to become involved and which would accomplish the same end: Howard's denial of me.

"But I did consent to act, and I acted. And the stage was set for your crowning psychological performance.

"For no sooner had I pawned the necklace and deposited the money in the Wrightsville railroad station, as instructed, than you struck.

"This time your tool was your brother Wolfert, Mr. Van Horn. Just as you knew Sally and Howard, so you knew Wolfert. What did Wolfert say? That you had told him you 'hoped' the Museum Committee wouldn't 'make a fuss' about your donation! To have expressed such a 'hope' to Wolfert, jealous, bitter, and malicious as he is, was to invite him to thwart that hope. Wolfert actually chortled, 'I was the one who put them up to it.' I remember his saying it at the breakfast table that morning. But Wolfert was only partially right. He was only the instrument — your instrument. You played on him, Mr. Van Horn, as you played on your wife and your son. To make you squirm, as he thought, Wolfert prodded the Committee to give you a testimonial dinner, a full-dress affair of the kind he knew you loathed. But this was precisely what you wanted him to do. Because it gave you the natural and innocent excuse for asking Sally *to wear her diamond necklace* — which you knew she no longer had.

"And so Sally would have to reveal that the necklace was gone. Would she tell the truth? Oh, no. To have told the truth Sally would have had to expose the whole mess of the blackmail, and its reason for being. You knew Sally would die rather than disclose that; you knew Howard would kill her before he let her disclose it. Again, it was a reasonable assumption that they'd invent some story to explain the necklace's being gone. Burglary was in the air; Howard had stolen the cash and made an attempt to make it look like an outside thief's work; theft of the necklace in another 'burglary' was indicated.

"And when Sally phoned you at your office to say that the necklace had been 'stolen' from the safe, you knew your calculations had been accurate and you exerted the last pressure: You called in Chief of Police Dakin.

"From that point, nothing could go wrong. Dakin would locate the necklace in Simpson's pawnshop, Sally and Howard would be confronted with the necklace, I would be identified by Simpson as the man who had pawned it, in sheer self-defense I'd have to reveal that Howard had asked me to pawn it — and Howard, to keep the story of his adultery with Sally from coming out, would deny it — would bear false witness," said Ellery, "against a particularly witless neighbor."

And Ellery said: "Nine crimes against the Sinaitic decalogue, only two committed by Howard as a free uninfluenced agent, the other seven imposed by you upon Howard as your dupe or actually perpetrated by you physically in the guise of Howard.

"Nine crimes, and when I recognized the grand pattern and so foresaw the inevitable tenth crime, Mr. Van Horn, you were prepared for me, your stage was fully set for your climax.

"Because it was murder you were leading up to, Mr. Van Horn," said Ellery, "double murder to satisfy your cold fury for revenge . . . the murder of your wife for having been unfaithful to you, the murder of your adopted son for having stolen your wife's affections. I include Howard among your murder victims, Mr. Van Horn, because whether he died by legal execution for a murder he didn't commit or by his own hand because he thought he had committed it, his death was murder just the same — and you were his murderer as surely as if your big hands choked his life out. As, in fact, they had choked the life out of Sally."

9

DIEDRICH's CHIN HAD sunk to his breast again, and again his eyes were closed. And, in the wheel chair, he appeared again to be asleep.

But Ellery continued: "When I telephoned you that night to warn you that your life was in danger, Mr. Van Horn, you knew your great moment had come at last. If you had any doubts, they were dispelled when I said it would take me forty or forty-five minutes to get back here. Nothing could have been better suited to your purpose. Forty or forty-five minutes were ample for what you had to do.

"I think, Mr. Van Horn, that you intended to kill Sally that night whether I discovered the Ten Commandments pattern or not. If I didn't discover it before Sally's murder, I could hardly have avoided discovering it afterward, with the evidence you manufactured. And if the very worst happened, and I stupidly failed to discover and name the pattern, no doubt you were prepared for that, too: Simply by revealing the pattern yourself, or making some subtle suggestion to me which would finally open my eyes. God knows you left little or nothing to chance. You'd kept throwing 'tens' at me all through the case — even going to the exquisite trouble of using Room *1010* for the blackmail rendezvous at the Hollis and Room *10* as the depository of the four letters at Upham House and designating Locker *10* at Wrightsville station for the second twenty-five thousand dollars!

"The time I allowed you, as I said, was ample. Wolfert wasn't home — or was it at your suggestion, Mr. Van Horn, that your brother suddenly found he had urgent and important work at the office so late at night? Your mother would probably not leave her room or, if she did, you could easily have handled her. Laura and Eileen were asleep — Wrightsville domestics retire early. So there was little or no danger of interruption. In the phrase which has served similar purposes since it was first used in 1590, Mr. Van Horn — the coast was clear.

"So while I was risking my silly neck speeding back to Wrightsville in the interests of your 'safety,' you calmly went up to Howard's quarters, again had a nightcap with him, again drugged him. Then you went down to the second floor and you asked Sally to come to your bedroom and you strangled her there and placed her body in your bed. And then you went back upstairs and planted four of Sally's hairs in Howard's hand and with a tweezer inserted minute shreds of bloody tissue from Sally's throat under Howard's fingernails. And then you returned to the study here, locked yourself in as I had instructed, and simply waited for my arrival.

"The thing was done. The final brush stroke on a classic canvas. All that remained were a few more lies, another demonstration of your histrionic ability — no great matter for a man of your extraordinary imagination and gifts. As a matter of fact, you outdid yourself that night. Your lies to me, particularly the one about Sally's insisting on waiting up for you in your bedroom to tell you 'something important' — with the implication that she intended to confess her adultery — were nothing short of inspired. And the *way* you led me around to the discovery that Sally was waiting in your bedroom was sheer genius.

"And I was completely taken in, Mr. Van Horn," said Ellery dully, "taken in on all ten counts. You set up the victim for me and I, Ellery Queen, little tin god of cerebration, furnished the *coup de grâce*. My 'brilliant' deductions, plus the indubitable evidence of Sally's hair and the shreds of her flesh in Howard's hand, left no loophole for Howard . . . or for me.

"Because the truth is," said Ellery slowly, "I implemented your heroic frame-up of Howard, Mr. Van Horn. Without me it couldn' have been the perfect thing it was. So I helped you kill Howard, you see. I was your little-tin-god-accessory before, during, and after the fact."

Now Diedrich's great head came up, and his eyes opened, and his loosely fleshed hand made a gesture of impatience.

"You accuse me of this enormous crime," he said with a certain liveliness, "and I must admit — as you put it, it sounds pretty plausible. But — just in the interests of truth, you know — it strikes me your argument fails to take into account the one thing that destroys it."

"Does it?" said Ellery. "Mr. Van Horn, I'd be overjoyed to hear it. I've never before in my life made an analysis I'm more anxious to tear down."

"Well, then, Mr. Queen, relax," said Diedrich with almost the old boom in his voice. There was a slight flush in his desiccated cheeks as he trundled the wheel chair closer to the desk. "You say Howard didn't kill my wife — although, of course, the boy did, thinking he was killing me. But if Howard was innocent, Mr. Queen, when you charged him with murder *why didn't he deny it?* That's what an innocent man would have done. And then what does he do? He takes his own life! Don't you see? It doesn't wash. Howard was guilty, all right. The poor boy knew you had him with the goods; he *couldn't* deny it. And when he committed suicide he admitted his guilt."

But Ellery was shaking his head. "No go, Mr. Van Horn. Like so many elements in this case, the two you bring up now are true, but only partially. You've employed the half truth, and the appearance of truth, to tremendous advantage throughout.

"Howard didn't deny guilt, true; but not because he was guilty in fact. He didn't deny being guilty because he *thought* he was guilty!

"Howard didn't know you'd drugged him, Mr. Van Horn; he thought, as I thought, that he'd gone through another amnesic episode. What happened during his blackouts always worried Howard. When he came to me in New York, that was uppermost in his mind. And when he asked me to come to Wrightsville, it was for precisely that reason: to keep watching him, to follow him when he went into another blackout, to find out what he did during episodes — whether he was, as he put it, a Dr. Jekyll and Mr. Hyde — because a feature of his blackouts was that *he remembered nothing afterward.*

"You knew all about Howard's amnesia, Mr. Van Horn; it was the keystone of your arch. Howard's mind was obsessed with the fear that during his blackouts he committed criminal acts. You knew that, and you knew that when he recovered from what would seem to him — and to me and to everyone else but you — another blackout and discovered that during his blackout Sally had been strangled and some of her hairs and flesh had been found on his hands . . . you knew Howard would believe himself guilty. The entire psychological history of his amnesia had prepared Howard for the unquestioning acceptance of any evidence of his criminality.

"As for his subsequent act of self-destruction, Howard was always a potential suicide, Mr. Van Horn. The suicide climax is implicit in psychological patterns like Howard's. He told me, for example, that when he snapped out of the blackout he suffered in New York — the one that sent him to me — he seriously contemplated throwing himself out of the flophouse window. As a matter of fact, in my first talk with Howard, I suspected suicide as an unconscious pattern, and I asked him point-blank if he'd ever come to — come out of a blackout — in the act of trying to kill himself, and he admitted to three distinct experiences of that sort.

"No, there was nothing remarkable about Howard's act of self-destruction after I demonstrated his 'guilt,' Mr. Van Horn. He was convinced he'd murdered Sally, he knew he was through, and he chose the way out which anyone who knew his make-up well — as well, say, as you knew it, Mr. Van Horn — might quite conceivably have predicted.

"While I'm on the subject," Ellery added suddenly, "it occurs to me that virtually every clue pointing to you as the god of the machine was known to me last year, when I obligingly sent Howard to his death for you. There was even a clue in my possession to your knowledge of psychology — a knowledge without which, as

I've already said, you couldn't have begun to plan your crimes. You handed me that clue very coolly the first night I met you, during our dinner-table conversation. You introduced the subject of books and their relation to practical living. And you included, among the few books you said had had practical value to you, 'certain studies of the human mind.' Which ones, Mr. Van Horn? I'm afraid I didn't look your library over carefully enough."

Diedrich was still smiling a little, but Ellery noticed now that there was a resemblance between his smile and Wolfert's, a resemblance which had not been apparent when Diedrich's face had been fuller.

"I think you know, Mr. Queen, what an admirer of yours I've always been — your work in fiction and in real life," Diedrich said. "I should have told you last year, while you were visiting here, that in spite of my admiration I've always considered your method — that justly celebrated 'Queen method' — extremely weak in one respect."

"In more than one, I'm afraid," said Ellery. "But which one do you have in mind?"

"Legal proof," said Diedrich pleasantly. "The kind of proof policemen with no imagination and district attorneys with factual training and judges with rules to judge by demand when a man is accused of a crime. The law, unfortunately, isn't impressed with mere logic, no matter how brilliant. It asks for admissible evidence before it's willing to put a defendant in jeopardy."

"Nice point," nodded Ellery. "I'm disinclined to defend myself beyond saying that I've always left the gathering of evidence to those whose business evidence-gathering is. My function has been to detect criminals, not to punish them. I admit that occasionally someone I've put the logical finger on has given the evidence-gatherers a run for their money.

"However," and Ellery's tone grew grim, "I don't think they're going to find this particular job too much for them."

"No?" said Diedrich, and now his smile was remarkably like Wolfert's.

"No. Your feat has been tremendous in sweep, but here and

there you've left a hole. The whole concept of yourself as the blackmailer, while daring and imaginative, was also exactly the sort of thing by which men hang. Last year the various pawn-brokers in whose shops you pawned Sally's jewelry could only attempt to describe a free-floating image; they had no frame of reference. Now it will be possible to show these people a photograph of you, or better still to face you with them. While time is on your side, I think it not unlikely that one or two of the pawnbrokers will identify you as the man who pawned that jewelry.

"Then there was the business of the room at the Hollis and the room at Upham House which the blackmailer engaged for the pur-pose of collecting the first twenty-five thousand dollars. I didn't follow that up at the time because I was pledged not to endanger the negotiations — something, of course, you counted on. But now a thorough checkback will be made. You must have signed two registers. Experts will identify your handwriting. The clerks may even be able to identify you as the man who engaged those rooms.

"The photostats may have been a bluff, but there's a good chance you had at least one set made in case you had to prove you still held a real threat of producible letters. If that's true, the photostats will be traced back to you. Could you have used the facilities of the *Wrightsville Record* you own, I wonder?

"The money itself: Fifty of your five-hundred dollar bills were taken by Howard from your safe here, turned over to me, and I turned them over to the 'blackmailer' — which is to say, back to *you*." Ellery leaned forward and said softly: "Did you destroy that twenty-five thousand dollars, Mr. Van Horn? I doubt it. The great weakness of your plan was that you were positive you would never be suspected. To have burned fifty five-hundred-dollar bills — your own money — would hardly have occurred to you, a man who came up the hard way, from poverty, a man of big business. But I doubt that you've yet dared to use them. So you probably have those bills hidden somewhere, Mr. Van Horn; and, I assure you, you'll get no opportunity to destroy them now. By the way — I still have your memorandum of the serial numbers of those bills. I saved it . . . as a memento of my most spectacular 'success.'"

Diedrich was pursing his lips now, frowning.

"I can't say what you did with the second twenty-five thousand dollars, J. P. Simpson's money, which I left for you on the lockers in the Wrightsville station; but maybe the bank still has its record of those bills, and if you've put them where you keep the other bills, that's another nail in your coffin."

"I'm trying to follow you, Mr. Queen," said Diedrich, "with respect, believe me! But am I wrong in pointing out that, even if all this is true, all it would do would be to connect me with the blackmailer?"

"All, Mr. Van Horn?" Ellery laughed. "Proving you were the blackmailer would be the prosecution's important job. Because it would establish that you knew all about the adulterous relations between your wife and Howard. It breaks down the one defense you had, psychologically, throughout the whole affair: the presumption that you were ignorant of what was going on. It gives you motive, Mr. Van Horn; it sets the whole case up against you.

"I should imagine the prosecution's case against you," continued Ellery, "difficult as it would be, would set out to prove two things: That you knew your wife was unfaithful with your son, and that you planned to punish both of them — your wife by outright murder, your son by framing him for her death.

"Proof of your knowledge will be established by proving that you were the blackmailer; proof that you planned to punish them both will be established by showing that you were behind all the events which apparently proved that Howard had deliberately broken all Ten Commandments — that is, that you framed Howard. In this connection, I'm afraid my testimony will be crushing. Your lie about having put the Connhaven Detective Agency to work tracing Howard's parents — I'll nail that one, and so will Burmer (who, incidentally, has an excellent reputation in this State). The nonexistence of 'Dr. Southbridge' — I'll nail that lie, too, squarely to you as the liar. And there's always Wolfert to corroborate my testimony — and that's something I'll watch with a great interest, Mr. Van Horn; I mean the spectacle of Wolfert succumbing to his lifelong hatred of you.

"There are numerous other angles for the police to work on,

Mr. Van Horn. Such as the drug you must have used to put Howard to sleep on at least two occasions. It may even be necessary to exhume Howard's body to test for the existence of the drug in his remains; if that can be done, it might not be too difficult to connect you with the purchase of such a drug. And so on."

But Diedrich was smiling faintly again. "A great many conditional clauses, Mr. Queen. But even granting everything you say, I haven't heard a syllable connecting me with the act itself . . . the murder."

"No," said Ellery, "no, that's true. That may well be impossible. But Mr. Van Horn, very few murderers are convicted on direct evidence. A case will be scraped together, a circumstantial case, admittedly, and you'll be tried for murder . . . Yes," said Ellery, after a moment, "I think that's the important thing, Mr. Van Horn. You'll be indicted, you'll stand trial, the whole story will come out, and the great Diedrich Van Horn, who until now has been the object of public sympathy, the betrayed husband and father, will stand revealed for what he is — the supreme egocentric who committed murder for revenge. Not murder on impulse, in the emotional explosion of betrayal discovered, but coldly deliberate, plotted, premeditated murder.

"You're an old man, Mr. Van Horn, and I don't imagine death as such has many terrors for you — you being what you are. But I do think public exposure has. And that will be a far more painful death for you. A much more terrifying punishment. That's the kind of punishment a man suffers even when he's lying in the bottom of a grave."

And now Diedrich was not smiling, nor did he smile again. He sat very quietly in his wheel chair. Ellery did not disturb him. He merely stood there looking at the old man.

But then Diedrich looked up, and he asked almost bitterly: "And if my purpose was to kill the bitch and frame the dog, why didn't I do just that? Why this high-flown, fancy business of the Ten Commandments?"

When Ellery answered, it was in the same even tone; but there was a deep flush on his face.

"A detective would have one answer," he said, "and a psychologist another. The truth is a combination of both.

"For all your physical structure and the practical affairs of business that occupied you all your life, you're essentially a man of the mind, Mr. Van Horn. Like all tyrants, you think. You've never acted on impulse. Everything must be thought out, planned, like a battle, or a political coup. You molded Howard from his infancy to a preconceived shape. You planned Sally as deliberately as Howard planned a statue; she thought you fell in love with her suddenly — she was wrong; she didn't know that you determined to marry her from the day you plucked her out of Low Village and started doing her over into the woman you intended to share your kingdom with years hence.

"Your Ten Commandments idea was in many respects the culminating inspiration of your intellectual life. It had scope, sweep, power. It was gigantic. It was worthy of Diedrich Van Horn.

"It began where all logical processes begin: with a premise. Your premise was twofold: You must punish your betrayers; and in punishing them you must yourself be unsuspected. Or, to put it more crudely, you must get away with murder. The injury you suffered was fundamentally to your ego, the ego of a megalomaniac. So the affronted all-powerful had to avenge the affront to his power; and he had to repair the injury to his ego by avenging with impunity — showing that he was above the laws governing ordinary men, that his power was greater than the power of law.

"But it isn't easy to commit murder and frame an innocent person for the murder and remain safe from suspicion. If you had murdered Sally simply and directly, Howard would have been no more a suspect than you; in fact, you would have been the preferred suspect. And if you had framed Howard simply and directly, Howard may well in sheer panic have blurted out the whole story of his relations with Sally, in which case you'd have been revealed as possessing the strongest motive — almost the exclusive motive.

"So your problem, plan-wise, was to make Howard appear to be the only *possible* suspect. But if Howard had a motive to murder anyone, under the circumstances, that one was you, not Sally. Therefore you had to arrange a crime in which apparently Sally had been murdered by Howard *in mistake for you*. And, what's more, Howard himself had to be convinced he'd done it!

"All this, Mr. Van Horn, as you saw, cut your work out for you. It made a complex plot unavoidable. I imagine you rather enjoyed the prospect. The Napoleonic mentality thrives on difficulties; it even seeks them; and sometimes it creates them.

"You took your time. To cover your discovery of the letters in Sally's jewel box you took the necessary steps to set up the illusion of an outside thief. But thereafter you rested and schemed. Between June and early September you thought, you analyzed, you crystallized your knowledge of your intended victims. You made tentative plans, but you took no action.

"I think what held you up was your realization that the more complex a crime-plan is, the more dangerous for the planner. Every added complication increases the chances for slips, loopholes, unforeseeable accidents of what Thomas Hardy called 'happenstance.' You were groping toward some solution of this very major difficulty when Howard himself gave you your opportunity."

Ellery suddenly caught Diedrich's eye. Their glances locked, and after that the two men held on in a sort of death grip.

"Howard phoned you from New York that he was bringing me back to Wrightsville, or rather that he was coming right home and I was following within a couple of days.

"Instantly you grasped what that could mean to you. The cover of innocence you required, and which your thinking had not been able to evolve, would be amply provided *by me*. How could anyone doubt your innocence or suspect your guilt *if a well-known detective solved the case your way*? It was the answer to everything.

"Oh," said Ellery, "it had its risks. Greater dangers in some ways than not involving me at all. But the beauty of this conception of Ellery-Queen-the-murder-accomplice, its breadth, its *kind* of risk, thrilled your imagination. Here was a campaign and a struggle worthy of Napoleon himself.

"I daresay you never hesitated."

He stopped; and Diedrich, his great eyes unwavering, said coldly, "Go on."

"Howard phoned you on a Tuesday morning. I arrived in Wrightsville on Thursday. You had two days. *In those two days, Mr. Van Horn, you conceived the Ten Commandments idea and you prepared every phase of it for my arrival.* You invented the story of the Connhaven Detective Agency and its 'investigation.' You worked out the Yahweh anagram, found the graves of Aaron and Mattie Way in Fidelity, added the *E* to the surname. You set in motion the whole business of the Art Museum project — you told me about that on Thursday evening, saying you'd offered to make up the Museum fund deficit '*yesterday*' — which would make it Wednesday, the day *after* Howard's phone call! You went into action with your long-perfected blackmail plan; need I remind you that the blackmailer's first call to Sally also came on Wednesday, the day after Howard told you I was coming to Wrightsville?

"Everything started to move with the announcement of my visit.

"Yes, Mr. Van Horn, you handed me the part of accomplice and I accepted it as gullibly as you knew I would. And I did everything you planned for me to do — danced to your tune at every step of the way. And that was really your greatest triumph, Mr. Van Horn, because I was really your most obedient puppet."

Ellery paused again. He went on with some difficulty.

"The Ten Commandments business was wholly for my benefit. For me to solve the case your way, you had to prepare the kind of case I have a natural affinity for. You knew me very well. Oh, we'd never met, but you told me yourself how you'd read every book I've ever written, how you'd followed my career in the papers — I think you actually used the phrase, 'I'm a Queen expert.' And so you are, Mr. Van Horn, so you are — in a way I didn't dream of until today.

"You knew me better than I knew myself. You knew my working method. You knew my weakness. You knew you had to give me the kind of case I'd fall for, the kind of solution I'd fight to bring to a triumphant conclusion — that I'd believe in!

"You knew I'd choose the subtle answer to the obvious, always; the complicated rather than the simple; the pyrotechnical over the commonplace.

"You knew I possess a rather grandiose psychological pattern myself, Mr. Van Horn. That I like to think of myself, whether I ever admitted it or not, as a worker in mental marvels. And that's exactly what you gave me—a sort of marvel to perform. A grandiose concept. A steep, labyrinthine trail. A blinding, stunning climax. And I performed for you, Mr. Van Horn. I worked out this stupendous solution for you, and everyone fell flat on his face being impressed with my cleverness—and you were never once suspected.

"The Ten Commandments," said Ellery. "What did the newspapers say? 'Ellery Queen at his greatest.'"

And Ellery continued in the same even, colorless tone: "But it's interesting to note that, in judging me accurately, and as a result of your analysis giving me the Ten Commandments idea to play with, you betrayed something of fundamental importance about yourself, Mr. Van Horn."

A glitter of curiosity came into the eyes.

"All along I'd diagnosed Howard's emotional troubles as being tied in to his psychoneurotic worship of the father-image. I don't think there can be any doubt of that. But when I extended that diagnosis to include Howard's whole conception of the violation of the Ten Commandments as a deliberate revolt against the greatest Father-Image of all, the Fatherhood of God, I was obviously in error, since the Ten Commandments concept wasn't Howard's at all. *It was yours.*

"Why did your brain conceive and hold to that idea, Mr. Van Horn? How did you come to *think* of it? Why the Ten Commandments? You might have conceived a hundred other ideas possessing the attributes you required to impress me into your service. But no—you chose the Ten Commandments. Why?

"I'll tell you why, Mr. Van Horn—the only thing I'll have told you tonight that I think will come as news to you. *Your very choice of the Ten Commandments idea was a clue to you as the guiding mentality if only I'd had the brains to see it.* Not to Howard, but to you.

"I attempted last year, in expounding my pompous little thesis to Prosecutor Chalanski and Chief Dakin and Dr. Cornbranch, to explain that *Howard's* choice of the Ten Commandments weapon —breaking the Father-Image of God in breaking the father-image of you — must have been rooted in his environment as a child . . . in a home where a foster grandmother was obsessed with religion, and so on. But when you really dig into it, that was a pretty weak point — *as it applied to Howard*. Your mother, Mr. Van Horn, according to your own version, has never been an active influence in your household — at least, in Howard's lifetime. She was hardly ever seen; nobody paid much if any attention to her when she was. And Howard was brought up by nurses and tutors; it was their influence which would dominate, not your mother's. And certainly, aside from your mother, this was not an oppressively religious household.

"But how about *you*, and *your* boyhood environment, Mr. Van Horn? — the environment *you* were raised in during the impressionable childhood years? *Your father was an itinerant evangelist, a fundamentalist fanatic who preached the anthropomorphic, personally vengeful, jealous God of the Old Testament — who, as you told me, used to 'beat the hell out of' you and your brother; you were, you said, scared to death of him.* Howard loved his father, Mr. Van Horn, but you hated yours. And it's out of that hatred that your Ten Commandments idea was born . . . a means by which, unknown to your conscious self, you employed your father's own weapons to kill him fifty years after he dropped dead of apoplexy."

And now Ellery said rapidly: "I think this brings us up to date, Mr. Van Horn. You murdered Sally and framed Howard for it, and so Howard's death is also on your hands; I helped you commit these crimes; and we've both, in our fashion, got to pay the penalty."

"Penalty?" said Diedrich. "Both?"

"In our fashion. Mr. Van Horn," said Ellery, "you've destroyed me. Do you understand that? You've destroyed me."

"I understand that," said Diedrich Van Horn.

"You've destroyed my belief in myself. How can I ever again play little tin god? I can't. I wouldn't dare. It's not in me, Mr. Van Horn, to gamble with the lives of human beings. In the kind of avocation I've chosen to pursue there's often a life at stake, or if not a life then a career, or a man's or woman's happiness.

"You've made it impossible for me to go on. I'm finished. I can never take another case."

And Ellery was silent.

Then Diedrich, nodding, asked with a sort of humor: "And my penalty, Mr. Queen?"

Ellery pushed back the swivel chair and with his gloved hand he opened the top drawer of Van Horn's desk.

10

"Because, you see," said Diedrich, watching Ellery's hand, "there's no good can come from telling the truth to *them*. The truth won't bring her back, Mr. Queen, or him.

"You just think you're finished, Mr. Queen, but I *am*. I'm an old man. I don't have much time left. I've built something in my lifetime. I don't mean this," his gaunt hand waved vaguely, "or my money, or anything unimportant like that. I mean, a *life*. A name. The sort of thing that makes a man go to the grave with just a little less sense of waste.

"You're a man of considerable insight, Mr. Queen. You must know that what I did left me with no sense of triumph or satisfaction. Or if you didn't see it, you can see it now simply by looking at what's happened to me. What's that line in *Lear*? *'Tremble, thou wretch, That hast within thee undivulged crimes, unwhipp'd of justice.'* To a man who's three-quarters dead already, Mr. Queen, isn't that penalty enough?"

And Ellery said: "No."

Diedrich said quickly, "I'm a very rich man, Mr. Queen. Suppose I offered you — "

But Ellery said: "No."

"I'm sorry," said Diedrich, nodding. "I spoke on impulse. That was beneath both of us. We can do a great deal of good, you and I. Name a charity and I'll write out a check for one million dollars."

Ellery said: "No."

"Five million."

"Not fifty."

Diedrich was silent.

But then he said, "I know money as such means nothing to you. But think of the power it could give you—"

"No."

Diedrich was silent again.

Ellery, too.

And the study. There was not even a clock.

Finally Diedrich said: "There must be something. Every man has a price. Is there anything I can offer you to keep you from going to Dakin?"

And Ellery said: "Yes."

The wheel chair rolled forward quickly.

"What?" asked Diedrich eagerly. "What is it? Name it, and it's yours."

Ellery's gloved hand came out of the desk drawer.

In it glittered the snub-nosed Smith & Wesson .38 safety hammerless he had seen there on the night Van Horn had shown him the rifled safe.

❧

DIEDRICH'S MOUTH TWITCHED, but that was all.

Ellery laid the revolver back in the drawer.

He did not close the drawer.

He got to his feet.

"You'll write out a note first. Give any excuse you think will ring true—grief, ill health.

"I'll wait outside the study. I don't think you'll demean yourself further by trying to take a pot shot at me; but if you have any such thought in mind, forget it. By the time you can wheel that chair around to this side of the desk to get the gun, I'll be in the other room; and I'll be in the dark.

"I think, Mr. Van Horn, that's all."

Diedrich looked up.

Ellery looked at him.

Diedrich nodded, slowly.

Ellery glanced at his wristwatch. "I give you three minutes." Then he glanced at the desk, the chair, the floor. "Good-by."

Diedrich did not reply.

Ellery stepped quickly around the desk, passed the silent old man, crossed the study, and walked out into the darkness of the room beyond.

He sidestepped and waited, careful not to lean against the wall. He had his wrist close to his face.

And after a few seconds the illuminated dial of his wristwatch began to take form.

A minute passed.

The study was quiet.

Another twenty-five seconds.

He heard the scratching of a pen.

The pen scratched for seventy-five seconds. Then it stopped, and there was a new sound — the slight squeak of the wheel chair.

The squeak of the wheel chair stopped.

And there was another new sound, a clicking sound.

And, very quickly, a shot.

Ellery backed away from the wall and skirted the edge of the area illuminated by the study until he stood in the darkness beyond.

He glanced into the study.

Then he turned and walked unhurriedly through the dark room to the foyer and the front door.

As he eased the front door open he heard a door open upstairs, then another, and a third. Wolfert? Laura? Old Christina?

He heard Wolfert's thin sawing voice cut through the house. "Diedrich! Was that you down there?"

Ellery closed the front door noiselessly.

Lights were springing up in the house.

But he set his feet on the Van Horn driveway and began the long night walk into Wrightsville.